A WOMAN UNDONE

A WOMAN UNDONE

TB MARKINSON

Published by T. B. Markinson

Visit T. B. Markinson's official website at lesbianromancesbytbm.com for the latest news, book details, and other information.

Copyright © T. B. Markinson, 2018

Cover Design by Erin Dameron-Hill / EDHGraphics

Edited by Kelly Hashway

This book is copyrighted and licensed for your personal enjoyment only. All rights reserved. No part of this publication may be reproduced, stored in a retrieval system, or transmitted in any forms or by any means without the prior permission of the copyright owner. The moral rights of the author have been asserted.

This book is a work of fiction. Names, characters, businesses, places, events, and incidents are the product of the author's imagination or are used fictitiously. Any resemblance to actual persons, living or dead, events, or locales is entirely coincidental.

CHAPTER ONE

The buzzer of the doorbell echoed throughout the house.

Sarah and I locked eyes, each of us on one side of the island in the kitchen. I'd been in the process of prepping afternoon tea and coffee, a mug in each hand. She had Demi on her hip, nuzzling the top of the baby's head. Fred and Ollie were hanging out with Maddie at the art table in the family room. Maddie, with Gabe in tow, had rushed back to Fort Collins from their ski trip with Maddie's parents as soon as they heard about Peter's arrest right after Christmas.

The presence of someone or some*ones* on the front porch was a terrible reminder of seeing my older brother hauled out of my house in handcuffs in the middle of the night less than twenty-four hours ago. Once, I'd insinuated my family was something television audiences may see on *The Jerry Springer Show*.

Ironically, the comment had been made *before* my mother passed and I'd learned that for nearly two decades my father had a secret second family and I had a half brother and stepbrother.

Now, Peter was out on bail for what I assumed was financial shenanigans reminiscent of something you'd see in the movie *The Wolf on Wall Street*. I'd stayed far away from the family business, not because I suspected unsavory tactics, but because for years I simply didn't like my family. Although, it was clear to me Peter was up to his neck in shit, and I truly didn't understand how it would impact my father's company. So far, all I knew was Peter had to surrender his passport and all his personal assets had been frozen. Fortunately for him, his house was paid for, and I'd learned it was in my father's name. Had Dad foreseen something like this happening? Or was that the benefit of being the firstborn son who shared the business gene? Given the outcome, I was thrilled to have my own mortgage and nothing to do with their company. Peter's arrest had solidified this desire. To be blunt, I didn't want to know the nitty gritty details involved. My personality had a hard time seeing past the black and white, and if I learned too much, I feared it'd permanently destroy my connection to Peter.

Tie, his wife, had been kicked out of the family on Christmas after her attempt to frame Peter for an affair he didn't have. Or did. Jesus, it was hard to know what the men in the Petrie family did or didn't do. Tie had done everything she could to make the holiday miserable, and I'd threatened to kick her out on Christmas Eve. My father, though, managed to remove her from the premises with the one thing she wanted: money. Even though I'd only talked a big game about getting her out of my house, since Peter's arrest, I worried I was next on her hit list, so to speak, since the woman was evil. Would she sic the police on me as well? I couldn't imagine on what trumped-up charges, but I was willing to bet she'd come up with something maddeningly hard to refute. Not that I thought the charges against Peter weren't completely legit, or was my knowledge of Peter's money-grubbing character playing a factor? Was Tie clever enough to know this if she had set him up? With Peter—it was difficult to know what was what. Every time I tried to figure out what I believed, my mind started to spin like a crazy carnival ride, resulting with me wanting to puke my guts up.

Knocking sounded on the door. Whoever was on the other side seemingly getting impatient.

More cops? Tie? Reporters? Mormons? I wasn't in the mood for any of those options.

"I'll get it," I finally said, setting the mugs onto the countertop. "You okay with the kids?" It sounded odd to say that, but having cops rush up your stairs to arrest a family member made me more jittery than usual. And, I used to have to contend with a blackmailing and alcoholic ex. I missed those simpler times.

Sarah nodded solemnly as if in tune with my concern.

I sucked in a deep breath and rolled my shoulders before answering the door.

There stood my father, in a Burberry coat, slacks, gray cashmere sweater, and tie. By his side was his second wife, Helen, the woman who'd been in the shadows most of my life.

"Hey," I said in a meek voice.

"How are you?" Helen pulled me into her arms, the snow on her London Fog splattering me and the floor. Not that I minded. It was the type of embrace I'd never received from my own mother, but I'd been learning, even in my thirties, no one was too old for a mom hug. It reinforced my pledge to hug my children at least once every day and to tell them how much I love them. Words I'd never heard from the Scotch-lady.

"We're hanging in." I pulled apart. "You two?"

Dad bobbed his head, stroking his chin, which was speckled with stubble. Had he had a moment's rest since hearing the news? From the hollow look in his eyes, I didn't think so. "We should sit down and talk," he said.

I'd called Dad when Peter was shoved into a police car. His team of attorneys had leaped into action and succeeded in bailing out my brother, who was now in his home, virtually in hiding. While the Petries weren't at the level of Bernie Madoff, my father and brother were well-known in the finance world, and it wasn't unusual for me to see their photos in the business section of prominent newspapers.

Peter's arrest had spurred a lot of chatter, which I couldn't stomach and tried to tune out. I was a history professor, and buzz words like *insider trading*, also known as black edge, *IPOs*, and other terms and phrases, were mostly meaningless to me since I'd done everything in my power to keep my nose out of the family business. I could hold my own discussing how the Treaty of Versailles and the subsequent disastrous inflation led to the rise of Hitler, but my brain shut down when it came to modern finances.

I waved for them to go ahead. "Maddie's with the kids in the front room. We can talk in there. I'm sure she'd like to know what's going on."

Again, Dad bobbed his head.

When I'd met Maddie many years ago, she'd been engaged to Peter. Just days ago, on Christmas, she got engaged to my stepbrother Gabe. Part of me wondered how Peter's arrest would impact her latest engagement. It wasn't a big secret that Peter was still in love with Maddie, and despite her assertion she was over Peter, I suspected she reciprocated, but I didn't know if that was because a part of her would always love Peter or if her feelings went deeper. Maddie was the type who liked putting people back together. I knew this because she'd done it for me in the past, and she wasn't good at staying away from the center of shitstorms.

Maddie had mentioned she wondered what Peter would have been like if he wasn't a Petrie, raised by parents who weren't loving and taught from a young age that cheating was a normal part of life. I'd been shielded from my father's affair, but Peter hadn't and hindsight was proving it'd warped his mind. Furthermore, Maddie said being with Gabe was easier, since Gabe wasn't as insecure as Peter. Also, Gabe gave her an *in* to the Petrie family, something Maddie desired for some insane reason. In spite of all the problems the Petries encountered, Maddie felt like she belonged, adding to her desire to marry Gabe. Another connection to the family without the actual Petrie DNA.

Then, there was the complication of Peter rushing into a marriage to Tie after his relationship with Maddie collapsed on their wedding day. Fuck, it was hard to keep everything straight. To add yet another wrinkle, Tie had been one of Peter's mistresses when he'd been engaged to Maddie, which Maddie didn't know until well after Peter married Tie. That must have hurt like hell. I'd never figured out Peter's reason for marrying Tie. Simply as a *fuck you* to Maddie for humiliating him on their wedding day? Or had he been afraid to be alone and Tie was ready, willing, and able? Or even more nefarious reasons? The last option seemed more plausible, considering Peter and Tie were involved.

Honestly, did Jerry Springer have such complicated family dynamics as the Petries on his show? I needed one of those boards you see on crime or conspiracy shows, with photos and strings leading to various suspects and scenarios. Or would that be too depressing? Would all the strings circle endlessly? I just wanted a normal life.

We trooped into the family room. It seemed to dawn on Maddie a family powwow was about to begin. She kissed the top of each twin's head. "I'll help Sarah get drinks."

"I should get Demi." I left the twins under the watchful eyes of their grandparents.

Sarah must have heard Helen's voice because she was

pulling down more coffee mugs from the cupboard when I entered the kitchen.

I relieved her of Demi, who had been at our house when Peter was arrested. There hadn't been a sighting of Tie, Demi's mom, and no word from her either. It was as if she'd vanished into thin air, although, none of us believed that. Tie wasn't the type to go away silently.

Demi giggled when I tickled her belly. Sarah grinned at me, our eyes in agreement. No matter what, we'd ensure our niece was loved and happy. Peter hadn't been a great brother and turned out to be an even worse fiancé and husband. But he'd started to change after the birth of his daughter. I'd spoken to him briefly on the phone after he'd been bailed out, and we were going to talk later today to firm up plans. He'd been clear; my main goal during this entire ordeal was to take care of Demi. Shield her from everything, something I agreed with completely.

Having been a child who didn't have anyone to take me under their wings, I was determined to ensure Demi wouldn't be impacted by any of the shit swirling around her. She was innocent. Probably the only one out of the three in her immediate family who was.

"Earl Grey or herbal?" Sarah asked me.

"Earl Grey. Strong."

She nodded, understanding. I had barely slept in what seemed like days, but it'd been less than twenty-four hours.

"Go. We got this." Maddie shooed me out of the kitchen.

Dad and Helen, sitting on the couch, conversed quietly. Ollie continued coloring her masterpiece with a massive red crayon while Freddie, his head cocked to the right with one eye squinted, stacked some blocks.

"I'm really starting to wonder if he'll be an architect or engineer," Helen observed.

"He loves to build things." I took a seat on the leather chair closest to my children, settling Demi in my lap. She was much clingier than either of the twins.

"How is precious little Demi?" Helen spoke to the child in her grandmotherly voice.

Demi reached out, cooing.

Helen rose, taking the excited Demi into her arms. "You're such a sweet girl."

Demi giggled.

Retaking her seat next to my father, Helen said, "She seems to be doing well, considering."

"We're trying to keep things as calm and cheerful as we can for all three." I shrugged.

"Peter misses her, but he doesn't want to subject her to the…" Dad settled on, "hoopla."

It was odd, hearing my father, Charles Allen Petrie, the finance whiz who'd built a successful company from the ground up, use the word *hoopla*. Although, Helen affectionately called him Cap, so he must have a playful side. Maybe there'd always been the hoopla side to my father that I'd never witnessed while my mother was alive. The Scotch-lady had a way of sucking anything good out of the air around her.

I'd lived with it for so long I didn't know there was another way to exist.

It wasn't until I fell in love with Sarah that I learned what it was like to be happy.

Of course, I'd fought it in the beginning, with my specialty being sabotage. I'd never been a happy child. And the beginning years of my adult life had been complicated by my relationship with Meg, an alcoholic who'd turned out to be toxic like my mother. The pre-Sarah me craved what I'd considered normal: pain and suffering. That was what I knew and understood.

Then Sarah had entered my life.

Everything changed from the moment I stared into her dark chocolate eyes.

Going from toxic to normal wasn't an easy adjustment for the likes of me. Most who knew me well called me clueless. Not surprising since I'd always considered myself a bit of a social experiment, having grown up with a conniving mother and a mostly silent father. Maybe I'd been cursed, being born into the Petrie family.

Sarah, with a tray in her hands, entered the room, knocking me out of my dark thoughts.

I smiled, knowing I wouldn't change anything. No matter the pain of growing up, the path I took, with so many speed bumps along the way, had led me to Sarah. She was my rock. My love. My life. The mother of our children.

We locked eyes, and she flashed her confident smile that always conveyed, *No matter what, I love you and I got you.*

"Who wants coffee or tea?" she said in a soothing voice. "We also have cinnamon rolls." Sarah set the tray down on the coffee table with a hand motion indicating, *Have at it.*

Dad fixed cups of coffee for Helen and himself. "Roll?" he asked Helen.

Her eyes darted skyward, and she released an anguished sigh. "I really wish I could since I don't like turning one down, but I'm still recovering from the shrimp fiasco."

He grinned slightly, not being the type to express full emotions. "You do like a good roll."

They shared a mischievous look, hinting to an inside joke that made me cringe. While I was happy for them, suspecting they had a healthy sex life was simply too much for me. In my world, my father wasn't a sexual being and his offspring had magically appeared on the planet. Thinking otherwise caused my brain to short-circuit.

Sarah, on the other hand, seemed to appreciate their closeness. If she knew my thoughts, she'd reprimand me for being too stodgy. However, she secretly loved my stick-in-the mud side. I was sure of it even if she wouldn't admit it.

Sarah handed me a cup of Earl Grey, perching on the ottoman in front of me, sipping her coffee. Craning her neck, she said, "That's beautiful, Ollie."

"Beau-ful." Ollie said her version of *beautiful*, followed by giggling, continuing her coloring with more determination on her face.

"What movie are Allen and Casey seeing today?" Sarah asked Helen.

"A superhero one. I can't remember which. Gabe's going as well."

Casey, Ethan's daughter, had been staying with us while her parents dealt with the death of Lisa's mom, Casey's grandmother. Poor Casey hadn't learned of her grandmother's passing yet. The last I'd heard, Lisa was going back and forth about wanting to fly Casey out for the services, and Ethan was doing his best not to put his foot down completely due to the expenditure and wanting to protect his daughter from the sad reality all of us faced: death. Both Gabe and Allen, who'd recovered remarkably well from the food poisoning, had volunteered to fly with her if need be. Sarah and I would foot the bill if Ethan would agree.

Everyone had been stepping up in their own ways to help the younger people. The way it should be. A new thing for the Petrie family, though perhaps not for my father and his newer family.

Maddie came out of the bathroom, her eyes looking a bit puffy, and was the last to sit in the remaining leather chair, after fixing a cup of coffee. "How's Peter doing?"

Dad cleared his throat, as if not ready for the discussion but knowing it was time. "He's doing as well as expected. He's still weak from being ill and..." He brushed lint or something off his trousers, and I had to wonder if he needed to do something to stay strong.

"Has anyone heard from Tie, yet?" Sarah asked, her eyes on Demi.

Helen shook her head, holding the baby closer. "Only word from her attorney. She seems happy to leave Demi with you two for the time being."

"And she's afraid to confront me." Dad's voice was gruff.

"Good," Sarah said in a tone that made it clear she had zero confidence in Tie's ability to care for her daughter during this time. Or ever. She turned to me. "We should go shopping. Get her more clothes and her own things. We have hand-me-downs from the twins, but…" Sarah's go-to when stressed was shopping, and when I nodded, Sarah pivoted back to Helen. "Has there been any mention of parental rights? Whether or not Tie will surrender hers? She left on Christmas with what I'm assuming was a bundle of money from you, Charles. And she hasn't called once to inquire about Demi. Clearly, being a mother isn't at the top of her list of priorities. I never thought I'd recommend or encourage any mother give up their child, but considering everything we know about Tie, I do think it's best for Demi."

I blinked.

Was surrendering rights even a thing?

"Not yet, but I'm hoping we can get her to see the light. Shouldn't be too hard since she didn't put up much of a fight on Christmas after our *heart-to-heart*. During the conversation, not once did she mention Demi, which didn't surprise me much given the type of woman she is." Dad sipped his coffee. If he and his attorneys had their way, I doubted Tie would ever be allowed back into Colorado, if she'd indeed been ferried away like I suspected. Considering my dad had been the one to uproot her out of Peter's life, like a pesky but determined dandelion, I didn't have much doubt she was far away. Physically at least.

But giving up Demi completely?

Was I the only one who hadn't considered this possibility?

Why would Tie do such a thing? Didn't the connection keep her tied to Peter's life? Continue her torment of him? The Scotch-lady had used me and Peter against my father, a fact I hadn't learned until after her death. Tie reminded me so much of my mother. Just the thought made my skin crawl. Of course, this may be the reason why Sarah and my father were already bringing up the subject, knowing full well how damaging a woman like Tie could be to a child.

As a mother, though, the mere thought of giving up my kids was abhorrent.

"Where is she?" I asked.

Dad shifted on the couch. "With Samuel."

"Peter's associate?"

"And *friend*," Helen added with emphasis on the last word.

"Why would Tie be with Samuel of all people?" Maddie asked. "He's kinda creepy."

I'd only interacted with Samuel once at a party hosted by Peter and Maddie when they were still engaged, but I hadn't forgotten the meeting. The thing that stuck out in my mind was his odd smile. Like an animal whose lip got caught on a canine. The man exuded zero typical human emotions, making him a great candidate for Peter's friend and business associate. Apparently, my opinion of my brother and his profession had hit a new low. Hard not to, though, after seeing him in handcuffs.

"The investigation is in the beginning stages, but it's becoming clear that the two are in a relationship." Dad let those words sink in. "And both have a vendetta against Peter, apparently." He reached for Demi's hand. "Their relationship can be used for her benefit."

The fact that he was holding Demi's hand and claiming Tie's alleged infidelity would help Peter's case made my stomach roil. Not that I didn't agree with Dad. That compounded the sickly feeling swirling inside. "You believe, then, that Peter's innocent? Given his…?" I struggled for the polite way to say *greed*.

Dad rescued me. "He's always been fond of money. That's no secret. But Peter isn't a fucking moron."

Fucking.

My father said the word *fucking*.

This was a bigger deal than using *hoopla*.

"They're trying to pin him with insider trading. Everyone knows he's friends with Reggie Whitcomb, whose hedge fund doesn't have the cleanest record," Dad said.

"It was Gabe who introduced them," Helen offered with an air of sadness.

Dad squeezed her thigh. "It's not Gabe's fault. Everyone knew Reggie's returns were too good to be true. Peter wouldn't have tied himself to a sinking ship. No one with half of Peter's understanding would do such a thing."

"Has Reggie been arrested?" I asked.

"He's being questioned. It's the way the world operates. Authorities pluck the hanging fruit off the branch and work their way up."

"But how did Peter get swept up into this?" Maddie's complexion was ghostly-white.

"Samuel had access to his accounts. We suspect he made the transactions in Peter's name. A private account. Not one through the company, which would have triggered our compliance department to get involved. Word has it there are incriminating emails and texts Peter swears on his life he never sent."

"I never suspected Samuel had it in for Peter. He was weird, but to do this?" Maddie tapped her forehead with a finger, looking lost.

"We may not know what set him off. My gut says Tie turned Samuel against Peter. I have no idea when she started plotting his demise, but she took great pains to reach this goal." Dad inhaled deeply.

"But how did they actually execute everything? And to coordinate Peter's arrest days after Christmas?"

"Careful planning. Ever since Madoff, prosecutors have been wanting to nail other white-collar crimes. To prove they're capable. The majority of the world hates corporate types. And dragging out a corrupt corporate raider during the holidays—headline gold." Dad grunted.

"We're not in New York City." Maddie covered her eyes. "Peter can be an asshole, but I agree with Charles. He's not an idiot. Greedy, yes. But a smart money-grubber."

Like when he'd told my homophobic uncle I was gay to get my inheritance.

It was difficult for me to ascertain what I thought about the Peter debacle. Did I believe without a doubt Peter was innocent? Guilty? Somewhere in the middle?

He'd been acting cagey on Christmas. I'd chalked it up to his troubled marriage. But what if he'd known he was under investigation and his freedom was at stake?

Judging from my father's expression, he didn't think that at all.

Neither did Maddie.

Helen was the type to always see the good in people. I'd never been able to figure out her true thoughts about her husband's firstborn simply because I'd never asked. My desire not to know anything grew stronger with each new development in my life.

I couldn't see Sarah's face, but I suspected she may not be completely on Peter's side. Dealing with me and my insecurities that nearly derailed our relationship, she'd known firsthand how messed up his childhood had been. Unlike me, Peter hadn't found his Sarah to help steer him to normalcy. I wondered if Peter would ever be able to fully trust a woman, or had the Scotch-lady permanently damaged him?

"What's next?" I asked.

"My lawyers are doing everything they can," Dad said.

I didn't clarify I'd meant what was next to befall the Petrie family.

CHAPTER TWO

That night, after everyone had left and we'd put all the kids to bed, including Casey, Sarah and I retreated to the library for a glass of wine.

She had her back against the arm of the couch, her feet pressed into my thigh. "How are you doing?"

I blew out some air. "I have no frigging idea." I mimed my head was exploding.

She laughed. "Okay, I wasn't expecting that answer. Can you elaborate? You know, use some of those fancy words you store in that impressive brain of yours when you want to woo the chicks?"

I feigned being hurt. "Not sure I should woo any chicks. Look where that got Peter."

"Did you just compare me to Tie?"

"Wh-what?" I stuttered. "N-no. Not at all."

She didn't blink.

"How could you even think that?" I pressed.

Still, she didn't blink.

"Oh my God!" I pitched my hands up.

Sarah laughed. "God, I love how easy it is to get you all riled."

I groaned. "This is when you show your true colors."

She quirked one of her eyebrows. "If you don't know me better than that, I don't even know what to say."

"I was… Wait, are you doing it again?" I slanted my head to query her expression.

Her evil grin confirmed she was indeed pulling my leg.

"You really are evil."

Sarah shoved her legs into my thigh, the pressure providing comfort. "It's how I help you."

"To have a heart attack? Not sure I need much help in that department these days."

Sarah's smile morphed into consternation. "I keep forgetting to up your life insurance."

"Hardy har har. Given the current situation we're in, that's not the seed you probably want to plant in my mind."

"Why? Are you considering bumping me off first?"

"And raise the kids on my own? Are you fucking insane? You left me alone with the twins for one weekend, and I nearly lost my mind. And, given you and Dad are set on getting Tie to give up Demi—I'd be left taking care of three." While I had no doubt Peter loved his daughter, he wasn't exactly the caregiving type. I'd lost track of how many times he'd left us with changing her diaper or feeding her. Demi had a nanny, but would the woman stay in the picture now? Not a pressing question at the moment, so I filed it away in my brain.

She nodded solemnly. "What if the number was four?"

"Is Casey staying? Long-term?" That made zero sense to me. "I know Ethan and Lisa are on the rocks and their finances are iffy at best, but to farm out their only child…" I tapped the side of my head. "Doesn't compute."

Sarah pinned me with a thoughtful look. "No, I wasn't insinuating that."

"That's good. I love Casey and she's always welcome here, but Lisa and Ethan are fantastic parents." I tapped her shin. "Isn't it funny that Ethan turned out to be a great dad, considering his quirks?"

Sarah's expression softened. "Your brother has been different since Demi's birth."

My thoughts clouded my brain. While I agreed with her, I still couldn't pin down my feelings about the pickle he was in. Not for the first time, I wondered if Peter's softening exterior was wrapped up in his guilt. Maybe he didn't do everything the authorities suspected, but believing he was undeniably innocent on all fronts…? Did becoming a better father wipe away everything else?

"Are you ready to sort the emotions swirling through you yet?"

"And drop the four children conundrum?" I counted on my fingers: Freddie, Ollie, and Demi. "If Tie actually gives up her parental rights, which I'm not entirely convinced she will, and Peter goes to jail, obviously, we'll take care of Demi. But, is Peter looking at years? If convicted, that is?"

"No idea. Right now, let's focus on the present. Talk to me. About Peter. It's got to be a mind fuck for you."

I rested my head against the back of the couch cushion. "I know Dad is absolutely convinced Peter's been set up, but what if he wasn't? Tie is a piece of work. I have no doubt about that. But to connive with Samuel to set Peter up for insider trading… That is hard to fathom. I know she's been reading and watching a lot about financial crimes and tomfoolery. I also know Peter's obsessed with wealth. He has been since birth. Or, maybe it was the Scotch-lady's so-called child-rearing." I juggled my palms up and down in the air. "I don't know what or whom to believe, and I'm not sure I want to figure it out."

"Do you have to know everything to support your brother?"

I scrunched my brow. "What do you mean?"

"Sometimes loving someone means accepting them even during the worst of times."

"You think Peter's guilty?"

"Most definitely," she said without hesitation.

"Does that mean you think he's setting up Tie to get Demi away from her? Is he trying to protect his daughter?" A small part of me could get behind this given my childhood.

She waved me off the scent. "No, you misunderstood. I have no idea if Peter is guilty of the crimes he's been charged with. Yes, I think your brother is greedy as fuck, but I have to side with Charles some. Peter's smart. From what I've gleamed from a private chat with your father and news accounts, the bread crumbs left for everything seem to be the size of bread loaves."

"Wouldn't the authorities see through that?"

"Possibly. As your dad said, Peter isn't their main target. He's a pawn."

"A pawn of the government. Tie. Samuel. Good grief. But I'm still confused. You said he's guilty."

"Of many things. Being a serial cheater. Terrible brother. Horrible husband. Shitty friend and coworker, if Samuel really is in cahoots with Tie."

Covering my eyes, I said, "I'm not following. Are you saying since he's all these things, he deserves to go to prison?"

Sarah sighed. "Not at all. I'm saying your brother has made a lot of bad decisions, treating people like shit along the way. Things are catching up with him. This is his Ebenezer Scrooge moment."

"Did you just toss out a Charles Dickens reference?"

"I did. Thought my classics buff would appreciate it, and it's the season for it." She pressed her feet into my thigh again.

I smiled. "I love when you do things like that. Even during times like this. You never forget about me."

"It's not possible to forget about you, sweetheart. I adore you."

"That's been Peter's problem. He can't love the way a normal person can."

"Are you sure about that?"

"I'm not sure he has it in him." I turned my upper body to face her. "Do you think he can?"

"I'd hate to think any person, who isn't a sociopath, can't learn to open their heart. It'd be a truly terrible world if that were the case."

I let out a bark of laughter. "The world *is* terrible. I've dedicated my academic career to studying the Nazis."

"You've also shared with me one courageous story after another about the resiliency of the human spirit and kindness during the worst of times."

"Peter isn't the type to sacrifice himself to stamp out Nazism. He's the one who'd say the right things to seem aboveboard while smuggling artwork and gold from the victims."

Sarah seemed to mull this over. "He may have been, but I don't know if I believe that anymore. It's not just Demi's birth that's changed him. It's you."

I clutched my sweater over my heart. "Me? How have I affected my brother?"

"Ever since you two have grown closer, he's changed. You were all alone growing up. Your mom didn't hide the fact that she preferred Peter over you, but have you considered this made him even lonelier than you?" She examined my face. "Let me put it this way. Say you were in a loveless relationship. Would you rather be alone in a relationship or alone on your own? Me"—she tapped her chest—"I'd leave the relationship to build a healthier foundation for when I found someone I could spend my life with."

"I didn't do that, though," I whispered to my lap.

"I disagree with you. You didn't make all the right decisions, getting involved with Meg proves that, but you did leave her and you learned how to survive all on your own. Peter went into the family business. Catered to your mom until her death not so long ago. You weren't even in touch with your family for years. You, my dear, learned how to survive. Now, when shit hits the fan, you can rely on the skills you've learned to pull up the drawbridges to survive. To become whole."

"Peter doesn't have any drawbridges? Is that what you're saying?"

"Not on his own. That's where you come in."

I contemplated her words. "No matter what, then, I should be there for him?"

"Yes. That's family."

"Is it weird or terrible that part of me is...?" I didn't know how to complete my thought.

"Do you mean happy about the situation?"

I squirmed. "I don't think that's the right way to put it, but I won't lie. It's kinda nice to see Peter fall apart. Mom had always crowed I'd amount to nothing and Peter would always be heads above." I shifted again. "I don't mean I was jumping for joy when the police led him out of our home. I was terrified for him. But, I don't know. I seem to have everything. Things I didn't even allow myself to imagine before you. Wife. Children. Friends. Career." I ticked off each on a finger. "What does Peter have? His fancy house? Money? We're taking care of Demi. When we spoke earlier, he mentioned he'd call me about Demi, but I think deep down he knows he doesn't have the tools to raise Demi on his own."

"I can't blame you, really, for thinking that, but I know you, Lizzie. You have a big heart. If you go too far down the path of relishing Peter's fall, it'll tear you up inside."

I nodded. "Can I just take a few more minutes to enjoy the feeling?"

Sarah whipped out her phone. "Shall we set a timer?"

I laughed. "I don't think I need it. I'm already feeling guilty about it."

Sarah waved for me to come to her. She repositioned, allowing me to rest my head on her shoulder. Stroking my forehead, she said, "We'll need to be strong for both Peter and Demi. The Petries haven't always been a cohesive unit. We can change that. It's time to circle the wagons. Complete the family's perimeter to protect everyone."

* * *

WE'D GONE TO BED, but while Sarah snoozed with her head on my chest, my eyes were wide open, staring out the window.

Was Peter asleep?

Or was he staring into the same black sky?

I reached for my phone on the nightstand, and without jostling Sarah too much, I punched out the words *Are you awake?* and hit send.

Not even seconds passed before he responded with a yes. Quickly, he followed up by asking about Demi.

I slithered out from underneath Sarah. I eased into fleece-lined slippers, one of my Christmas gifts, and a robe, and plodded downstairs to the library, where I dialed Peter's number.

"Hey," he answered after the first ring as if he'd been waiting for someone, anyone, to call.

"You sound like shit."

"Getting arrested tends to do that to someone."

"I imagine so. How are you doing?" I paused. "I'm sorry. That's probably the worst thing I can ask right now."

"It's okay. No one has asked me that, actually. Not since…" His voice trailed off.

I wasn't entirely sure if he meant not since his arrest or

getting bailed out. Did it really matter? Both events were intricately linked.

He pressed on. "I'm sorry I didn't follow up on our conversation about Demi. Dad said he'd talk to you and Sarah, and I don't know what to expect right now. I keep thinking the police will barge in at any moment, and then what? Will social services get involved? I can't stomach that thought."

"We won't let that happen to Demi. Ever."

"I knew I could count on you. This is such a nightmare. A complete and total nightmare."

"Peter, did you do it?"

He laughed. "That's the other question no one has asked me. I understand why the lawyers haven't, but even Dad hasn't."

I waited, using silence as a way to prod him to answer. It was a technique I used when teaching.

"No, Lizzie. I didn't do the thing they're claiming."

I believed him. At least, I really wanted to have faith my brother wouldn't do such a thing, because if he did, what would that say about me? But I also knew he'd done some things he wasn't proud of. Not that I wanted to push, because I wasn't like Sarah. I had a hard time divorcing certain pieces of information from my mind. While Sarah swam in the gray areas, I was a black and white person. When it came to the Petries, ignorance wasn't just bliss; it was my survival technique.

"I don't expect you of all people to believe me," he continued, "but you are the one person I want to."

"Why?"

"I respect you. I don't feel that way about many. Not even Dad. Not entirely. God, I used to resent the shit out of you. The way you didn't let Mom get to you." He sighed.

I laughed. "Oh, I did. Just not the same way you did."

He chuckled quietly. "I know that now. But you came out

stronger when you shouldn't have. I admire that about you." He sucked in a deep breath. "I don't know if I can do this."

"Do what?"

"Come out stronger." His voice quavered.

"Do you know how I became stronger?"

"No. How?"

"I learned to trust those around me. Lean on me. Dad. Helen. Sarah."

"Maddie."

I should have seen that one coming, but it still took me by surprise. "Has she reached out?"

"Yes."

His one-word response wasn't that comforting, leading me to believe he was holding back on something. I wasn't all that surprised considering we were talking about Maddie, the Petrie Whisperer. "Poor Gabe," I said aloud without thinking.

"Don't get ahead of yourself, Lizzie. Nothing has happened, and he's my stepbrother as well."

"So, you've thought of all the implications on the Maddie front?"

"I've thought of all the implications on all fronts." He let out another sigh. "I've been doing a lot of thinking. Getting arrested really made me take a hard look at my life. I don't like myself. I don't even know why you're on the phone with me at two in the morning."

"When you put it that way, I have to go."

He laughed.

I remained quiet.

"You aren't really hanging up, are you?"

"Not a chance, Peter. Earlier, a wise woman told me you're my family and family members circle the wagons."

"Too bad Sarah doesn't have a sister."

"Yes, the Petries like to keep everything within the family."

He laughed. "God, you make us sound like the *Flowers in the Attic* family."

I cringed. "I didn't mean to, but we do have a weird dynamic. I mean even Allen is dating my nanny."

He remained quiet for several moments before conceding. "That we do. My therapist—"

"You're in therapy?"

"I recently started. He seems to think I crave the crazy because I was raised by crazy."

"We crave what we know. That's how I ended up with Meg."

"Tell me about that. If it's not too hard to."

I rubbed the top of my head. "Oh, gosh. Okay. Prepare yourself, though. It's a long story."

"I have all the time in the world for you these days."

"Geez, if I'd known that, I'd have set you up years ago."

"I was a shitty brother, wasn't I? Don't answer that. I do want to know more about you and Meg. My therapist keeps asking me questions I don't know how to answer. Maybe learning about what you've been through will help me piece my own life trajectory together."

CHAPTER THREE

It was December thirtieth, and I was entirely done with this year.

Sarah rolled over in bed and scrunched her face. "I wasn't expecting to wake to such a serious expression."

I swiped hair off her forehead, allowing me full access to her stunning eyes. "I was just thinking about this year and what next year will be like."

"By your furrowed brow, I'm guessing you don't have high hopes for the upcoming three hundred and sixty-five days."

"I don't know about that. I was more contemplating the cruelty of New Year's Eve."

Sarah bunched a pillow under her head. "This I have to hear."

"Are you mocking me?"

"Not at all. I love Lizzie wisdom. It really opens my eyes. Please proceed." She motioned for me to continue.

"For your bemusement."

She playacted being hurt. "I would never." Planting a kiss on my cheek, she said, "Seriously, talk to me about what's waking you so early in the morning."

"I don't think I actually fell asleep. I may have, but..." I shrugged.

"Talk to me, Lizzie. Please." Her voice was sincere.

"It's nothing really. I was just contemplating the false hope a new year offers: tantalizing anticipation the upcoming months will be better than the ones before. Perhaps the explanation is simple. Many of us are limping over the finish line at the end of a calendar year, battered beyond belief, and we want to believe there's more than surviving, but I don't think there is. We move from one episode to the next. I'm trying to convince myself this isn't true."

"That's pretty dark. Even for you."

"I didn't always take the time to think about this. Before you and the twins, I was firmly in the camp life would always suck. And it did. At the time, it didn't stand out to me all that much as being terrible. It was my life. I got up every day, battled my way to the next time I could crash in bed in hopes of getting some rest. Day in and day out, that's how I lived."

"I know," she whispered. "You weren't very kind to yourself. The pressure you put on yourself—no one could live up to it."

"I thought I could. And I thought if I actually accomplished what I wanted, it would signify I was better than... them."

"Your family?"

I nodded.

"And now? Are you still trying to be better?" She arched her brows.

"I know I'm better and not for the reasons I thought would get me to this point."

She placed a hand on my cheek. "Why?"

"You. Ollie. Freddie. Our friends. I talked to Peter the other night—"

"You did?"

"Yeah. Sorry I didn't mention it earlier. I was—" I tapped my forehead.

"Processing. You've always needed time to do that."

"I know it can be one of my frustrating traits."

Sarah smiled. "Not frustrating, sweetheart. It's you. It just took me time to learn that about you. Once I did, I understood. You spend so much time locked in here." She tapped a finger on my forehead. "Tell me about your talk with Peter."

"He was telling me how he resented the fact that even with Mom hating me and his ganging up on me, I was the stronger one. He wants to know how he can come out of this stronger than before. I told him the only way I did was by letting myself love and trust others, but I don't think that's the only reason." I rushed to add, "I don't mean you didn't—"

She kissed me on the lips. "Don't worry about that. Keep telling me the thoughts that have been keeping you up."

"Well..." My voice choked up, and my eyes teared. "I had to confront the old Lizzie. The scared Lizzie. The angry Lizzie. I had to realize that no matter how hard I pushed myself, I'd never be perfect, but in my own way I was weirdly perfect because I was me. I just needed to embrace me, which is odd to admit, because it sounds so selfish, and you know better than most how I can be self-involved."

"Everyone can be. And everyone has to be at certain points in their life. The danger is not being able to overcome being self-involved when you no longer have to insulate. You, my dear, stopped thinking only of yourself and let me in." She climbed on top of me, her weight on me easing the swirl of emotions inside.

I cupped each side of her face. "Thank God for that. I can't imagine life without you."

She stared deep into my eyes. "I feel the same about you."

I pulled her lips to mine, kissing her sweetly. "I adore you, Sarah. I'm the person I am today because of you."

"Not solely me, though. Or the twins. One of the things I admired most about you right from the start was your strength. It's always been there. I'm so happy and relieved you finally see it."

"I'm going to need to dig deep to get through this."

"True. And for all the other bumps in the road life can bring."

"First order of business, what's on the agenda for today?"

"Are you in a hurry to get out of bed?" Her eyes darkened with desire.

"I'm never in a hurry to get out of bed when you're on top of me. Just wanting to know what the schedule is, considering we have four kids under our roof."

Her eyes darkened further, but I couldn't place the new emotion. "Your turn. What's bugging you?"

"N-nothing," she stammered.

"So not convincing, Mrs. Petrie." I dragged out the pronunciation of *so*.

"It's nothing, really. There's enough stuff we're dealing with."

"You're always at the top of my concerns. Please talk to me," I implored.

"It's selfish, though." She looked away.

"I'm used to your selfishness," I cracked, swiftly following it up with a peck on her neck, admittedly taking advantage of her weak spot.

"It's just that… I finally got you to agree to having another child, and then all of this happened. Casey will only be here a few more days, but Demi…"

"You think we can't handle four kids?"

"How? The twins ran me ragged this year. Demi is a sweetheart and easygoing, but that doesn't mean it won't be work to provide all the love and attention to help her through this time. Right now, she has no idea what's going on, but kids grow up quickly." She heaved out a breath, all the while biting down on the right side of her lip. "I'm not getting younger. If I want to get pregnant—"

"The window of opportunity is closing."

Her ghost of a smile chilled me some. "You do have such a way with words sometimes."

"I didn't mean to sound so... however that sounded." I pulled her down onto my chest. "Let's not focus too much on the... issues... logistics... No, I can't seem to find the right word. What I'm saying is, let's focus on us. You've wanted another baby since before we probably had the twinks. Let's do it."

"What if we end up with twins or more this time?"

"You're starting to sound like me." I tightened my grip on her.

"I know. It's terrifying."

"Sounding like me or having more than one child?"

"Yes."

I laughed. "Don't ever change. I love that you can make me laugh even on the darkest of mornings."

She rested her chin on my bare chest. "It wouldn't be too selfish to make a doctor's appointment? Because I kinda already made one. Right before Christmas, on the twenty-second to be exact, you suggested we should chat about making an appointment, and when you left to run errands, I took the initiative. Just for a consultation. And then the Christmas from hell happened, followed by Peter's arrest, and I've been somewhat nervous to tell you about the appointment in January, which is much sooner than I anticipated since they just had a cancellation right before I called." She took a deep breath after getting all this out in one go.

I smiled. "I should have known."

"You aren't mad?"

"No, honey. We can't put our lives on hold just because

Peter's fell apart. Don't we already have what we need from the donor?"

"Yes."

"Can the appointment be changed from a consultation to the next step?"

"I don't know. I can call, but Demi. We can't turn our backs on her."

"I'm not suggesting that at all. Demi is very much a part of our lives." I pulled Sarah so she was now on her back and I could stare into her beautiful face. "And so is whoever is to come." I placed my hand on her stomach. "I want us to have a baby sooner rather than later."

"Again, I have to wonder how we'll manage."

"The same way we manage now."

"Are we managing now?"

"I think so. It's not always pretty, but there are three sleeping babies in the nursery who are happy and healthy."

"And two exhausted moms not wanting to get out of bed." She wrapped her arm around my midsection.

"Don't forget the nannies, grandmother, aunt, and uncles."

"You're forgetting another grandmother and two grandfathers."

"Two grandfathers?" I asked.

"Troy."

"Troy is their grandfather or will be when they officially tie the knot. Wow, I'm not sure if I made that connection. Is he okay with that?" It was difficult to reconcile the man who wasn't that much older than I was embracing the title.

"He seems to be. The man is weird like that."

"Men are."

She nodded. "Are you really serious about getting pregnant soon? You aren't just saying that because I've been badgering you about it for months?"

"You have been badgering me, but it's not why I'm saying it.

I wouldn't agree to kids unless I was one hundred percent sure."

"I'm not sure I'm one hundred percent sure." The determination in her expression didn't match the doubt in her statement.

I gazed into her dark eyes. "I don't believe that for a second. You've always had your heart set on three."

"It's scary to think about. Really."

"It should be. We're talking about being responsible for another human life. It's not something that should be taken lightly."

"What if we end up adopting Demi?"

"She'll never be lonely, and Ollie will have more siblings to protect. Something tells me she'll like that. Having a gang of Petries to boss around."

"Dear Lord. What have we unleashed on society? Think about this, Lizzie. If we have four kids, you may never be able to retire."

"Let's be honest. Odds are I wouldn't be able to anyway. I don't know how to stop."

"Does that include this? Am I supposed to be the rational one and say no more kids?"

"Is that what you want?"

She shook her head.

"If we need to hire a full-time nanny or two, so be it. Is Casey too young to work for a living?"

She chuckled. "I doubt we can afford Casey. Besides, she needs to be a kid for as long as she can be. Someone with her brains in such a tiny body—it'd be hard."

"I think the thought keeps Ethan up at night."

"It keeps me up sometimes. Have you heard from him?"

"Mostly texts to see how Casey's doing. You know about the FaceTime sessions with Casey since they use your phone. Everyone assumes I'm an idiot when it comes to technology." I ran a hand through her silky locks. "They've decided not to fly her out for the services." She started to speak, but I placed a finger on her lips. "Yes, I offered to pay for the flight. Lisa doesn't think it'd be good for Casey to attend the funeral. I'm not sure Ethan's been completely upfront about all the dynamics of their family's acceptance of Lisa and Ethan adopting a black child. Not to be Captain Obvious, but they're both from Mississippi."

"It's still hard to grasp Lisa lost her mother while all of this has been going on. Can you hold me until we absolutely have to get out of bed?" She raised her head to look at the clock on the bedside. "We may have thirty minutes until one of the kids wakes up."

I yanked the covers up over us. "Of course."

"Are you sure you aren't mad about the appointment?"

"Not at all. If I was the type to believe in signs, I'd say all of them are pointing to us having another."

"That's how I feel."

I kissed her forehead. "Close your eyes."

She mumbled, "You too, promise."

I did.

* * *

I STAGGERED INTO THE KITCHEN, feeling like I'd been riding my bike for days, when in fact I'd only just woken a few minutes earlier to realize while I'd slept, Sarah had been on kid patrol all on her own. "I'm so sorry. Why didn't you wake me?"

"Wow, you look like sh—" Maddie stopped herself due to little ears and settled on, "Shiitake."

"Interesting recovery," I said.

Sarah, with Demi on her hip, filled the teakettle. "I didn't wake you because you needed sleep. Maddie was here, and we managed the kids. Gabe just left for work. Casey is hosting one of her famous tea parties." She jerked her head to Casey and the twins sitting at the table in the family room. "And, Little Miss Demi is enjoying a cuddle." Sarah tickled Demi's side, causing her to giggle.

"Do you know who really needs a cuddle?" I held out my arms. "Come here, baby girl. I need some magical baby power."

"Whose car should we take today?" Maddie asked Sarah.

"Where are we going?" I snuggled Demi's head under my chin.

"The kids have been invited to a party. Since Maddie cancelled her ski trip, she's volunteered to go with me in your place." Sarah put a tea bag into my *I'd rather be studying history* mug.

"Am I watching Demi?"

"Nah. We'll bring her."

I furrowed my brow. "Why can't I go?"

Sarah and Maddie shared a look that seemed to convey, *Did I hear that right?*

Maddie took the bait. "You want to go to a party for toddlers and elementary school-age kids."

"Are you going to two parties?"

"Kinda but at the same place."

I glanced down into Demi's blue eyes. It was like staring into my brother's eyes so many years ago, but Demi's were much kinder. "Are you following this?"

She smiled.

"The twins have music lessons with Mia, the daughter of Claire and JJ Cavendish. Claire's son, Ian, is in Casey's dance glass. Claire and JJ are having two groups over for a holiday bash."

"Claire's the publisher of the local paper. I'd love to talk to her about some of her articles. Every news organization should have a historian on staff."

Sarah goggled at me, nearly spilling hot water all over the

kitchen island. "Are you going to ask Claire for a job to fill the spare time you don't have?"

"Not at all. It might be a good program to have some history grad students work with the paper. Some may want to beef up their résumés."

Sarah tapered one eye, squeezing a dollop of honey into my tea, our latest compromise on sweetener since she was against sugar. "Like an internship?"

"Yeah. I mean, I wouldn't broach the topic at the party, but it would be helpful to meet her in a social setting—" I flicked one hand in the air.

"To prepare her for the Lizzie train wreck?" Maddie mocked.

"That was lame. Even for you."

"Oh snap! Lizzie's bringing her snark A-game. I like it." She jabbed a finger into my free shoulder and then pretended to gobble Demi's tiny fist.

"I've been going easy on you all these years. No longer."

Maddie laughed, heading to the tea party, taking a seat between Fred and Casey.

"Coward," I muttered after her.

Sarah took Demi from my arms. "Enjoy your tea, and then hop in the shower. We're leaving in an hour or so."

"Do you think it's a good idea?"

"We need to stop at the store to buy more clothes for Demi. And, with the post-Christmas sales, we might as well get some clothes for the twins. They seem to grow every day."

I smiled. "Always finding an excuse to shop, but I meant the internship. Getting students some real-world experience."

"Oh, that. Yes. Don't forget JJ is also in the media business. Her website is becoming the next big thing."

"I hadn't thought of that." I smothered my jaw with my palm, tapping my index finger right under my eye.

"Just be careful, Lizzie. Both are in the media, and your brother just became a big story. Watch your back."

"Are you serious? Who's going to care about me? Peter, I understand, but I'm just his sister." I gestured to my history mug, bathrobe, and slippers. "I'm not exciting."

Sarah regarded me in the way she did when she thought I was being extremely naïve. "For someone who reads the *New York Times* every day, you'd think you'd know some of the first sources reporters chase for developing stories is interviewing friends and family of the subject of the news."

"Peter isn't the news," I defended.

"What is he, then?"

"My brother."

CHAPTER FOUR

Ethan's number flashed across my phone. Excusing myself so Casey wouldn't overhear me, I stepped into the library and closed the door. "Hey."

"Hey." He sounded like he had one foot in the grave.

"I'd ask how you're doing, but I can tell from your voice it's been rough. How can I help?"

"Take care of Casey."

"Who? Oh, shoot. We forgot all about her." I snapped my fingers near the phone in hopes he could hear it on his end.

He chuckled. "Stand-up isn't in your future."

"Not so sure about that. My students think I'm a riot." I rushed on to avoid a snarky comment. "How's Lisa doing?"

"She's hanging in. It's amazing how resilient she is."

"Moms are. We have super powers."

"I believe you. I'm flying back tomorrow, hopefully. There's a storm here, so we'll see. Lisa's staying to help her dad adjust, if that's possible. Don't tell Casey I may be back. I want to surprise her."

"Roger that. Do you want to stay here for the night? We aren't doing much for New Year's, but we'll have food and drinks. Casey packed you a bag just on the off chance you wanted to move in with us."

"Of course, she wants that. You have Netflix, and I had to cancel ours." It was difficult to determine if he was laughing. "Is it safe to stay there? Your texts haven't mentioned anything to worry about, but…?"

I glanced around my library, as if there were marauding Petries lurking. "I think so, why?"

"I heard about Peter's arrest on the news. I didn't want to ask you via text since that seemed kinda cold, but it's been crazy here and I'm hardly ever alone to call you for the dirt."

"Not sure I know more than you."

"How are you doing? Has the press descended upon you yet?"

"Nope. Rest assured, if they had, I would have made arrangements to get the kids away from it all. I don't suggest going to his house, though. That's one of the reasons Demi is still with us." The others included Tie missing in action and Peter not being single dad material. "Oh, we brought your cat over here. She seemed quite lonely. Surprisingly, she adores Hank, and my little bugger has finally taken to her."

"Don't let her get pregnant." His voice was stern.

"Is that possible? She's not fixed?"

"Is Hank?" He attempted to sound alarmed, but I detected a giggle.

"Yes. Oh, forget I said anything." Given he and Lisa had been fighting about expanding their family, I failed to mention I had the baby-making process in the forefront of my mind.

"Lesbians. Honestly, you need to study the reproductive process. But, don't fret. Minnie's fixed as well." He chuckled. "Sorry, no one here seems to be in the mood for my weird sense of humor."

"I've always appreciated it, well at least eighty-seven percent of the time. Besides, my idiocy does have some benefits during these spells. Do you want me to pick you up from the airport?"

"Nah. I know you two have your hands full with everything. I've scheduled a shuttle. I should be there around four in the afternoon. Lizzie…"

"Yes?" I prodded with a gentle voice.

"Thanks again for everything. You saved my bacon."

"Are you and Lisa okay?"

"We're talking like adults. That's a good sign. Oh, hey, I've got to go."

"See you tomorrow. I promise not to spill the beans. Not intentionally at least."

He laughed, and then there was dead air.

Sarah slipped into the library. "Everything okay?"

"We're not supposed to tell Casey, but Ethan's coming home tomorrow."

"Not Lisa?"

"She's staying with her dad for a bit." I pulled Sarah into my arms, one hand cradling the back of her head. "Don't die ever, please."

She held me tightly, her jasmine perfume enveloping me like a security blanket. "Oh, sweetheart. You aren't getting rid of me that easily."

"Thank goodness for that. Ollie scares me a bit."

Sarah laughed. "She has a mind of her own. Fingers crossed she uses her powers for good. Time will tell." She broke away. "How are Ethan and Lisa?"

"Talking."

"Talking is good."

"I've never been fond of it myself."

Sarah drilled her chocolate eyes into my blues. "I remember. Do you remember the trouble you caused by not opening up?"

"I don't cause trouble anymore. You won't let me." I captured her lips to silence whatever was about to fly out of her mouth. "I was serious earlier. I don't know what I would do if anything happened to you. And, I didn't think this was a possibility, but given recent events, don't get arrested."

"Hey now, it's not my family that has the criminal element."

"Low blow, Mrs. Petrie, considering you're the one who encouraged me to reconnect with my blood relations."

Sarah's grin was the one she wore when I was being ridiculous. "Yes, it's all my fault. Don't forget one good thing may come out of all of this."

"Uh, possibly raising four kids?"

"Not what I had in mind, but that's also something good." Her fingers held onto the locket I gave her for Christmas.

"What did you mean, then?"

"Your brother may become a better man."

"Nothing seems to dent your belief in people."

"Not true. I have zero hopes for Tie. Or desire to help her see the error of her ways. But Peter, he..." She placed a finger on my lips. "Don't take this the wrong way, but he reminds me of you."

"How could I take that the wrong way? Being compared to a man hiding in his house because the press wants a winning photo before he heads off to the slammer?"

"Glad that went over as well as expected. Come on. Let's get the kiddos ready for shopping and then the party. Casey wants to cash in on the microscope you promised her on Christmas Eve. And, apparently, Ethan asked for all of the Harry Potter books for her. Am I correct in understanding no one wanted to go caroling, so you bribed every last one?"

I peered into her eyes to see if I was in trouble. Not detecting a clue either way, I opted for honesty. "Yes, aside from Troy. In good news, I owe you, your mom, and Helen a massage—not by me. Or, that's not what I agreed to." I cringed, thinking of rubbing—nope. *Don't go there*. I pressed on, "At the salon."

"You really are amazing and so very sweet."

"It's good you're finally seeing this."

"I've known for some time." Sarah rubbed her hands together. "Given everything, I'm really looking forward to my treat. Is it just massages or a full spa treatment?"

I playfully groaned. "Jesus, I can't win in this family. Is Maddie wanting to cash in on her panorama lens soon?"

"She added it to the *family's* online wish list, but given we're going to Best Buy, there's a chance she'll hit you up today. At least she's sticking with this hobby."

"Vultures. Every last one of you." I wrapped my arms around Sarah again. "I wouldn't change any of you, but don't tell the rest. They already have my number. I don't need them to figure out how much they can get from me."

"Oh, I think you get what you want in return."

"Which is?"

"Love."

"Was it always for sale?"

She rolled her eyes but ended up laughing.

* * *

SARAH PUSHED the twins in their stroller, and Maddie guided Demi onto the sidewalk.

"How did armies in World War Two manage? It took us ten minutes in the parking lot to get our crew ready," I said to no one in particular, because as soon as the glass doors of Best Buy glided open, Maddie, with Demi, took off like a shot to the camera section. Sarah headed for the phone section, leaving me with the twins.

"The microscopes are this way." Casey placed a hand on the stroller.

There were only a few options. "What do you plan to do with a microscope anyway?"

"Find a cure for cancer."

"Oh," I said, part of me believing that if anyone could, it would be Casey. "Do you know which one you want?"

She pressed her lips together, shuffling her feet.

"I see." I looked over the options. "I'm guessing this one." The most expensive option had an LCD and digital camera for images and video. "Remember me when you become a famous scientist." I patted the top of her head.

Her eyes tripled in size when she realized I wasn't going to put up a fight for the cheaper version. "Are you for real?"

"Can you tell your father there was a fantastic sale or that we won it in a raffle?"

"That wouldn't be true, though."

I loved her dedication to honesty even if Ethan was going to rip off my head and feed it to the cats. "Right. Let's go get the crew before they find... things."

Of course, by the time I corralled Maddie and Sarah at the register, they had a stack of items.

"An Apple Watch?" I posed to Sarah. "You want them to track your every move?"

She rolled her eyes. "They already do, and if it'll help me lose weight after..." She didn't finish the thought, but I knew she meant after having another child. "And before you say anything, I ordered a rowing machine for the gym."

"We don't have a gym."

"We do now. Or we will once I'm done with the basement."

Maddie clutched Sarah's shoulder. "We should get a mountain climbing machine. To train for climbing one."

"Neither of you hike!" Even though my voice crescendoed, I also knew it was useless to argue with these two. Once an idea took root, it was impossible to dislodge it. "That's the other problem with New Year's—resolutions both of you will forget by the third week, if that long." I waggled a finger at Sarah and Maddie.

Maddie took Casey's hand. "Come on. You're too young to learn this side of marriage. By the way, I found the lens I wanted, and it's one hundred dollars cheaper than the one I found online. You're welcome." With that, she left with Casey and Demi.

I turned to Sarah. "I want a spin bike in this so-called gym." If you can't beat them, join them.

"Yes, dear." She kissed my cheek. "Can you manage this? I'll track down Maddie and get everyone loaded into the car so we're not too late for the party."

"Sure. Give me your credit card."

"We have joint accounts, wiseass. I love you for trying, though."

I got into line, behind two husbands, all of us with dazed looks.

One, with a black puffy jacket, said, "'Tis the season."

"For greedy family members?" I asked.

Another man flipped around, chuckling. "Tell me about it. Be glad you don't have teenagers yet. That's when it gets really expensive." He eyed the microscope. "I have two of those in the basement." He inspected the box more closely. "Wow! They've really improved. I may like this one."

"Are you a scientist?"

"Plumber. You wouldn't believe the stuff I see."

I tried to control my revulsion, but I feared my face scrunched.

"What about you? What do you do?" he asked.

"History professor."

His face puckered.

"Let me guess. You hated history in school?"

He nodded.

The guy in the puffy jacket volunteered he was a civil engineer.

There seemed to be a holdup at the register, and the three

of us continued our conversation. By the time I returned to the car, everyone was seated and Sarah had loaded a video for the kids, all of them fully engrossed, aside from Demi, who dozed in her seat.

"What took so long?" Sarah flipped the visor back into place, her lips shiny with a fresh coat of red.

"Price check or something. I made some friends."

Sarah laughed but stopped. "Really?"

"A plumber and civil engineer."

Maddie popped her head between the seats. "That's not the way any jokes start. Usually, it's a rabbi—"

Sarah flashed the universal *stop right there* sign. "Little ears." Her attention back on me, she asked, "Do they have names?"

"Ralph and John."

She smiled. "You're growing up right before my eyes."

"Careful, I can actually see smart-ass smoke coming out of your ears."

"Little ears," Maddie chided. "Let's get this on the road. I'm dying to meet The Miracle Girl."

"Please don't embarrass me." I backed out of the parking spot.

"Yeah, I'm the one who embarrasses us in public." Maddie patted my shoulder and settled into her seat.

Sarah shook her head, failing to cover a guilty smile.

"Careful, or I'll take back your watch."

She gave me her full attention. "No, you won't. You're not as curmudgeonly as you aspire to be."

"Is that a challenge?"

She groaned. "Let me save you time. That won't impress me. Not one bit."

"Now you tell me. All the wasted effort."

CHAPTER FIVE

I parked the SUV at the end of the drive, whistling. "Why don't we live outside city limits like this?" My eyes scanned the snowdrifts. "Not a house in sight. My idea of heaven."

"Not everyone craves social isolation." Sarah unbuckled her seat belt, a look of glee in her eyes. "Let's get this party started."

"Prepping for D-Day, part two," I muttered, heading to the back of the vehicle to free the twins.

Maddie helped Casey out and then gathered Demi in her arms. "You ready for sugar overload, Demi?"

"I am," Casey crowed, darting her arms in the crisp air. "I'm parent-free."

The thought stilled my heart. What would it be like inside, once the sugar high set in? A flaw in my plans to have a private chat with Claire.

"I don't know about that, Casey. We can always video your mom and dad if you don't listen," Sarah threatened, although her soft shoulders and smile didn't appear all that intimidating.

"They have too much on their plates with Grandma being

sick. You wouldn't dare. Ian!" She waved a hand and ran toward a boy roughly her own age who stood in the open doorway.

"Let's hope nothing ever happens to Ethan and Lisa," Sarah whispered into my ear. "She's smarter than both of us put together."

"Did you know her microscope has an LCD and digital camera? I'd never be able to figure it out. I'm pretty sure she'll actually use it for some scientific miracle." She had scientific detachment down given her lack of concern for her grandmother. Although, how many kids factored in death when dealing with sickness? Casey was brilliant, but also still a child in so many ways. I reached for Freddie's hand. "Careful, little man. Lots of ice." Freddie cautiously took a step, while Ollie zoomed past, pulling Sarah along, who gripped a cheese and cracker basket for the hosts.

Inside, after wrangling snow boots off the toddlers, who immediately sought out the other kids their age, I took in the scene. Kids. Parents. Christmas tree. A table set up with snacks and drinks. "Which one is Claire?" I asked Sarah.

She scanned the people. "At the punch bowl. Her wife is next to her."

I blinked. "Is her wife a little person?"

"She's over five feet."

I mentally measured her. "Not by much."

Sarah placed a hand on each of my shoulders. "Please don't ask her if she's a little person. Do I need to have Casey explain to you why that would be bad? Especially since you plan to hit on her wife—*hit up*, I mean."

I chuckled. "You have zero faith in me. I made friends earlier when left alone. Why do I have to keep pointing this out? But now that I think about it..." I tapped my chin. "Hearing Casey explain it would be humorous. I've always thought you should write a book for the clueless, but maybe

Casey might be the better option. Gives you more time to pen children's stories."

"Not that I've had much time for that." Sarah placed a hand on her belly as if reconciling her lack of writing time for her desire to have another baby.

Maddie added, "Maybe we can start a podcast with Casey explaining things to the Clueless One."

"Who?" I asked.

Maddie and Sarah exchanged an *oh boy* look before Maddie said, "*You*, Lizzie. You really do worry me sometimes." She whirled around to Sarah. "Please, don't let anything happen to yourself, because I can't take on Lizzie. I would have to find her a home. Do they have facilities with staff to handle the likes of Lizzie?"

"Or for the likes of Maddie? I'm not the one who's ex was arrested and who's engaged to the ex's stepbrother." I stuck out my tongue.

"Hello," the little person—er, JJ Cavendish said.

"Oh, hi," I shook her hand. "Lovely home."

"Thanks. We haven't quite mastered Sarah's zeal for decorations."

I slanted my head. "You've been to my house?"

"Uh, no. Haven't had the pleasure, but I saw pictures online."

"Of my house?"

JJ, Maddie, and Sarah gawked at me as if I really were the Clueless One.

Finally, Sarah explained, "Maddie snapped photos and submitted them for a local contest. I'm pretty sure I mentioned it."

"Oh, maybe." I had no recollection, which wasn't unusual since it was hard to keep up with Sarah and Maddie. "With Peter's arrest and taking care of four kids, I can't remember much these days."

Sarah gave me her *zip it* expression, casually jerking her head to JJ.

Maybe due to her vantage point of peering up at everyone, JJ picked up on it immediately. "No worries. We're all friends today, and I'm not on the clock. You're safe until January second."

"Because that's when the contest ends?"

JJ laughed. "I like you. Not many appreciate the finer art of snark. Can I get any of you a drink?"

"I'm Maddie. Thanks for allowing me to crash your party." She stepped in front of me.

"The more the merrier." JJ's smile seemed sincere.

"I'm a huge fan of your show," Maddie gushed and took the basket from Sarah before handing it to JJ. "We brought you a gift."

JJ shifted on her feet. "Thanks. I've seen you at some of Mia's music lessons. Which rug rat is yours?"

Maddie pointed out Demi. "I'm in charge of that one today, and I'm the twins' aunt."

JJ observed Demi, clearly the tiniest on the floor with other babies ranging from twelve months to two years, rattling maracas.

"Isn't that Peter's favorite instrument?" I asked Sarah.

Again, she gave me her *stop talking* look.

For years, I never mentioned my brother's name, but today, standing in the home of two media people, I couldn't stop. "Maybe I should go for a walk," I whispered in Sarah's ear. "I doubt any foxes would give two shits about Peter."

She seemed to mull over the choice but didn't respond to me. "I'd love some mom juice if you've got any."

"Red or white?" JJ asked.

"Red."

JJ turned to me. "Lizzie?"

"I'm driving. Water?"

"I'm sure we can do better than tap water. Sparkling?"

I nodded.

JJ motioned for Maddie to place her order.

"Red."

"Two reds and fancy water for the driver." JJ departed for the kitchen.

Maddie whacked the back of my head. "What's wrong with you?"

"Besides the sudden headache?"

She flung her eyes to the ceiling. "If I wanted to do serious brain damage, I could. That is, if you had a brain."

"Why are you threatening me?" I rubbed the back of my head. "Go mingle or something. Making me nervous will only cause my diarrhea of the mouth to become much worse."

Sarah shoved Maddie in JJ's direction. "She's right. Go get our drinks, and cut Lizzie off from the source."

When alone with Sarah, I whispered in her ear, "This is why you didn't plan on bringing me today."

"Partly."

"What's the other part?"

"You aren't really the parent that takes the kids to parties." Her matter-of-fact tone made it clear she wasn't teasing.

And it stung.

Sarah's expression softened. "I know it's hard with your work schedule."

I puffed out my cheeks.

JJ thrust a glass into my hand. "Everything okay?"

So much for Maddie's attempt to keep JJ from me. "Apparently, I'm the opposite of a helicopter parent." The words tumbled out of my mouth.

JJ bobbed her head. "I understand. Claire's hidden all my electronics so I can't answer messages during the party. Speak of the devil."

"Hi," the woman said.

"Claire, this is Lizzie. Be nice. Sarah just reamed her for"—JJ appraised my hangdog expression—"working too much, I'm guessing."

"You make me sound terrible. I just said I'm usually the one who takes the kids to parties." Sarah accepted the wineglass from Maddie.

"It's true. Besides the twins' party, I haven't been to any. I need to do better. Maybe that'll be my New Year's resolution. Be a better parent."

"You're a wonderful parent." Sarah kissed my cheek, with a look in her eye that she'd make up for the comment later.

"JJ beats herself up as well," Claire said with a kind smile.

Not letting go, I added, "I would like to note you said I don't go to birthday parties."

"You hate people." Sarah again spoke the plain truth.

I could feel my cheeks burn. "That's not entirely true. It's just from my studies and my fa—" I stopped myself from mentioning my family again. "Uh, people can be terrible."

"Tell me about it." JJ raised her water in a cheers fashion.

I clinked my glass against hers. "If you ever want to know how terrible, I can tell you all about the Nazis."

Sarah shook her head. "Oh, no. It's a holiday party for children. No talk about Nazis. Not today. Not until your first day of classes, which isn't for a couple more weeks." She shook a teacher-like finger at me, her smile quite becoming.

"Actually, I'd like to pick your brain about something." JJ hooked her arm through mine. "Care for a bit of fresh air?"

"That's code for JJ is stressed and needs a cigarette," Claire teased.

We left via the front door, JJ guiding me around to the back of the house, along a shoveled path. She fished a pack of smokes out of her cardigan, offering me one.

"No, thanks. Sarah's been on a health kick since before she got pregnant."

"Was it hard quitting?" She shook the pack, as if saying the word *cigarette* made her feel guilty.

"Oh, I've only smoked once and got enough hell for that." Feeling like an ass, I rambled, "Actually, she didn't yell at me much. She was more surprised than anything. She used to smoke. Not a lot, but..." I shrugged, praying I could get my brain to kick in and stop me from speaking for the rest of the afternoon.

"I wish I could say the same, but I have an addictive personality." Her laugh clued me in she wasn't kidding at all.

"Is that why they call you The Miracle Girl?"

"Kinda sorta. I'm starting to like you even more if you haven't read my memoir. I hate when people want to talk about it." She shook her cigarette, ash falling to the ground.

I chuckled. "No one reads my books either." It hit me what I'd implied. "I don't mean no one has read yours. I was just—"

She waved me off. "I wish no one read it."

"Why'd you write it, then?"

JJ rubbed her thumb along her fingertips, indicating money. "Isn't that why any of us does anything?"

"I guess so. Not a lot of money in history, though."

She sucked on her cigarette. "You have the look of someone with passion. Is that why you study history?"

"It does get my blood going."

"You teach at the university, right." It wasn't a question.

"CSU, yes." I got the feeling she knew more about me than I would have liked. Was she fishing because of Peter? If she was, she was taking the long route.

"I won't beat around the bush, because who has time for that these days? After Sarah told me a few weeks ago what you studied, I was curious and read your books. I want you to write articles about the rise of Nazism for *Matthews Daily Dish*. I'm not asking you to compare any modern politicians to their rise, because I don't think that's helpful to the conversation. Given all the pundits on TV, I may be in the minority. I do, though, think readers should be informed how authoritarian regimes in the past have captured total control. And, we could always use a historian on our broadcasts. I'm thinking of a Sunday morning show we're cooking up. Ease you into the role and see if it's a good fit. What do you say?"

I burst into laughter.

She cocked her head. "What's so funny?"

"I came here to ask your wife to allow some of my students to intern at the paper, and here you are, hitting me up to write for you."

"Intern?" JJ furrowed her brow.

"Historians are great fact-checkers."

"Ah. Now, I'm following. Claire's always looking for a way to give back to the local community."

"And, you're always looking for a way to support the family. I think our wives are very similar." I added, "We are, too."

"True. I'd be lost without Claire." She put out her cigarette with the snow. "Give my proposal some thought, and I'll be in touch soon. I know our wives have exchanged contact details, which is a good thing, because I don't even have a pen and paper." JJ chuckled but didn't seem too put out to have family time, even if she had just offered me a job. "We better get back to the party before Claire sends the posse out."

Inside, the kids were singing "Santa Claus Is Coming to Town." Freddie banged on the drums. Ollie laughed. Casey and Ian, along with three other kids their age I didn't know, danced. Demi, in Sarah's arms, was wide-eyed, and I wondered if she'd ever had the opportunity to attend classes or any lessons with kids her age. I knew she had a nanny, but I didn't know much about Demi's socialization and that worried me.

JJ grinned at me.

"This is the stuff I hate missing," I confessed.

She reached up and placed a hand on my shoulder. "Me too, Lizzie. Me too."

I sidled up next to Sarah, kissing her cheek and then taking Demi into my arms. "You won't believe what just happened," I said.

"The Easter Bunny arrived?"

I rolled my eyes. "Something like that."

She shoved my shoulder. "What?"

"JJ offered me a job. Writing articles and possibly making TV appearances."

"No, seriously. What happened?"

"I just told you."

"You? On television?"

"Does that sound preposterous?" I attempted to mask my hurt feelings.

"What? No, I just never contemplated it. That's all." With her upraised palms, she gestured she meant no offense.

"It could be a good thing for the department. Not to mention my career."

"Lizzie!" Casey rushed toward me. "Can Ian sleepover?"

"Uh…?" I whispered in Sarah's ear, "Do boys and girls have sleepovers?"

Sarah's eyes wandered to our twins. "I haven't considered that possibility, yet at Casey's age…"

Casey had busted us in the past about our take on gender identity. Sarah didn't want to force boy or girl things on our children, but a sleepover? How would that factor in when the time arose?

"We'll have to talk to your parents, Casey, before making any plans." Sarah settled on the logical answer, while I stood dumbfounded.

Casey accepted this, zipped back to Ian's side, and continued dancing, the two of them chatting up a storm.

"I didn't know you could dance to Christmas carols," I

commented.

Sarah's eyes were on Ian. "He seems like a sweetheart."

I studied the boy. "He does. Luckily, though, Ethan will be back tomorrow and he can deal with this problem. But it does raise the issue what to do when the twins have friends over."

"Clearly, we need a bigger house. With well-defined areas for Fred and his guys and Ollie and hers. We can patrol the borders like lions."

"I seriously hope you're joking."

"Which part? Patrolling or a bigger house?"

"All of the above."

"Considering how quickly our family is growing, we may have to move to a bigger place. Or turn your library into a bedroom."

I smothered my chest. "You wound me. Why don't we convert the basement into bedrooms instead of a gym?"

"Tell you what. Our next house, I'll ensure you get an even larger library. You just need to triple your income. How many TV shows can you sign up for?" She waggled her brows.

"Says the woman who so recently claimed I don't do enough stuff with the kids. Besides, you love our house. No way would you ever move."

"True, but I do foresee some home projects on the horizon to accommodate the changes, and I don't want to go back to work, meaning the burden falls onto you."

"What about your writing? Get cracking on that."

"You too, dear. Get your novel published. I challenge you." Her eyes pierced mine.

"You're terrible."

"Because I know you can't turn down a challenge?"

"Yes." I leaned closer. "And your chest is heaving. You aren't playing fair."

"I want to win, Lizzie. Always."

I tossed my head back, laughing. "When do you ever lose?"

CHAPTER SIX

I stared at the laptop screen, not believing the email I'd just read.

Sarah, in her pajamas, strutted into the library and stopped in her tracks, nearly spilling her tea. "Everything okay?"

"Wh-what? Oh, yeah. JJ is serious. That's all."

Somewhat relieved, Sarah placed her tea down and crashed on the couch facing my desk, her arms out. "Come here. Tell me about it."

I shut my laptop but didn't rise right away. Sarah, used to my processing ways, didn't press. "It's just when we talked earlier today, I thought she was blowing smoke. You know, shooting from the hip to make me feel more welcome in her home."

"Yes, that's how I welcome guests. Would you like something to drink? And, how about making TV appearances for my company?" She laughed, blunting her barb.

"I know, I know. It would be an odd thing to say to someone unless you were sorta serious. But, I was watching a clip she sent. Three experts yelling at each other. Do people really like to watch that? No one was making sense. Just shouting to be heard."

"The people who like those shows do, I suppose, or they wouldn't be produced. You've watched enough of CNN to know that."

"I like to have it on mute and read the news ticker."

Sarah sipped her tea. "Are you considering it?"

"The money might be nice." I fiddled with a pen, hitting it against my thigh.

Sarah gazed at me with a curious expression. "You do know that's the last reason why I would want you to take on any job."

"And yet, it's one of the main reasons most people accept jobs. It's not like teaching is the highest paid job available."

"It's not like we're poor, either."

"True." I dropped the pen onto my desk, steepled my fingers, and rested my chin on them. "It would be a challenge. Get me out of my comfort zone."

"How different is it from the panels you attend? Academics love to argue."

"It's in our DNA." Still resting my chin on the tips of my thumbs, I tapped my index fingers against my bottom lip.

Sarah, shaking her head, smiled. "You're really considering this as a challenge, aren't you? If JJ actually offers you the job, you might as well say yes just to prove you can do it. I know that look in your eye."

"Shouldn't we discuss it further, though? Like how this will impact you? I'll be working more, maybe. Although, I'm fairly certain I can record in the studio on campus, and JJ mentioned the segments would be prerecorded on Fridays, a day I'm already at CSU. But there's the JJ angle."

With her eyebrows arched, she asked, "Which is what?"

"Getting an inside track to Peter. Even out in Mississippi, Ethan's heard about Peter's arrest."

"It was on the national news. A finance guy being pulled out of bed while celebrating the holidays with his sister is bound to make headlines. It seems like an extremely elaborate con for JJ to offer you a job and then try to wheedle snippets from you about your brother, who won't be in the headlines that much longer. Something else will happen to capture America's interest. A potato in the shape of SpongeBob, perhaps. A sound that half the population thinks sounds like looney and the other half tooney."

I leaned back into my seat. "Are you saying no matter what I say or do on a show, it won't really have consequences because of the ridiculousness of some news?"

"Oh, not at all. People have been fired for saying the wrong thing on TV or social media. Think Megyn Kelly."

"Not sure I'd ever advocate for blackface. I'm not really the one who advocates for anything, except to learn things. Read books. Think."

Sarah laughed. "True. On occasion, you prefer arguing even when you know you're in the wrong. It can be cute, sometimes, the lengths you go to not see the obvious."

"Am I missing anything at the moment? That's obvious?"

Her brow crinkled. "Not that I can think of."

"Too bad. I thought you came in here to seduce me."

Sarah glanced down at her navy long sleeve Grinch shirt that asked if it was too late to be good and matching pants with neon-green grinch heads with the words *Define naughty*. "You have strange fantasies."

I flicked the pages in one of the open books on my desk. "Doesn't the Grinch turn everyone on?"

"That would be a perfect example of something to never say on camera."

My smile fell. "You don't think I can do it, do you?"

Sarah lurched up, placing her mug down on the coffee table. "I never said or implied such a thing. I happen to know when you set your mind to something, you do it. And you do it well.

I've seen you in action at a history conference. You'll be in your element."

"But?" I motioned for her to get out whatever she was holding back.

"It's just not something you've ever mentioned being interested in. I mean, when I found out about your novel, that took me by total surprise, but it wasn't entirely out of left field, either, given the historical angle."

"You didn't handle the novel news all that well."

"That's not entirely—" She stopped her rebuttal. "Okay, you're right. I didn't. That was a bad night."

I cupped my ear. "Can you repeat the important part of your statement?"

"I didn't handle the news well," she said with a sheepish smile.

I rose from my desk chair and made my way over to her. "That wasn't the part I wanted to hear again."

"It's the only part I plan on repeating."

"Is that a fact?" I took a seat next to her, nuzzling my nose into her neck. "What if I say pretty please?" I licked her earlobe.

Her breath hitched. "Don't stop there."

"With a cherry on top," I whispered into her ear.

"I meant the licking part."

"I know, but you aren't giving in to me, so why should I give in to you?" I licked her lobe again, easing my tongue into her ear. "Why are you being so stubborn when we both want the same thing?"

"I want to admit you were right?"

"You just did." I peppered her neck with kisses.

"You tricked me."

"Perhaps. I'm working on my TV skills. Getting an opponent to see things my way."

She released a full-throated laugh. "Do you plan on telling your television audience how you honed your debating skills?"

"By seducing my hot wife? I'm trying to picture a conversation where that would come up."

"Put your mind to it, and you'll find a way."

"A terrible way to waste brain power. I've been using too much of it these days. I want to disappear into you."

"You really do employ the strangest seduction techniques."

"Shut up and kiss me."

Sarah swiveled her neck, planting her soft lips onto mine.

The kiss started off slow. Deliciously so. Neither wanting to ruin the moment after the frantic days of holiday prep and then the Petrie fallout.

I threaded my fingers through her hair. "God, I need you, Sarah. I always need you."

She stared into my eyes. "I remember a time when that thought scared the bejesus out of you."

"I do as well. I was an idiot who didn't know how much in love I was with you. Now, the thought of losing you sends my mind spinning."

"I know you have abandonment issues, given your upbringing, but Lizzie, I'm not going anywhere. Your crazy is just what I need."

"You promise, no matter what happens? I have a feeling things are going to get much worse before we see the light at the end of the tunnel. How can I avoid ending up in divorce court like Peter?"

"Just be you."

"Maybe you misunderstood. I don't want to lose you."

Her smile was sweet, with a hint of sadness. "You aren't the old Lizzie anymore. The one who shuns human contact and emotions. You've grown into an amazing wife, mother, daughter, sibling, and friend. When I met you, I knew you were special—no, not special ed, so don't crack that joke like you do. I just didn't know how incredible you'd become."

I rested my forehead against hers.

"But, if you don't take me upstairs right now and make love to me, you'll be in trouble." Her eyes glistened with desire.

"And you say *my* seduction techniques need work? Threats? Really?"

"Do I need to get the whip and handcuffs out?"

"Oooh, so not scared." I jumped to my feet, offering her my hand. "Let's go fuck."

Sarah shook her head but allowed me to help her off the couch. I took advantage of the situation by pulling her into me and kissing her hard. "Last one naked and in bed has to feed the kids in the morning."

"A story we'll never tell the kids. Or anyone. Don't share it on TV, either. On your mark. Get set." She ran before saying *go*.

"Cheaters will be thoroughly punished," I called out.

"Counting on that," she said, not breaking her stride on the stairs, taking two at a time.

"Not sure you need a home gym. Lugging kiddos around seems to be working for you." I eyed the outline of her ass cheeks. "The view is doing wonders for my libido."

"Nice attempt at distracting me." She cleared our bedroom door, yanked off her top, and cast it onto the floor.

I stilled her hands before she could strip off her bottoms. "Just give me a moment to appreciate these." I kissed the outer edge of her areola.

"Do you concede that I won and you're feeding the kids in the morning?"

"Yes. Now shut up and let me focus." I nudged the door closed, not wanting any intruders, although the kids were spent from the party and were snoozing in their beds.

"Yes, ma'am."

I gently shoved Sarah onto the bed, allowing her to

scramble up closer to the pillows, making room for me to climb on top, still clothed. "Now, where was I?"

Sarah eyed her right nipple.

I took her left into my mouth.

She laughed. "That works as well."

With her nub in my mouth, I said, "You can't stay quiet, can you?"

"I thought you liked it when I was loud in bed."

I bit down on her nipple.

She groaned.

"Those are the sounds I want," I said, biting it again, eliciting another satisfying groan.

My hand trailed down her stomach, slipping under the band of her pajamas, enjoying the feel of her pubic hair.

"It's funny how much you love that considering you usually shave all of yours."

"I'm a conundrum; that's for sure. And, you're right, I love the way it feels." My hand made its way slowly back up her torso, tweaking her nipple, before pulling her head to mine for a slow burn kiss, our tongues enjoying the pre-fuck dance. I moaned into her mouth, "You feel so incredible."

Sarah tried to remove my sweater and shirt, giving up and opting to use her eyes to implore me to strip.

I did, of course.

There wasn't anything else on the planet that felt this incredible. Her skin on mine. The healing power. The sensuality. The way it brought the inner animal out to play.

And hers.

She started to ride my hip.

Both of us breathed heavier.

Our kissing reached the *fuck me* stage.

I relished it for a few more minutes before I made the next move, shedding her bottoms and then mine. I needed all of me on her. To possess her and vice versa in the only way lovers could. This was the facet of marriage I never truly understood until we'd made love on our wedding night. Staking my permanent claim. It hadn't been the first time we'd made love, but it had been the first time after signing a document proclaiming she was the only person I'd be with for the rest of my life.

Every time since then reminded me of that night.

The security in knowing we were made for each other.

The completeness in my life.

And hers.

Experts may disagree about believing a partner completes you, thinking it only fitting in rom-coms.

They'd never known Sarah.

How her capacity to love all of me, including my quirks, allowed me to love myself. Without that, I wouldn't be a wife. Mother. Daughter. Sibling. Teacher.

Sarah made everything possible.

I stared into her eyes. "I love you."

She didn't blink, gazing deeply into mine. "You're amazing."

"Let me show you how amazing I think you are."

My body snaked down hers, leaving a trail of kisses.

This time, I didn't stop at her hair, the urgency of needing to taste her too much to deny.

My tongue separated her lips, both of us releasing moans.

I flicked her clit, while slipping in two fingers.

"God, you feel so good. Don't stop."

I didn't.

CHAPTER SEVEN

"Daddy!" Casey zipped across the family room as soon as she spied Ethan's lanky frame.

He bent down and opened his arms. "I missed you, peanut."

Peanut?

I didn't recall a time I'd heard Ethan call his daughter by that nickname.

Sarah beamed at me, which I was sure I returned with the same emotion. The bond between parent and child should never be severed. Unless the parent was toxic like the Scotch-lady or Tie.

"Where's Mommy?" Casey asked, still clinging to Ethan.

"Mom will be home in a week. She had to stay behind to help Grandpa."

Casey yanked away. "Why? I miss her."

Grief supplanted his happy feelings. He laid one hand on her shoulder, still hunched to her level. "Because... his wife died." Ethan's voice caught, and it was clear by the turmoil in his expression he didn't know the best way to break the news. How does one explain death to someone so young? Even Casey, who wanted a microscope to cure cancer, to the best of my knowledge didn't have much experience with the awful side of life.

"Grandma died?" Casey whispered, putting everything together much quicker than I think Ethan wanted.

Ethan nodded.

Casey didn't move, and she had her back to me, so I couldn't see how she processed the information. If Ethan's pained grimace was a reflection, though, it hit Casey hard. She hadn't seen too worried about her grandmother's illness on Christmas Eve, but now that she'd passed, it was a whole new ball game.

Finally, Casey said in a shaky voice, "Can I talk to Mom?"

Ethan stood. "Of course. Let's go into the library and FaceTime her." He gripped her tiny hand with his.

Sarah sniffled.

I cuddled Demi closer to my chest.

The twins continued with their art project, bringing an odd smile to Sarah's lips. "It's amazing. One life can end so easily, and yet everyone else keeps on going. Death can be so cruel on many levels."

I nodded, unsure what to say. "Shall we get the baths out of the way before our guests arrive for the non-party?"

Sarah had sworn she'd never host another party, but somehow Rose, Troy, Maddie, and Gabe were expected to ring in the New Year with us. Maybe she'd meant no more parties for the Petries, and given how Christmas had played out, it was for the best. My family could ruin just about anything. Dad and Helen planned to spend the night with Peter, while Allen had a date with Bailey. It was fitting that Allen was the one with a date, because no matter what happened, life marched on.

She nodded. "I'll start with Demi. Why don't you see how things go with Ethan?"

My eyes must have bulged.

"It's okay. You can handle it."

"B-but? What should I say?"

Sarah squeezed my shoulder. "Times like these, it's best not to talk much. Listen."

"I'll never figure things out. Usually, you're telling me to bare my soul. Now, I'm supposed to keep my trap shut. And, yesterday, at the party, I wasn't supposed to mention Peter."

Sarah nodded sympathetically. "Try to be better today. I'm surprised you didn't mention the skid marks in Peter's boxers to JJ. That would be gold for a newshound, considering his predicament."

I shuddered. "Why does everyone insist on bringing that up?"

She laughed. "It's funny to think your immaculate brother doesn't know how to wipe his ass properly."

I stuck my index fingers into my ears. "Please, for the sake of everything under the sun, never say that again. I'm still processing the news he got clipped with Maddie present." I yanked my fingers out since it wasn't all that comfortable.

"Don't forget that he can't get it up."

I sucked in a deep breath, closing my eyes.

"You're still a prude." She whispered in my ear, "Even though you do dirty things with me."

"That's allowed. We're married. All other things of that nature—off-limits, even more so when discussing family members." I slapped my palms together to indicate the matter was closed.

"That's cute, but you should know better than most when it comes to your family, nothing is ever said and done." She grinned at Demi on her hip. "Come on, baby girl."

After Sarah was out of sight, I wheeled about to the twins. "Your mother loves to drive me crazy."

"Talking to yourself?" Ethan took a seat in the leather chair, stretching his long legs out onto the ottoman. "Oh, man. That feels good."

"Long—" I stopped, but Ethan's curious expression propelled me to forego Sarah's advice about not talking. "Day or days?"

"You can say that."

"Where's Casey?"

"Still talking to her mom. They wanted privacy."

I nodded. This seemed like the perfect time to employ Sarah's advice to keep my mouth shut.

"You look weird. Constipated?" he asked.

"Nope. Not a problem I've ever had, actually."

"Way too much information." He showed his palms.

"Just giving you the facts."

"That you're a poop machine?"

"Gross!"

"You brought it up."

"You did!" I said much too loudly.

Ethan chortled. "I've missed you. It's amazing how much you keep me grounded by being you."

"By picking on me?" I perched on the arm of the sofa.

"Teasing. How'd Casey do?"

Was this the time to mention Casey was worried about her parents divorcing? Or that she wanted to have a sleepover with a boy? Or the insanely expensive microscope I'd purchased?

With one look at Ethan's drooping eyelids, I opted to lie. "Nothing to report."

"That's not entirely true."

Did Casey already blabber? About what, though? "Uh...?"

"Peter. How's he doing?"

"Good question. Dad's lawyers are trying to work their magic. None of us has seen Tie since Christmas. I would have sworn she'd be the type to flock to TV cameras, spilling her guts. Her silence is making me nervous." Was she worried about incriminating herself, if it was true she had played a role in setting up Peter? Or had Dad's team somehow made it clear it'd be in her best interest to keep her trap shut? "Honestly, I don't know what to think about any of this."

I shared the details about Peter's case, with Ethan occasionally asking a question or offering an opinion with a snort or groan.

Sarah reentered the room with a freshly bathed Demi. "Ah, Ethan, you look like you could use a snuggle." She handed off Demi. "Okay, Twinks. Bath time!" Sarah clapped her hands together in her *you should be excited about this* fashion.

Freddie gave her his serious once-over.

Ollie continued working on her drawing, shaking her head.

Sarah's pleasant expression morphed into drill sergeant. "On the count of three, you two will follow me upstairs."

That got their attention.

Once the coast was clear, Ethan stage-whispered, "She really does scare me sometimes. I almost got up for my bath."

I laughed. "Usually, I'd help round up the kids, but she thinks you need to talk to me."

Ethan's sigh was the best indication he really didn't want to talk.

"It's okay. I"—I placed a hand over my breast—"think talking is so overrated. We can flip on the television and pretend we're bonding."

"Deal. I never got a chance to watch my favorite holiday film this year." He tapped his fingertips together.

"What movie should I cue up?"

"You honestly don't know my favorite holiday film?" He squinted one eye.

"*It's a Wonderful Life?*"

"No."

"*Miracle on Thirty-Fourth Street?*"

"No." He was enjoying himself now, watching me come up with films.

"*The Nightmare Before Christmas?*" This particular one baffled me completely. How did the king of Halloween Town end up in Christmas Town? There was nothing similar between the two holidays, unless you counted all the people who dressed up as Santa or elves on Halloween.

Ethan cleared his throat.

"Oh, sorry. I can't think of any other Christmas films."

"*Die Hard.*"

"That doesn't sound overly cheerful." I entered the name and hit play.

Half an hour into the movie, Sarah, the twins, and Casey returned. Sarah took one look at the television and glared at me as if I'd been the one that chose a movie about terrorists seizing a building on Christmas Eve. I mean, I did study the Nazis, but it wasn't like I lived and breathed them.

Gabe and Maddie arrived soon after.

"Are you watching *Die Hard*?" Gabe asked.

"Nope," I said.

Gabe looked at the screen again as if he'd never seen a television before. Finally, he stuttered, "Y-yes, you are."

"You knew that when you asked," I waggled the remote at him.

He sat down next to me, taking the remote from my hand. Leaning over to make eye contact with Ethan, he asked, "Mind if we restart it?"

Maddie pitched her hands in the air. "Men." Although her shit-eating grin was proof she was putting on a show, but for who's benefit? Ethan's? Gabe's? Surely not mine. She eased Demi into her arms.

Sarah's glare had lost its venom. She probably realized this was exactly what Ethan needed. "Shall I make popcorn? And move the children to a safe zone?"

I took the last part as my cue to move the craft center, but when I rose, Sarah motioned for me to stay seated.

Casey came into the room, handing Ethan his phone. "Can I watch with you, Daddy?"

Ethan opened his arms, and Casey snuggled into the chair with him, falling asleep rather quickly, much to my relief since I didn't deem the movie appropriate for her. I suspected Ethan knew she'd crash sooner rather than later.

Next to arrive were Rose and Troy. Much to my surprise, Troy opted to watch *Die Hard*. How did the man who hummed "Twinkle Twinkle Little Star" all the bloody time like this flick?

For the third time, we restarted the movie.

CHAPTER EIGHT

"Ten, nine, eight, seven…"
Everyone was on their feet, cheering on the drop of the ball in Times Square.

Sarah squeezed my hand.

The little ones were in bed, but Casey hopped up and down on her feet, squealing and clapping her hands, proving how resilient children can be during times of grief. Also, Ethan was doing his best to put up a brave front for the sake of his daughter, and the rest of us wanted to be there for the both of them.

"Happy New Year!" everyone shouted.

Maddie pulled the string on a party popper, the confetti spraying Gabe.

He retaliated with his own, while Casey and Ethan added to the destruction of the family room.

Troy kissed Rose, and I had to control my gag reflex. Seeing my mother-in-law doing the tongue tango with her much-younger fiancé wasn't in my comfort zone.

Sarah wrapped her arms around my neck. "Happy New Year, sweetheart."

"Everyone knows it's not actually midnight in Colorado,

right? We're two hours behind the east coast. Do we have more party poppers?"

"We do, but if they don't know or care, I don't plan on offering more. I'm ready for bed, and my gut says everyone wants to be on their own for the stroke of midnight." She kissed me. The sweet kind that implied I wasn't getting lucky later.

Not that I could blame her.

From the tired expressions on everyone's faces, it was time to put this year to bed once and for all.

Rose and Troy, looking lovey-dovey, made their way over. Rose said, "We're heading out."

Sarah gave each a hug.

Gabe sidled up to me. "How's Peter hanging in?"

I found it odd he was asking me, not Maddie. Then again, had Maddie confessed she'd been in contact with Peter? And if she did confess, was it causing problems between her and Gabe? Peter seemed to be her blind spot, and I was surprised she was in my house right now, not Peter's. "I think okay, but I really don't have a benchmark for how to judge his state of mind during situations like this."

He nodded. "Yeah, it's hard to..." His voice trailed off, and I didn't have the energy to press. "Maddie's worried for him."

"Same here." I locked eyes on him to try to figure out the purpose for this line of questioning.

"Me too," he said, and I had to give it to him because he seemed sincere.

I would hate to be in his shoes at the moment, given the history between Maddie and Peter.

Maddie slid her arm through Gabe's and rested her head on his shoulder. "Are you ready to go to your place? I'm beat."

"I was just thinking that." Gabe kissed the top of her head. "Hopefully Peter can avoid getting arrested again and not ruin another holiday." He laughed but stopped abruptly when

Maddie pulled away and flung a death glare that made me tremble in my socks. "Sorry. That was in bad taste."

Sarah stepped in and gave Maddie a hug.

Maddie mumbled something in Sarah's ear. I wasn't able to make out the words, but given Sarah's supportive shoulder squeeze, I think Maddie made it known she was ticked off about Gabe's ill-timed joke.

Gabe gave me his hand to shake, baffling the shit out of me.

After they left, I let out a relieved sigh. "Can you talk to Gabe?" I whispered to Sarah.

"He's your stepbrother."

"I'm calling *not it*, though. Completely legit tactic."

Sarah shook her head, but she couldn't curb an adoring smile.

Ethan announced, "Casey, let's hit the road. I want to sleep in my own bed tonight."

"Are you sure?" Sarah asked.

Ethan nodded. "You two have been wonderful, watching Casey, but I think it's time."

Sarah placed a hand on his shoulder. "I understand. Don't worry about grabbing all of Casey's stuff tonight. We can pack it up and get it to your place soon."

Translation, I would be driving to Ethan's place tomorrow. Not a bad tradeoff given it'd be the first time in days we'd have the house completely to ourselves.

After twenty minutes of hunting for Minnie, their cat who didn't seem to want to leave our house, we saw them off.

Closing and deadbolting the front door, I turned to Sarah, "And, then there was only us."

She fell against me. "Bring on the new year. I'm ready for a fresh start."

"Does that mean you're going to bed now?"

"Did you have anything else in mind?"

Her dubious expression spurred me to think quickly on my feet. "I'm going to soak in the tub."

"I'm down with that."

"Let's go upstairs so I can get you wet."

"I'd tell you to up your seduction game this coming year, but I don't think it'd help much."

"Mock all you want. You fell in love with this version of Lizzie, and you're stuck with it." I ran my hands up and down in the air, implying take it or leave it.

"Does that mean you aren't making any resolutions?"

"This is a conversation for the bath. You coming?"

"Before I get wet? You're ambitious."

"It's so not fair how you can make these jokes, but I can't."

"Humor can't be taught." She winked. "Come on. I'm ready to get naked with you."

We ascended the stairs, our gait slower than usual.

"Maybe I should ride my bike more," I huffed.

"I'm serious about the exercise room."

We crested the landing and turned left toward our bedroom.

Finally in the bathroom, I started the water for the tub, while Sarah collected fresh towels and robes. "It's going to take ages to get caught up on laundry. And, now with Demi…"

"What are we going to do? Keep her in the room with the twins?" I tested the water, kicking the cold tap up a bit. I'd always been fond of extremely hot baths, but Sarah didn't take to my *all or nothing* ways.

"For now, yes. They're all so young and sleeping through the night, so I don't think it'll be much of an issue." She yanked her sweater over her head. "We'll have to wait to see how long she'll be here. At some point, it might be best for the girls to share a room."

"Ah, Freddie finally has an advantage. He's been outnumbered since day one."

Sarah unhooked her black lacey bra, slipping the straps over her arms. "Unless we manage to have a baby boy."

"I'll get right on that, learning DNA coding in my free time."

"That would be helpful." She stripped off her jeans. "Why are you just sitting there? Are you not getting in?"

"Sorry. I was distracted by your strip tease."

"Or your heart was racing waiting for me to broach the *we need to move to a bigger house* topic. It's your favorite topic."

I waggled a finger in my right ear. "What'd you say? Got water in my ear."

"It'd help your schtick if you were already naked and in the water."

I snapped my fingers. "The details always fuck me."

"They get the best of many, so don't let it get you down."

I tossed my head back, laughing. "You're on a roll tonight. It bodes well for the new year. You've been such a wet blanket since we met."

Sarah eased into the water. "Just for that, I may deny you entry."

Perched on the side of the tub, I shrugged. "Maybe I'll add voyeurism to my hobby list. Right now, I'm seeing the appeal."

"Get undressed and get in here before I pull you in fully clothed."

"You wouldn't dare. You were just complaining about laundr—"

There was a splash followed by Sarah's laughter.

I spit out water.

She continued laughing. "You look like a drowned rat."

"There's a reason for that. I think my phone is toast."

Sarah slapped her hand over her mouth. "Oh, Lizzie! I'm sorry."

It was my turn to laugh. "Kidding. It's on the counter."

She splashed water at me.

I splashed back.

Her eyes smoldered.

My sweater weighed me down. I stood in the water, failing to get my soggy jeans off. "This always looks so sexy in movies." I shivered. "But it's heavy and cold."

She got to her feet. "Let me help you."

The two of us got all my layers off.

"Add hot water. You're shivering even more."

"Uh, I don't think I'm cold." I hopped out of the tub and headed for the toilet with both hands over my mouth.

* * *

THE BED LURCHED to the side, and I cracked one eye open. "What happened?"

"Your end-of-the-semester ritual of puking up your guts finally kicked in."

"When Gabe was acting weird on Christmas Eve, before I knew he was freaking out about how to pop the question, I thought he had the flu and wished he'd share. Could this be Karma?" I rolled onto my back, causing the room to spin for a brief spell. "I'm sorry."

Sarah's smile was kind. "Don't apologize for getting sick. Given everything that's happened…"

"What time is it?"

"Noon."

"Noon? How long have I been asleep?"

"More than twelve hours."

"Then why do I feel like shit?" I whined.

"The wonders of the flu."

"Did you cancel with the Marcels?"

"Yes." Sarah brushed hair off my forehead. "They hope you feel better soon. Maddie whipped up homemade chicken noodle soup with your favorite thick egg noodles."

The mere idea of food made my stomach flip, and I clamped my lips tightly.

"Okay. You haven't hit the food stage. Can you drink some water, or do you need ice chips?"

"Not thirsty. Just tired."

There was a commotion out in the hall, and then the twins burst into the room, repeating, "Momma!"

"Sorry, they insisted." Maddie had Demi on her hip.

Sarah hoisted Freddie onto the bed and then Ollie. "Be gentle. Mommy doesn't feel good."

The twins hugged my waist, resting their heads on my stomach. I did my best not to breathe too much on them, as I wrapped my arms around them and pulled them close.

"Okay, you two. Time for your lunch." Sarah scooped them up and eyed me with concern. "I'll check on you in an hour."

* * *

THERE WERE MUFFLED VOICES, and I rolled over, covering my head with a pillow.

Someone gently removed the pillow. "Lizzie, how are you feeling?"

It was Sarah's voice.

I groaned.

More muffled voices.

"Here, honey, I need you to drink this."

I grunted, which I hoped conveyed *No way in hell; leave me alone*.

"You don't have a choice, so sit up." Sarah's voice was sweet but also firm.

I sighed. "Can't you just leave me to die?"

"Sadly, no. Let me help you up."

I motioned for her to give me a moment.

Maddie had extra pillows to prop me up. "Come on, champ. It's not like you to quit."

Usually, this type of goading would spur me on. In the moment, I couldn't even muster the energy to say a word. It was as if my batteries were deader than dead.

The two of them managed to get me into a sitting position, and Sarah held the mug with what I assumed was Theraflu for me to take a sip. I grimaced.

"Just a bit more, sweetie."

Sarah hardly ever called me *sweetie*.

Not wanting to worry the mother of our twins, I choked down more of the vile concoction.

"Do you want to lay flat again?" Sarah set the mug on the bedside table.

I answered by closing my eyes, not budging.

She swiped hair off my brow, placing a tender kiss on my sweaty forehead. "I'll be back in an hour."

I tried to say I love you, but my throat was sore and constricted.

* * *

ON DAY THREE, I ventured downstairs.

"It lives!" Maddie announced.

I squinted. "Why is it so bright out?"

"It's overcast and snowing. You've been in a dark room for days." Sarah put the kettle on. "Tea and toast?"

I nodded, plopping onto the barstool, out of breath. "What'd I miss?"

"Where to start?" Maddie tapped a finger on the countertop.

Sarah tossed shade at Maddie before saying, "Nothing at all. How are you feeling?"

"Like your mom finally ran me over with her Caddie." I propped up my head with a sweaty palm. "How are the kids?"

"They're at Mom's."

"Because of me?"

She shook her head. "No, we haven't banished them. They've only been over there for a couple of hours."

Sarah busied herself buttering toast.

Maddie scanned her phone.

"Any word on Peter?" I asked.

"He's no longer on the front page of most newspapers."

That was progress.

"And Tie?"

"No word." Sarah's lip curled up into a snarl. "To not even call to check on her own daughter … that's just cold."

"My mom didn't have any issues with that," I said.

"Not exactly a woman anyone should aspire to emulate."

I nodded, loosening my robe. "Why are you blasting the heat?"

Maddie placed her hand on my forehead. "Go back to bed. We'll bring up your tea and toast when they're ready."

I started to mount an argument, but Sarah pointed in her mom fashion for me to do as I was told.

"So far, this year sucks." I moped upstairs and climbed back into bed.

CHAPTER NINE

An odd chiming sound woke me, and it took me several seconds to process someone was calling me on my phone. "Hello?" I croaked.

"Jesus, you sound terrible."

"Hey, Peter. It's nothing, really. Just the flu." I glanced at the clock and saw it was a little after eight. Given the darkness, I guessed it was nighttime.

"The best cure for that is getting arrested. Makes the flu seem like a dream."

I chuckled. "I'll keep that in mind, but maybe we should aim to only have one Petrie in the big house at a time."

"Can we have that motto on our family crest?"

"I'm sure some royal family or robber barons have already claimed it." I propped some pillows behind me. "How are you doing?"

"The press finally moved on, so that's good. I was wondering if I could see Demi."

"Of course, you can see your daughter. Do you want us to bring her to you?"

"I was hoping to come up there. This house—it's too big for

one, and I'm going insane. Besides, it's best to keep Demi in Fort Collins to avoid her photo appearing on the news. Do I need to bring anything for Demi?"

"Whatever you think she needs or wants. We went clothes shopping for her."

"I'm sorry. I should have sent some."

"Don't worry about it. You have enough on your mind, and Sarah loves to shop. She's dreaming of setting up a home gym. I feel for the delivery guys dropping off equipment, including dumbbells weighing fifteen pounds or more." I covered my mouth to stifle a coughing fit. "When should we expect you?"

"If you're up for it, tomorrow morning."

"Sounds good. Maybe we can have a movie marathon or something." I paused. "Do you like movies?"

He laughed. "It's so odd that we don't know shit about each other. I don't even know your favorite color."

"I'm pretty sure you don't know my birthday either since you scheduled your first wedding on it."

There was more chuckling. "Sorry about that. In a way, you got the last laugh. Maddie is one of your best friends."

"True. Thanks for fucking up that one."

"It's my specialty."

"Speaking of your terrible track record with women, any word from Tie?"

"Yep. She's living the life in New York City." He made a type of whistling sound.

"And?"

"She's filed for divorce."

Ouch. Having a vengeful wife set you up for insider trading would hurt. But not being the first to file for divorce after that would sting some, I'd think.

"She seems amenable to renouncing her parental rights," he continued. "She wants a clean break, according to Dad."

"Wow." I mulled over how to proceed. "How will this work, then? If you, uh, go to prison?"

"Good question. I've agreed to cooperate with their investigation."

I bolted up into a sitting position, regretting it when a wave of dizziness hit. "What do you mean? I thought you didn't do it."

"I wasn't in cahoots with Reggie, but I know a lot of the key players involved."

"Good God. They want you to be an informant."

"Essentially."

"I don't understand why you'd agree if you're innocent."

"I'm not innocent of everything. It's complicated, Lizzie. It's a dirty business, not that it matters anymore since part of my agreement is never to have anything to do with it again."

"Wow! What will you do?"

There was a pregnant silence. "That is a very good question."

Sarah entered the bedroom, her forehead crumpled.

I mouthed Peter's name, and she nodded, climbing into bed with me.

"Will they wipe out your accounts?" I asked.

"There's a fine involved, yes. And I have to plead to lesser crimes."

"If Tie put this in motion, why are you considering this? Have you told them everything about Tie and Samuel?"

There was a gulping of breath on the line. "It's hard to explain. Dad's irate, but a part of me feels like I have to do this. I don't know how to explain to my daughter, when she'll be old enough to understand, that I had her mother arrested for setting me up. Besides…" There were more deep breaths. "I haven't been a good man. I want to change. If this is how I do penance, maybe it could turn out to be a good thing. I have to try, so I can be the father Demi deserves."

It was odd hearing my brother, who once outed me to a relative to claim my inheritance, speaking about falling on a sword to protect his daughter.

"For both of your sakes, I hope it turns out."

He was quiet for many moments again. Apparently, both Peter and I were processors when it came to heavy shit. Finally, he said, "I should let you rest. I'll see you tomorrow. Oh, is there anything I can bring for you?"

Momentarily stunned, I managed to say, "Thanks, but Sarah's been taking good care of me, I think, at least. I've been in a coma. I actually don't know what day it is."

"January fourth."

"Is it really? I keep losing days with this illness. See you tomorrow, Peter," I said, disconnecting the call.

Sarah snuggled up against me. "How are you feeling?"

"Peter's going to be a rat."

She felt my head. "I don't think you have a fever." She started to get up. "Let me get a thermometer."

"No, I'm fine. Peter's going to work with the authorities for a lighter sentence. Not because he's guilty, or maybe he is. I don't want to know the full story. But he doesn't want to have the mother of his child arrested, and he thinks this is the first step to becoming a better man."

Sarah settled back down. "Hmmm."

"Uh-oh. What does that mean?"

"It's hard to believe he's only doing it to become a better version of himself, considering we're talking about your brother."

She had a point, but I couldn't see where she was going. "You think he has ulterior motives?"

"Yes."

"Care to fill me in?"

"You really haven't considered anything?" Her tone implied I was missing the obvious.

"I've been asleep so far this year."

Sarah wrapped her arm tighter around me. "I know. I've missed you."

"How have the kids been?"

"Perfect angels. Even Ollie."

"Is she feeling okay?"

Sarah's laughter echoed in the room. "I had the same thought, but whenever I check her temp, she's fine."

"Maybe she's learning from Peter how not to be an asshole."

She slapped my chest. "Olivia Rose is not an asshole!"

"Spoken like a true mother." I took a sip of water. "Tie's giving up her rights."

Sarah's lips pursed as she seemed to process the information. "I'll never understand that, but I do think it's for the best for Demi. The woman doesn't know how to love."

"I'm proof that family is what you make of it, not necessarily restricted to blood relatives. I know more about Ethan than I do about Peter. Hell, I know more about Ethan's cat. Earlier, I asked Peter if he liked movies. Then again, I didn't know Ethan's favorite holiday film."

"*Die Hard* is such a guy choice for a holiday flick. Did your family ever go to the movies together?"

I stared at her. "I think you know the answer to that."

She shook her head. "I do, but it's still difficult for me to wrap my head around your childhood. How lonely it must have been. How do we protect Demi from that?"

"We need to talk to Peter about his plans. If he doesn't go to prison, will he raise her on his own? Hire a live-in nanny? Keep her with us?" I yawned.

Sarah placed her head on my shoulder. "You need to rest."

"Does that mean you won't tell me what nefarious plan you think Peter's up to?"

"Not tonight." She released a puff of air. "I'm not even sure I'm right. You Petries have a way of keeping me on my toes. For now, I'll try to give him the benefit of the doubt. I'll try to learn from you, considering you have way more skin in the game and you're hoping for everything to turn out."

"I'm not sure I'm hoping for the best or just willing to let it play out the way it will. I've learned not to expect much from Peter, so this isn't that hard, except for the Demi factor." I sat up. "Speaking of, do you think it'd be okay if I went into the nursery?"

"Why wouldn't it?"

"I don't want to spread my germs."

"Oh, right. I think standing in the doorway will be okay."

We both got out of bed.

All three children slept peacefully in their cribs.

I leaned into Sarah, who had her arm wrapped around my waist. "It's funny. Ten years ago, I'd thought I'd always be alone. I used to wake in the middle of the night, crying from the crushing feeling of loneliness. Even when I was with Meg, I'd have these dreams. Sometimes, with her next to me, I'd wake from one of the nightmares, and I'd reach out for her, but I wouldn't be able to remember her name right away. I think even then, I was waiting for you." I jerked my head to the twins. "For them. And now, Demi."

"Hopefully you have more room in your life for more people to love. You're not even forty. Plenty more living and loving to do."

I smiled at her. "Oh, I know. But the thought doesn't scare the crap out of me. I used to pray for a short life because, really, how much could I take? Now, I want to enjoy every day to the fullest. Just saying that does my head in."

"Careful, Lizzie. People might start to think you're an optimist." She bumped her hip into me.

"Don't tell anyone and ruin my grouch persona."

"Your secret is safe with me." She sealed her promise with a kiss on my cheek.

CHAPTER TEN

The following morning, I woke alone in bed, although it was still dark out. I sniffled, rubbing the sleep from my left eye.

After getting out of bed and taking care of my morning routine, I made my way to the nursery to find everyone still asleep. Maddie, also sound asleep, was in one of the guest rooms—I assumed, since the door was shut. No one was in the spare room that Sarah had recently commandeered as her writing space.

"Where's Sarah?" I whispered to myself, scanning the hallway as if a magical bedroom door would appear.

Maybe she couldn't sleep and was in the office working on a story.

I padded downstairs in my slippers and robe, surprised to see the Christmas tree had been taken down. The living room seemed lifeless without it. Soon enough, Sarah would fill the house with Valentine's decorations. The thought brought a smile to my lips.

In the office, Sarah was curled up under a quilt on one of

the couches. Again, the absence of the tree made the room seem lonelier.

She stirred when I sat on the edge of the coffee table. "Are you okay? Do you need anything?"

"Just missed you. Why are you sleeping in here?"

"You were coughing pretty bad. I'm sorry. I should have stayed."

"Nonsense. I'll let you sleep. I thought you were writing." She closed one eye. "There's color in your cheeks again. That's a good sign. Just in case you were wondering, pasty white isn't really a good look on you."

"Aw shucks. I'll have to toss all my clown makeup away."

"What time is it?"

"Nearly six."

"Why are you up?"

I laughed, which turned into a coughing fit. "I've been in bed for days. Starting to get sores, I think."

"I doubt it's that serious."

"Does that mean you won't inspect my entire body?"

She rolled onto her back. "You really are feeling better. Sadly, the flu hasn't improved your flirting game."

"Good thing for you."

She rubbed both eyes with the heels of her palms. "Exactly how is that a good thing for me?"

"Less chance of other chicks digging me now that I'm on the precipice of becoming a television star."

"Yes. Historians are the new rocks stars of the twenty-first century. Do we need to stock up on sweaters with elbow patches?"

"There's an idea." I shook my hand, adding, "Make room."

Sarah scooted toward the back of the couch, her arms open for me. "I'm glad you're feeling better."

"I don't really have a choice. The semester will start soon.

And, I can't continue to shirk my duties here. The boss in this house is hard to please."

She ran her hand through my hair. "Do you think you'll get fired?"

"It's possible. Or punished."

"You sound kinda excited about that possibility."

"She has a special way of punishing me, although that may have to wait for a few more days. I may die." I started coughing again.

Sarah held me tightly in her arms. "No dying."

When my cough receded, she tapped my back. "Let's get some tea with honey for you."

"I can make it. Why don't you rest some more?"

"I'm awake." Her voice was gravelly with sleep.

"At least let me make you a cup of coffee."

"You can be stubborn."

"Says the woman arguing with me about who will fill a teakettle and coffee pot." I got to my feet. "I probably should shower before Peter arrives."

"I think all of us would appreciate it." She crinkled her nose. "Do you need help in the shower?"

"That desperate to see me naked? Maybe you should give me a sponge bath."

"You're right. You are feeling better and can manage tea and coffee on your own." She pulled the quilt over her again.

"I really do need to work on my game."

"Two sugars in mine, and no, I'm not stressed or sick. It just sounds like a good way to celebrate you getting out of bed."

"Is that how the sugar limitation works? If I don't die, you allow yourself a decent cup of joe to celebrate?"

"Yes. Can you manage to get sick and better on a regular basis? I really do like sugar."

"Great. Now I have to keep an eye on you to ensure you

aren't leaving the bedroom window open on winter nights so I'll catch a cold solely to increase your sugar intake."

"Why are you still talking and not making coffee?" She made a motion with her hand that implied I should shut my mouth.

I kissed her forehead and exited the library.

Maddie was already filling the coffee pot. "It lives."

"Barely. Sarah would like a cup."

Maddie added more grounds. "Gabe has to get to work soon."

"Did he stay the night?"

"You really have no idea what happens in your own house."

"It's how I continue to look myself in the mirror, ignoring the things people like you do." I fished a tissue out of the pocket of my robe and blew my nose. "Peter's coming over today to see Demi."

She nodded. "He texted."

I wondered how much she knew about Peter's plans to rat out the fat cats. I shook my head, glad I kept that terrible phrasing to myself.

"Well, look who it is." Gabe, freshly showered, clapped a hand on my shoulder.

"Morning," I said, still attempting to stop my nose from dripping.

"Can I get that to go, sweetheart?" Gabe kissed Maddie's cheek.

"I'm pretty sure you can pour it into a travel mug." There was a frostiness to Maddie's tone.

"Touchy!" Gabe laughed off her thinning lips.

"Are you getting sick?" I asked, concerned about the redness prickling her cheeks.

Maddie shook her head. "Don't think so. Some of us aren't weak like you. So far I've survived the shrimp debacle and your flu."

"You didn't eat any of the shrimp, so claiming you survived it is dubious at best."

Maddie grinned. "You really are feeling better if you're using words like dubious."

I wadded up the tissue. Too tired to get up to toss it in the trash can under the sink, I tucked it back into my pocket.

Gabe filled his mug.

"Are you working today?" I asked Maddie.

"No design projects at the moment, so Sarah and I are planning to work on a story. Are you going to stay out of bed today?"

I wondered if not having a paying gig was the reason behind her mood. "Peter's coming by, so I probably should."

Gabe, still pouring, spilled some onto the counter. Blotting it with a paper towel, he said, "I thought he was in hiding."

"The press gave up on him, at least for now." I shrugged. "He wants to see Demi."

Gabe examined Maddie's face. "Oh. I hadn't thought of that."

My brain was too muddled to figure out what that meant, but by the pinched expression on Maddie's face, Gabe was on her shit list. Perhaps she was still pissed at Gabe for the terrible joke he'd made about Peter ruining holidays.

He brushed his lips on her cheek, more perfunctory than tender, asking, "Would you like to do lunch today?"

"I can't. I have plans with Courtney." She didn't look up from her phone.

"Dinner?"

"I'll let you know."

Gabe stood frozen before responding, "Okay. I'll call later to see how you're doing."

Maddie nodded, still not glancing in his direction.

Gabe left.

"That was weird," I said. "What's going on with you two?"

"N-nothing," she stammered.

"Why don't you want to go to dinner with him? That's not like you."

"Who said I didn't?" She poured two mugs of coffee and scooted my tea over.

I blew into the mug. "Your hunched shoulders and the *fuck no* look in your eyes."

"You need new glasses."

"I'm wearing contacts."

"You need new contacts, then."

"I just went a month ago."

"To where?" Sarah stretched her arms overhead, her shoulder-length hair going every which way.

"I'm going to check on Demi and the twins." Maddie left.

I eyed her retreating back, not thrilled with the idea forming in my head.

"Are you going to throw up again?" Sarah asked. "You're pasty white."

"Last night, you didn't want to tell me that Peter may try to win Maddie back."

Sarah slumped against the counter opposite where I sat, with the mug in both hands. "It's just a theory."

"I think it's coming to life. Did you and Maddie plan to work on a story together today?" I rubbed my arms to combat a chill.

"Yes."

"Oh, maybe... You know, is it really my concern if Maddie and Peter rekindle whatever they had?"

"Gabe is family as well."

"Yes. That's the problem. It's been the problem since the beginning. Is it too late for me to take your last name?"

"It wouldn't change much, I'm afraid."

Ollie's wails trickled downstairs.

"I think Ollie knows you're feeling better." Sarah went upstairs.

"I'll get breakfast going," I said to no one in particular, but it made me feel better. I couldn't control the Peter/Maddie/Gabe show, but I could make oatmeal. I'd been dead weight for too many days.

CHAPTER ELEVEN

The doorbell rang at 9:03.
"Why can't Peter just waltz in like everyone else?" I rose from the sofa in the family room to make the short trek to the door, winded by the time I opened it.

"No need to ring—" I stopped, realizing I wasn't lecturing Peter but Jorie. "Oh, hi. I'm sorry. I was expecting my brother."

"Which one?" she asked.

"The one with one foot in prison." I swiped my brow. "I'm sorry. That wasn't supposed to come out of my mouth."

Jorie's smile confirmed she thought my verbal diarrhea was adorable. "Don't worry. I'd already heard the news."

A gust of frigid air blasted through me. "Shit, I'm sorry. Come in." I stood back to allow her entry.

She appraised my pajamas and bathrobe. "Have you been ill?" Worry lines creased her brow.

"Yes. Just a couple of days ago, I was praying I'd die." I shut the door.

"Was that supposed to be spoken aloud?" she teased.

"Probably not. It's possible I'm still delusional. More so

than normal, which is saying something." I led her to the family room. "Look who I found."

"A much-improved version of Peter." Maddie gave Jorie a hug. "How was your Christmas?"

"I was with my family, so…" She shrugged as a way to fill in the blanks. "I know it's late, but I got the twins a gift." She handed a wrapped present to Sarah, who called the twins over to unwrap it.

The twinks tore into the gift, which turned out to be two tambourines with dolphins on them.

"My dad took us all to Hawaii. When I saw these, I had to get them. My little brother Max loves his."

There were also two tiny drums with sea turtles.

"Oh, this is great. Like Freddie, Demi loves the drums," Sarah said.

"She does?" I asked.

"The kids had music class yesterday."

"They did?"

"You'll have to excuse Lizzie. She's been bedridden and is completely out of touch with reality these days." Sarah handed a drum to Demi, who took to it like a wolverine to a raw steak.

I covered one ear. "Sh-she's good."

Sarah swatted me playfully. "She's learning. Be nice."

"I am. I haven't taken it away. I'm going to make a cup of tea. Perhaps stuff a couple of tea bags into my ears. Does anyone want anything?"

"Just don't take two tea bags to the face," Maddie grinned.

"Uh, okay. Jorie, would you like some tea or coffee?"

"Tea would be great. I'm still adjusting to winter after being in Hawaii." She rubbed her hands together and then blew into them.

"Coffee," Maddie and Sarah chirped.

I bolted out of the room, my robe billowing out, but Demi's assault on my ears continued in the kitchen.

Sarah tailed me, rubbing my back as I stood at the sink. "How are you feeling?"

"Hanging in."

"Which means you feel like crap. You can go to bed. I can handle Peter when he arrives."

I laughed, which sounded like Hank hacking up a hairball. "You make it sound like we're awaiting a nuclear waste package or something."

"Well…" She flicked her hands in the air. "Oh, I bumped into JJ at the twinks music lesson. Claire also has the flu." Sarah announced this as if it was the most important thing she'd said to me in days.

"Oh, that's too bad." I wasn't sure why that was breaking news. Winter was known as flu season.

"It turned out to be a good thing, because I had a chance to chat with JJ and she peppered me with questions to gauge whether or not you're interested in the job. How's it feel to be wanted by The Miracle Girl?"

I yawned.

"Don't look too excited."

"Come on. You can't really think I'd be good at the job. It's fun to think about, but—me on TV? Jorie asked me which brother I was expecting, and I said the one who was on his way to prison. I have zero charm."

Sarah circled my waist with her arms. "I disagree. In case you haven't figured it out yet, people find the clueless ones endearing. I know I do."

"That's because you signed the dotted line, promising to love me until I die."

"Was that the deal? It sounds so long." She rested her head on my chest.

I had another coughing fit and broke free from Sarah to spit phlegm into the sink.

"Or not so long. Have you taken your medicine?"

I nodded, still coughing.

"I don't think I've ever seen you this sick. Go to bed."

"Not yet. I'm tired of bed. I'm tired of sleeping. I'm tired of everything."

Sarah slanted her head. "Did you want to bang on the drums with Fred and Demi? Get out whatever"—she circled a finger in my direction—"this is?"

"I'm acting like a baby? Is that what you're saying?"

She held her forefinger and thumb half an inch apart.

I sighed. "Sucking it up."

"Who's being a buttercup?" Peter's voice shocked me considering he usually commanded a room with a booming one. Now it was barely above a whisper. Another surprise was the beginnings of a beard. Had it been deemed it'd be better to remove all sharp objects from his house?

"Me, apparently. How…" I was about to say are you, but decided that would be stupid and changed to "was the drive?"

"Not bad. The roads are mostly clear. It's been a bad winter. Snow-wise," he added, looking down at his shoes, a beat-up pair of sneakers. Another new development.

"I'm making coffee. Want some?" I focused on Demi on Peter's hip.

He nodded, snuggling Demi closer to him.

Sarah watched our interaction like a tennis fan, but there wasn't any joy in her eyes. "Are you hungry? It looks like you haven't eaten since…"

It was unusual for Sarah to step in it, and her face lit up like a firework.

"The shrimp fiasco," I rushed to say.

"Yes. The shrimp." Sarah flashed me a relieved look.

"Those were the good old days," Peter joked, almost coming across as sincere. "Thanks, but I'm not hungry."

"Why don't you two go into the front room and hang with the kids while I get the drinks?" Sarah shooed us out of the room, and I wondered if being around Peter would finally break her. Under normal circumstance, as normal as Petries can be, she was the rock when I acted weird. Perhaps she was coming down with my flu. That was the last thing we needed.

Maddie and Jorie sat with the twins, making some type of artwork with glitter and glue. For the life of me, I couldn't remember activities of these types when I was a kid and felt a bit out of place considering my lackluster skills in the creative department. My comfort zone was reading to the kids each night before bed.

"Where's the coffee?" Maddie barked.

"Sarah kicked us out of the kitchen." Peter settled into a chair, bobbing Demi up and down on his knee. "Have you been good for your aunts?" Peter asked in a singsong voice.

Demi giggled.

I wished I had my phone on me to snap a photo for Demi. *Hold on, Lizzie.* Peter wasn't dying or anything. Just possibly going to prison for hopefully a short stint. He'd survive that, right?

Maddie took a picture with her phone. "I'll text you this," she said to Peter.

He nodded his appreciation.

"Okay, troops. The caffeine is here." Sarah set down the tray. "Jorie, did you want honey or milk in your tea?"

"No, thanks. Black is fine."

Sarah sat on the sofa next to me. "Jorie lost her job at the toy store."

"Oh, I'm sorry to hear that," I said, once again befuddled why Sarah seemed pleased with bad news. I'd only been out of commission for a few days, but I was grasping for straws, trying to figure out all the changes.

"She's going to be our new part-time nanny," Sarah pressed on.

That was why Jorie was here. A job interview of sorts.

This captured Peter's interest. "What happened to Bailey?"

"Oh, she's still on the team as well." Sarah sipped her coffee. "Bailey will be back on the job when the semester starts in a couple of weeks. She and Allen are enjoying their final days of freedom—"

"Before the craziness of school starts again." Maddie came to Sarah's aid.

Peter grimaced slightly but focused his energy on bouncing Demi up and down, much to her delight.

I tried to recall if Sarah and I had decided to hire a second part-time nanny. I remembered tossing around the idea, but not an actual decision. Not wanting to question Sarah in front of Jorie, I remained mute.

"Welcome aboard," I said.

Maddie and Sarah exchanged a relieved look, making it known that this was a plan the two of them had concocted without me. Given we now potentially had three kids under the age of two, I couldn't blame Sarah.

Peter hoisted Demi into the air. "What do you think, goosey-goose?"

I wasn't sure what Peter was referring to. Jorie as a nanny? Living with Sarah and me? His legal predicament? And *goosey-goose*? Was that typical, or was my fever back and I was imagining things?

Demi ripped a fart.

It wouldn't have been my method of easing the tension in the air, but from the hilarity that ensued, it worked wonders.

"What are they feeding you?" Peter asked. His nose scrunched, but a smile appeared on his face, reminding me once again how much he cared for his daughter.

"The magical fruit, of course." Maddie patted Freddie on the head. "Do you have gas too, Freddie Weddie?"

Honestly, was this the only safe conversation with Peter in the room? Whether or not Fred had to break wind?

Freddie laughed and banged on the drum.

"Is there a party?" Gabe entered the room.

"Did you forget something?" I asked him.

"Nah, just decided to take the day off."

The fire shooting out of Maddie's eyes wasn't a good sign, and I sincerely doubted Demi could mount another diversion so soon.

"Peter, how's life on the outside?" Gabe pitched his palms in the air. "Just kidding."

Peter glared at our half brother.

Maddie sucked her lips into her mouth, looking down into her coffee cup.

Sarah tapped her fingertips over her right brow as if trying to force her brain to think of something. Anything.

A sound on the deck nabbed my attention. Whirling my head around, I thought I spied a figure, but why would someone be out there in more than a foot of snow? "Is it just me, or is there someone skulking in the backyard?"

"The press, maybe?" Sarah posed to Maddie.

Gabe, with his chest puffed, said, "I'll take care of it."

"I can do it." Peter handed Demi to Gabe.

"You're the last person who should go out there." Gabe tried handing Demi back.

Sarah huffed and took Demi from Gabe, holding the now anxious girl close to her chest. "She's not a baton." She glared at both of them in her *I'm so disappointed in you two* way. I'd been on the receiving end of that look a few times, and it stung. The men, though, seemed not to notice, too busy sizing the other up.

While Gabe and Peter flexed their muscles, Maddie stormed past them out onto the deck. "Who in the hell do you think you are?" she shouted.

If it was someone wanting juicy news footage, Maddie had just handed it to them on a silver platter.

"What in the world are you doing out here?" Maddie's voice softened. "Are you lost?"

Oh, please, don't be another kid for me to raise.

Gabe and Peter dashed outside to assess the situation. Or perhaps they decided they needed more space for their confrontation.

Soon enough, they all returned with George in tow.

"George! You aren't wearing a coat! Or shoes!" Sarah chastised.

"Who are you? Why are you kidnapping me?" George tried to break free from Maddie and Gabe, who each held an arm.

"It's okay, George," Sarah said in a soothing voice.

"Why doesn't he recognize us?" I asked.

"Stroke maybe," Sarah whispered.

"Over Christmas, when George was acting so odd, Ethan had pondered if he'd had one."

"What do we do?" Sarah asked.

"Uh…?"

Jorie retrieved Demi from Sarah's arms.

"That's a good start. Let's get the kids to the nursery," I said to Jorie, sweeping a twin onto each hip, using more energy than I had in days.

Upstairs, after placing the twins on the floor, I asked Jorie, "Any chance you can start work today and stay up here with them?"

"Of course, I can, but you don't have to pay me. Is he okay?"

"I have no idea." Without another word, I rushed back downstairs. "Never a fucking dull moment," I muttered through gritted teeth.

George sat in a chair, with two blankets on top of him, his teeth chattering.

Sarah was on the phone.

Maddie was talking sweetly to George, who resembled a frightened bird who'd fallen out of a nest.

Peter and Gabe continued to bicker in the corner, Peter shoving Gabe's shoulder, but I didn't have time for them at the moment.

I eyed George, wondering what it was like to be him in this moment. Cold. Scared. Utterly lost. His wife had died not so long ago, and all he had was his dog—

"Where's Gandhi?" I asked.

Gabe and Peter glanced about as if the dog would just show up. It was hard not to scream that they were useless when we really needed them to step up.

I rushed outside but didn't spy the Yorkie or any pawprints in the snow.

In the kitchen, I pulled out a spare key to George's house. "Gabe, go check, please."

"I'll go, too." Peter stood straighter.

"Fine, if it makes you feel better," I said, fed up with the macho bullshit.

"I'm sorry. Can you repeat that last number?" Sarah was jotting down what I assumed was a phone number. "Thanks, Betty."

I raised a questioning brow as to why Sarah was on the phone with the neighbor who hated me. Then again, Betty was the queen of the Whipple Street Gossips, and if anyone would know what was going on with George, she'd be the first stop for an inquiring mind.

Sarah said goodbye and informed me, "His closest relative is a brother in Wyoming."

"George has a brother?" I rubbed the top of my head. From my experience, brothers were pretty much useless in times of emergencies.

"Apparently." Sarah punched the digits into her phone. Soon enough, she said, "Is this Walter Newsome?" There was a pause. "Oh, I'm so sorry to hear that." Sarah made a throat-cutting gesture to inform me Walter wasn't a viable solution.

Shit.

Were we on the hook for George's care?

No.

I was putting my foot down.

Demi was family.

George was an old man.

Who was all alone.

Fuck.

We were on the hook for his care.

I groaned at the ceiling, shaking both fists.

Sarah continued. "My name is Sarah, and I'm calling about George." Another pause. "You're his nephew?" Sarah wandered into the library.

I returned to the family room, where George shivered under the blankets even though the fire was roaring.

"I think we should call an ambulance," Maddie whispered out of the side of her mouth.

The idea wasn't appealing since it would bring out all the neighbors, and my brother, who literally had his mugshot smeared all over financial websites and blogs, was currently under my roof—or hunting for a Yorkie. What would the headline scream if Peter was caught smuggling the dog from George's house? *Corporate Raider Turned Puppy Thief*? He'd truly become America's most hated man.

But, George had been wandering through the snow without shoes for God knows how long. How could I let an old man die in my home? If the press got word about that... I was turning into such a cynic.

I nodded.

"Is this a 911 thing?"

"How would I know? Is there a number we can just call to

say, 'Hey, there's a frozen old man sitting in front of my fireplace, so can you come get him before his toes fall off?'"

Maddie peered at me. "Sometimes I really wonder about you."

Only sometimes?

She must have opted for 911, because she didn't bother looking up a number. I'd been about to ask Alexa, but maybe it was better not to on the off-chance George was more lucid than he appeared.

Would anyone notice if I went back to bed? Or hid upstairs in the nursery? Or simply walked out the front door and returned a few days from now? Everyone had survived while I was in bed.

Sarah approached in her *momma general* way. "Okay, his nephew is calling George's sister."

I stuck a hand in the air. "Are you telling me George has a nephew and a sister?"

She nodded, her eyes clouding over with confusion.

"Then why in the fuck where we stuck with him on Christmas? The man kept talking about how much he liked dick in front of our children, and I'm still not certain he didn't sleep with Tie in the library."

"What?" Peter stood in the room, holding Gandhi in his arms. Once again, I worried about headlines, but I didn't see any strange vehicles on the street or whatever.

"Uh, an ambulance is coming for George."

"What were you talking about? What about George and Tie?"

"It was just a... a misunderstanding. You came in at the wrong time."

Which was becoming the story of my life.

Peter stared at George, who had his eyes closed, and then glanced at everyone else. "I don't know what to believe anymore. About anything."

I nodded, feeling fully connected to Peter at that moment.

"How long do you think the ambulance will take?" Maddie asked, and I was pretty sure she did so to keep all of us on the task at hand: not letting George expire in one of my favorite chairs.

Seriously, had the flu warped my brain entirely and made me less compassionate?

Or was everything colliding at once and my clueless brain had simply snapped like a twig?

"What should I do with this?" Peter held up the dog, who licked Peter's face.

"Put him in the library. I don't want him running about when the paramedics come. The last thing we need is to rush him to the vet for a plaster cast."

Maddie asked me, "Have you ever seen a dog with a plaster cast?"

"No. And I don't want to."

"You're grumpy."

"I'm tired. Of everything. Everyone seems to dump all their shit at our doorstep. I don't get it. You fucked Peter in our home and got engaged to my half brother in my backyard. Peter got arrested on Christmas. We just got rid of Ethan's high medical needs cat, and now we have George's Yorkie. And, George is dying in my favorite chair by the fire!"

Everyone stared at me.

Paramedics burst into the room.

Gabe asked Maddie, "When did you fuck Peter?"

Maddie scrambled out of the way of a woman checking George's vital signs. "I was engaged to him."

"Before Lizzie and Sarah bought this home." A vein in Gabe's forehead pulsed.

How in the world did Gabe remember that detail with everything going on?

"Did you sleep with Peter after he married Tie?" Gabe pressed.

Sarah waved her hands in the air. "Can we focus on one problem at a time? Which in case none of you can figure out on your own is the old man being attended to by these very kind people who don't really care who fucked whom and when."

From the curious expressions on the paramedics' faces, I think they were more than slightly interested, but they continued to take care of George. Soon, a gurney was brought in, and they loaded up George.

"Where are you taking him?" Sarah asked.

The female supplied the hospital name and then said, "We can't allow one of you in the ambulance, but you can meet him there."

I stifled a groan, knowing the George experience wasn't over and we'd be spending the rest of the day in a hospital. Or Sarah would. Leaving me with the twins, Demi, a Yorkie, and two brothers who could possibly end up in a fistfight.

Could the new year get any worse?

CHAPTER TWELVE

Maddie and Sarah headed to the hospital to attend to George as much as they could considering they weren't family members. I highly suspected their involvement would be coordinating between George's nephew and sister until they arrived. Sarah's motives I understood. That was who she was. If there was a person in need, she'd rush to their side.

Maddie, on the other hand, had a big heart no doubt, but I suspected it was limited to those in her immediate circle. She'd probably prefer dangling from the Empire State Building than face the Gabe inquisition. So far, her second engagement was crashing and burning much faster than the one with Peter. Seriously, I'd been a relationship moron for much of my twenties, but as it was turning out, I was heads above Maddie, who loved to counsel people about their flaws. Was that her flaw? Being able to see others quicksand but not her own?

At the moment I had a bigger problem on my hand. Two brothers, who both remained in my house, seething.

Jorie was still upstairs with the kids, who were not taking a nap, but I'd asked her again to keep watch over them and entertain them to the best of her ability. It was turning into a hell of a job interview for the poor woman.

Gandhi zipped around the house, yapping his head off, hunting for Hank, who I was willing to bet was hiding in my sweaters in the closet, his safe place when things got crazy here. Was there room for me?

I stood in between Peter and Gabe, still in my slippers and navy bathrobe.

"When did it happen?" Gabe demanded.

Peter released an evil laugh. "Like I'm the type to talk about that."

It struck me as odd, considering Peter hadn't exactly been careful about his philandering ways. At the same time, he'd never bragged about conquests, either. At least not with me. That didn't mean much since I still didn't know many things about my middle-aged brother.

"Before or after I met Maddie?" Gabe pressed.

"This is a conversation you should be having with your *fiancée*." Peter stressed the final word, punctuating the sentence with an exuberant hand gesture.

"I plan on it!" Gabe reached around me and shoved Peter's shoulder.

Peter returned the shove, jostling me.

I placed one hand on each brother. "Gentlemen!"

There was a knock on the door.

I ignored it, not comfortable leaving my post between the dueling brothers. "Can we keep this civil? We're all family."

"No, Lizzie, we're not. Gabe's an interloper."

"Interloper! I spent more time with your father than the two of you combined. At least I wasn't one of the forgotten children. Admit it, Peter, that rankles you."

It was an interesting argument I hadn't fully analyzed, focusing more on the fact that Gabe and Allen had grown up with an actual mother, not some monster who delighted in torturing her offspring. Was Peter jealous Gabe knew his stepfather better than Peter did? Was I? I'd wondered how Peter felt about Allen, who was a blood brother. But what about Gabe? It did appear he'd spent a lot more time with Dad. At least during his younger years. They even had a holiday tradition, which we didn't have in our home. Until recently, Peter worked alongside Dad. Had that turned the tables on Gabe's connection?

Dad had probably gone to their soccer games, if they'd played soccer. Attended school plays. Had he gone to parent teacher conferences for both of them? Could he have since the relationship was a secret? Had he worn a disguise? The image of my father in a false beard, wig, and large overcoat, attempting to speak with an English accent infiltrated my mind, and I started to laugh hysterically, bending over at the knees.

"Look what you did. You broke Lizzie!" Gabe sucker punched Peter in the gut.

Peter bent over, recovering much more quickly than I'd anticipated, and he plowed into Gabe, both of them ending up on the floor, rolling around, hitting and kicking. It was like watching two children who'd never learned how to fight.

There was a deafening whistle, and I quickly smothered my ears, turning to see Courtney with both pinkies in her mouth, releasing yet another whistle.

"What are you doing here?" I asked, dumbstruck.

"Maddie sent me over. We were supposed to have lunch, but she filled me in, worried that these two bozos would do—well, this." Courtney pointed to Peter and Gabe, both laying on their backs, breathing heavily. Gabe's nose was bloody, and Peter had a split lip.

"It's a new thing, apparently. Mortal combat Petrie style." I shrugged. "Can you teach me how to whistle like that?" With three kids, a cat, and possibly a dog, it may come in handy.

She smiled. "Sure. What should we do with these two?"

I glanced down at them. "Good question. If they want to act this way, I wish they'd go to their own homes and do it. I'm so over this shit."

It struck me I was standing in a room with three individuals Maddie had slept with during the last two years. Did either of the guys know that? And, if they found out, would they brawl with Courtney?

My money was on Courtney winning that fight.

"Did Maddie say anything about George?" Before she had a chance to answer, I plowed on, "I need tea. My throat is killing me. Would you like tea? Something else? Is it too early for wine?"

"Tea sounds great."

I stood over my brothers. "I'm going to the kitchen. If I hear one punch or whatever, I may call the cops. Peter, you'd be the big loser in that one, considering. Seriously, you two, my children are upstairs. As is your daughter." I jabbed my finger at Peter. "We might be fucked up because of our upbringing, but I'm doing everything possible to give my children a better chance in this world. If you two fuckwits can't get onboard with that, the front door is that way. Don't let it hit you in the ass on the way out."

In the kitchen, Courtney chuckled. "Fuckwits. I need to start using that word more with my subordinates." She continued laughing. "Maddie told me you've been on death's doorstep. You really do look like hell."

"I feel like it." To hammer the point home, I had yet another coughing fit.

"Not to be rude, but I think I'll make the tea. I hate germs."

I plunked down on the barstool. "No arguments here."

"Have you tried grog?"

"Like what pirates drank?" I contemplated this, wondering if Courtney knew the best way to get me to try something was to go the historical route. The nerd in me couldn't refuse most of the time.

"Kinda. A few years back, I had a hellacious cold, and Kit made me his version of grog. Lo and behold, it helped."

"Kit? Tie's brother took care of you when you were sick?"

"He can be sweet when he wants to be." She shrugged.

I shook my head, not entirely believing a word she said. "I can't picture Tie doing anything like that unless the mixture contained poison."

"They're two different people. Much like you and Peter."

I showed my palms. "Point taken." Although, Kit hadn't called once to check on Demi during this, and I wasn't holding my breath that he ever would.

"Will you at least try some grog if I make it?"

I started to say no but hacked up a chunk of what I assumed was my lung.

"I'll take that as a yes." She patted my head on the way out of the kitchen, presumably to stock up on grog ingredients from the bar in the library.

Soon enough, she returned with a bottle of rum and then rummaged in the pantry, locating cloves and sugar.

"Did pirates have a long life expectancy?" I asked.

"Probably not, but I sincerely doubt it was the rum. Swords, cannonballs, sinking ships, the English navy, and lack of vitamin C probably killed more of them than the drink I'm about to make you."

"Scurvy over grog." I chanted the word *grog* in my head, while Courtney prepped the concoction. "How do you know so much about piracy?"

"I get my history lessons like anyone else. From movies and TV."

I huffed.

She chuckled. "What caused the brouhaha between the stepbrothers?"

"Maddie and I inadvertently."

"I guessed the Maddie bit, but how do you factor in?" She added some cloves to the simmering mixture on the stovetop.

"It's possible I mentioned Maddie and Peter's tryst in my home when I was having a verbal meltdown while the paramedics were attending to George." My shrug implied, *What can I do?*

She laughed. "Sorry I missed that, Bottle Rocket."

I rolled my eyes at her nickname for me. "Gloating isn't a good look on you."

"Are you sure?" She batted her eyelashes.

"Lizzie?"

I whipped around. "Oh, Jorie! I'm so sorry. I forgot you were still here. It's been… interesting down here."

Jorie had three baby monitors in her hands, each showing a sleeping child. "I gathered from all the ruckus. Is it always this… eventful?"

Fearful she may quit her nanny position after one day, but not wanting to outright lie, I said, "It depends on the day and how many Petries are under one roof. Although, technically, Gabe isn't a Petrie, so there goes that theory."

"He's family, though, so I think it still counts. Hi, I'm Courtney." She extended her hand over the kitchen island for Jorie. "I don't think I've had the pleasure before." Courtney didn't attempt to hide the fact she was ogling Jorie's rack, which was hard to avoid looking at considering… *No, Lizzie, don't dwell on your new nanny's boobs.*

Jorie placed the monitors down on the countertop and shook Courtney's hand.

They both held on for a moment longer than necessary.

Just what I needed. For Courtney to seduce my newest nanny while my youngest sibling dated the other nanny. What happened to people finding love in the workplace?

"How'd you get the kids down for a nap?" I asked.

"It wasn't hard really. I sang some lullabies, and surprisingly, you can't hear much of what's happening down here, which helped. It wasn't until I saw them on the floor that I realized they'd been fighting."

"Ah, they're still on the floor. Good. Probably wore themselves out acting like fucking assholes." I closed my eyes. "My apologies."

"I'm making grog for Lizzie. Would you like some?" Courtney splayed her fingers on the countertop, pressing down on her hands, showcasing her cleavage, and even I took a gander, immediately feeling guilty.

"Uh, I think I'm still on the clock."

Courtney's eyes crinkled. "What clock?"

"My nanny clock," I declared as a way to say *hands off*.

"What?" Realization seeped into her eyes. "Oh, you're watching the bambinos. I thought Lizzie just got really interesting." Courtney winked at me.

Fairly certain she was implying I'd been paying Jorie for sexual favors, I stared, openmouthed, delighting Courtney further.

"Hey, is it safe in here?"

Rose and Troy stood in the kitchen entryway on the side of the dining room. Had they spied the stepbrothers in the family room and taken the long route?

Courtney waved them in. "I don't recommend the family room. Peter and Gabe may be gathering their strength for round two. Or is it three?"

"How are you feeling, Lizzie?" Troy asked.

"Like I want to die. And not just because of the flu."

Rose tutted sympathetically, while Troy patted my back.

"What caused this latest twist?" Rose asked.

Courtney and I said, "Maddie."

Rose nodded. "It was only a matter of time, considering."

"Really?" I said.

Everyone but Troy stared at me with *duh* expressions on their faces. I didn't have the energy to press for signs I'd missed. I knew the two weren't the best of friends, but literally fighting each other?

"We're here to take the kids," Troy said to Courtney as if she were the woman of the house. At the moment, I was fine with that. I had my head propped on my palm, trying to stay awake.

Courtney turned to Jorie. "Looks like one more for grog."

"I actually have to head out to pick up my brother from a birthday party." Jorie's gaze skittered over Courtney.

I couldn't have come up with a better excuse, and I was 87.56 percent sure Jorie wasn't fibbing.

"What are you going to do with…?" Rose jabbed her thumb to the family room.

"I'm ignoring them for the moment. It's a Maddie issue, and I have no desire to call in the authorities. It's becoming too common here," I explained.

Surprisingly, everyone nodded in agreement.

"Oh." Courtney snapped her fingers. "I hear congrats are in order."

Rose rested her head on Troy's shoulder. "Thank you."

"Have you two set a date?"

"Not yet," Rose said with a look that implied there was too much family drama to focus on that.

I felt terrible and wondered if I should talk to Sarah later to see if we could help in some way.

Courtney also seemed to pick up on it and nodded sympathetically, adding more rum to her brew. "You know, maybe everyone needs some today." She dumped the rest of the bottle in.

It was still early. Sarah had hired Jorie as our nanny. George had been wheeled out of my house. Peter and Gabe had tried to punch each other's lights out. Courtney was in my home, and even though I hadn't yet put my finger on how that factored in, I was certain it did. And, I was willing to bet we'd adopted the demented Yorkie, who was adorable, but loud and energetic, which wasn't helping the pounding behind my eyes. I couldn't imagine what the rest of the day would bring.

"Any word from Tie?" Rose asked Courtney.

Courtney, with a look of contrition, shook her head.

Rose spoke to Troy. "I hate to take the kids when they're sleeping, but it's probably still for the best."

"Sorry about this," I said.

"You have enough on your plate today. Sarah said she'd be home in a few hours. George's sister is on her way from Casper to take over there. Does anyone else want to hide in our home?" She surveyed everyone's face, even Jorie's, which was sweet considering the young woman had her own difficult family and I think secretly wanted to be adopted by the Petries. God help her. Probably for the best to get her out of the situation today, but how?

"Well, I should be going. I hope everything... Good luck." Jorie waved adios.

"I'll walk you to the door. No innocents will be injured on my watch." Courtney waved for Jorie to head through the dining room instead of the brawler's pit, also known as the family room.

The sparks between Courtney and Jorie were hard to miss. Would they stop in the library to cement the deal? It seemed to be the thing these days.

"Did they just meet?" Rose hefted her eyebrows.

"Yes, but... I don't know why everyone in my life has it out for me these days," I said. "I wish Sarah were here." I rested my cheek on the countertop, enjoying the coolness on my clammy skin.

Courtney sailed back into the kitchen, a big smile on her face. "What'd I miss?"

There was a scuffle in the family room.

Courtney headed for the fray with Troy tailing her.

Rose and I exchanged a surprised look. Did Troy plan on enlisting the men to sing along to "Twinkle Twinkle Little Star" to help them calm down?

There were raised voices.

I reached for my phone, contemplating following through on my threat to call the cops. But the neighbors were probably already dissecting the George drama, and this was after Peter's arrest.

Instead, I dialed Helen's number. "Hey, it's Lizzie."

"How are—?"

"You need to come get Gabe. Now. Before he kills Peter or ends up dead. It's a toss-up, really."

"Be right there."

"She's on her way," I informed Rose as I disconnected the call. "Now what?"

"Have you considered moving? I hear Alaska is quite nice this time of year."

"Tempting."

She laughed. "You know it's bad when you're considering moving to Alaska in the dead of winter."

CHAPTER THIRTEEN

Since the kids and Jorie were now out of the house, all the adults—and I was using the term loosely—were in the family room, nursing steaming mugs of grog.

"Oh, Gabe, your mommy's here," Peter scoffed. His lower lip still had blood on it and was puffed out, making the words difficult to decipher.

"At least I have one." Gabe's white shirt was splattered with blood. "Even when yours was alive, she wasn't much of one."

That seemed like a low blow to Peter *and* me.

Dad stepped in behind Helen.

"Uh-oh, Petey, your daddy's here." Gabe really seemed pleased with himself, and it was a side of him I didn't know he had.

Helen and Dad stared at their grown sons as if they'd never seen them before.

"I recommend the grog. It makes this much more bearable." I swayed my mug side to side as if in a Bavarian pub.

"Mental note, Lizzie can't handle rum," Courtney said, tapping her temple with an index finger.

"That's the least of our concerns at the moment. Does

anyone want to fill me in?" Helen crossed her arms, tapping one foot.

"It's my fault." I hiccupped. "I'm just so sick of all of you. Having your lives fall apart and expecting me to put them back together. It took me years to get my life together, while all of you"—I swung my mug to include everyone—"didn't give a shit if I was floundering. I survived alcoholic Meg. Grad school. Battled Graves' disease on my own. Then I met Sarah. Fell in love. And, even then, I was pretty much ignored.

"Then Mom died, and *voilà*, you two," I singled out Dad and Helen, "want me to accept your relationship at face value when, honestly, I resent all the lies and abandonment. Peter's unraveling and quite possibly going to prison. And he wants my help. Gabe is engaged to Maddie, when neither is ready for marriage because they don't really know each other. And, it's clear he's jealous of Peter and vice versa. Sarah is at the hospital taking care of our neighbor. His dog"—I petted Gandhi's head—"he's a pretty good cuddler. Courtney—you make great grog, although, I think you want to fuck my nanny." I hiccupped again. "That pretty much sums up everything."

"I see," my father said. "I'll take you up on the offer of grog."

Courtney hopped to her feet. "Helen?"

"Yes, dear. This isn't going to be pretty."

I tossed my head back. "Oh no! Is this going to turn into a family heart-to-heart? Can't all of you just leave?"

"Is that what you want?" It was Sarah's voice.

I sat up straighter, holding Gandhi tighter as if I needed protection. "Oh, hi. You're back."

"I heard I was needed."

"You have no idea," Peter said. "Lizzie's losing it."

"Says the man with a fat lip," I scoffed.

Courtney returned with two mugs.

"How much has she had?" Sarah asked.

"Not enough. Grog wench, more, please." I held my mug up for Courtney to refill.

"I kinda like that name." Courtney took my mug.

"Where's Maddie?" Gabe asked.

"At the hospital."

"Coward!" I shouted between my hands, bullhorn-like. "Hey, everyone who's slept with Maddie, raise your hand."

Sarah gave me her *not one more word out of you* glare.

Undeterred, I slurred, "S-ssory, but it's been a big fucking elephant in the room. This entire family has is-issues with keeping their pants on. And for some reason, everyone's pecca-dildos—dillos, rather, cause problems in my life when the last thing I really want to know about is who is s-screwing who. I don't give a sh-sh-shit." It took effort to get out the last word. "Jesus, I'm the lesbian of the family. Lizzie the Lesbian destroys all. If you listen to the family values sch-schmucks, I'm the downfall of society, but it's all you fuckwits who are ruining things."

Sarah set her purse down on top of the entertainment stand. "You want to have a *come to Jesus* meeting with your family to clear the bad voodoo or whatnot? Fine. Lay it all out, Lizzie."

I thought I had.

Sarah's eyes drilled holes into my forehead. "I'm waiting."

"What am I forgetting?"

"Raise your hand if you've kissed Maddie." She folded her arms across her chest.

All eyes turned to me, although I hadn't raised either hand.

"Really, Sarah? That's what you want to discuss?" I said, my voice wavering at first, but it gained steam by the end.

"It's only fair. You want everyone in this room to atone for some wrong they'd done without you atoning for yours."

"I have atoned for it! Couples therapy. Individual therapy. Apologizing repeatedly. What in the fuck do I have to do to get you past this?" I lurched forward in my seat. "I'm so tired of you throwing it in my face."

"I am past it. I wouldn't have had kids with you if I wasn't. But, I don't think people who live in glass houses should throw stones. I get you're angry with your father, mother, Peter, Gabe, Helen, Allen—"

I motioned for her to stop. "Hold on. I'm not mad at Allen. He had nothing to do with this. He's as much of a vic—" I closed my mouth, clapping a hand over it to ensure it stayed shut.

"Go on, Lizzie. Say the word," Helen prodded with a supportive smile.

I stared at her, trying to figure out the trap.

"You kissed Maddie? When did you kiss Maddie?" Peter asked, more baffled than angry.

Dad waved for him to pipe down. "You are a victim in this. All of you, are, including Peter and Gabe." Dad reached for his wife's hand. "Even Helen. If you want to hold anyone responsible for everything, it should be me."

I blinked.

The man never really spoke, so it took effort to get past the shock of him speaking and laying bare his culpability.

"It wasn't solely you, though. Was it?" I confessed. "The ghost of Mother." I swiped my eyes. "How do I excise the damage she's done? Why did I have a mother who never loved me? Hated me, in fact. Who delighted in torturing me for as long as I can remember. What did I do in a previous life to deserve this? Kill all the fucking unicorns or something?" I clutched my chest. "I have nightmares where she's on top of me, strangling me. I've had that lovely dream since high school. I wake in the middle of the night, terrified I'm all alone just like she said I would be. Whenever I reach a goal, one of my first thoughts is, 'it doesn't matter. She'll still think I'm pathetic.' I hate it. Even from the grave, she still has this power over me." I sucked in a ragged breath. "Sometimes I just want to stop trying. Stop pushing myself. Because it won't matter."

"I think that too," Peter confessed. "She always demanded more, no matter what I achieved. Being valedictorian. Not good enough. Graduating at the top of my MBA program. Not good enough. Making my first million. Nope. Keep pushing. Never rest. Never enjoy. Achieve more. Strive harder. Never relent. It's exhausting."

"Because she didn't enjoy a day in her life," I said. "And she pushed her disappointment onto us. My brain gets that. My heart, though. It hurts. A lot. I'm fucking terrified one day I'll wake up and be her. Hurting the ones I'm closest to." I stared into Sarah's eyes. "I know I'm not perfect. I know I've made egregious mistakes, but when you keep reminding me of them, it hits me more than if you slapped me across the face." I sucked in a breath. "I don't mean you can't ever tell me if I've done something that's upset you. I'm not that delicate. But, I would like to be able to move on once and for all."

"Me too." Peter rose from his seat and extended a hand to Gabe.

Gabe stood, swiping Peter's hand away and pulling him into a hug. "God, I hated you for so long. The perfect eldest son who was the finance world's golden boy."

"Thanks for tossing in *was* the golden boy." Peter laughed. "I never even wanted to go into business."

"You didn't?" I asked.

He shook his head. "I wanted to be a pilot. In the navy."

"I never knew that," Dad said, looking to Helen as if determining he was hearing the words correctly.

"*Top Gun* may have played a factor," Peter said, a sheepish grin sliding onto his face, making him look years younger. "I'm much too old now to chase that dream."

"I always wanted to be a historian."

Peter laughed. "I know. You were born wearing a sweater with elbow patches."

Everyone laughed.

"I never knew how you had the chutzpah to stay the course," he continued. "When I told Mom I wanted to be a pilot—the scream that came out of her. I dropped it right then and there."

"You can still be a pilot. Not in the navy, but you can get a license," I said.

"Do you think I can learn that in prison? Instead of making license plates, go to pilot school?"

"I hear the country club prisons for the likes of you aren't so bad." I shrugged a shoulder, knowing it was a weak attempt to allay his mind.

"I suggest finding a crew in prison. For protection." Gabe shoved his shoulder.

Dad's eyes misted. "Would you excuse me a minute?" He entered the powder room.

Helen stared off into the distance.

Peter sat on the ottoman, his hands pressed together as if he were praying.

Gabe perched on the edge next to him. "It's going to be okay."

I hunched down. "We'll visit you all the time. You may get sick of us."

Tears dropped from his eyes. "Take care of Demi. That's all I ask. She's all I have left."

"We will, but that's not true. Everyone in this room is pulling for you."

Maddie, still in her red wool coat, entered the room. "Uh, is everything okay?"

"Yes and no," Sarah said. "The Petries are having a family meeting, Petrie style."

Peter looked up. "When did you kiss Lizzie?"

Maddie stripped off her jacket. "Let's get this over with."

Gabe, Peter, and I queried each other's faces, before I said, "I think we're okay now. Too bad you weren't here earlier. You missed these two bozos fighting, my meltdown, and Dad's crying in the bathroom. Not a bad day's work. I do ask for the next Petrie meltdown, we meet in someone else's house. I'm tired of you fuckers under my roof." I tossed my arms around Peter's and Gabe's shoulders.

"I love this family. How do I become an honorary member?" Courtney asked, holding two mugs of grog that she'd been gripping while everything had been said.

"Sleep with Maddie. Oh wait, you already did that." Gabe tossed up his hands. "Welcome."

Maddie wheeled about to Sarah. "I'm not liking this."

Sarah smacked her lips. "I…" She didn't complete her thought.

Gabe got to his feet and spoke to Maddie. "Maybe we should go to my place. Talk."

"Sounds ominous but okay."

They left.

"This calls for more grog. I made it to help Lizzie's flu, but I think it has even more powers than I realized. Who wants another cup?" Courtney asked.

We all raised our hands, aside from Peter who said, "I'm going to spend some time with Demi."

"Have the kids had lunch?" Sarah asked.

I started to rise but collapsed back into the seat, Gandhi yapping at me for disturbing his snooze.

"I got it." Sarah left.

"I'll help her." Helen followed.

I closed my eyes to stop the room from spinning. Were pirates always drunk? Perhaps if one of Courtney's ancestors was in charge of the grog. "I need water." It was time to snap out of the fugue.

CHAPTER FOURTEEN

"Do you think we should go back to couple's therapy?" Sarah asked, getting under the covers.

"If you'd like. It's pretty high on my list of things that I love to do." I pulled her closer to me.

"Sarcasm isn't the best form of communication when discussing the state of our marriage." She placed her head on my shoulder.

"Is our marriage in such a state that we have to avoid sarcasm? I didn't think we'd reached that level… again."

"I tossed you under the bus in front of your entire family."

I let out a bark of laughter. "That you did. Luckily for you, it worked. I actually feel somewhat better in an *I can't believe I said all that shit* kinda way."

"You never told me about that dream you have about your mom."

"It's not something I like to talk about. Thinking my mom wanted me dead because I was such a huge disappointment. That's a hard thing to live with."

"I don't think it's true, though. I think you terrified your mom."

I leaned down to look into her eyes. "How so?"

"She knew you were better than she was."

"Ha! I sincerely doubt that."

Sarah's head popped up. "No, seriously. She tried to beat you down. In every way possible, aside from actually killing you, and you didn't let her. Yes, you struggled. You made poor decisions. But, once you righted the ship, you stayed true to yourself. Look at Peter. He went into the family business instead of being a pilot, and we need to stick a pin in that, because that was weird. But, you chased your history dream, incurring the wrath of your mother. Not many would have been able to give your mother, who was a force to be reckoned with, the middle finger like that. It wasn't like you knew your father and perhaps Peter in his own way were silently cheering you on. You did it all on your own. By the time I met you, you were nearly done with your PhD. No one can ever take away your accomplishments, Dr. Petrie. I think deep down, your mother may have admired you."

This thought struck me. "Do you really think so? I mean, I'm not still seeking her approval. Or, I don't believe I am, but that would be ironic—no, that word is misused all the time. It would be interesting if that were the case."

"Only you would toss in how *ironic* is misused while contemplating whether or not your mother actually loved you."

"Loved?"

"Yes. In her really fucking bizarre way." Sarah climbed on top of me. "Women like your mother don't truly understand the feeling, but I can't imagine your mom not loving you, because you really are the most amazing person."

"Aw." I cupped the right side of her face. "You're projecting your feelings onto her. It's something we all do, according to my therapist."

"Let's find a new therapist."

"Do we really have to go to couple's therapy?" I sighed. "I think we're doing okay."

"You didn't tell me until today how much it hurts you when I don't let things go."

"It's not something that's easy to say, especially knowing how much my idiocy hurt you."

"It was years ago."

"I'm aware. Years are kinda my thing. It's all part of that historian gambit."

"Interesting word choice."

"Gambit?"

"It was a risk you took. Who knew a woman would find historians sexy?"

"Are you trying to seduce me?"

She kissed the side of my neck. "Can you blame me when you toss out words like gambit?"

"Why do you think I do it?" My breath hitched when she nibbled on my earlobe.

"Do you use these fancy words when lecturing?"

"Absolutely. I'm pretty sure all my students are madly in love with me."

"It's not just the words or historical knowledge." She continued peppering my neck with sweet kisses.

"What else?"

"Your sweater vests. You wore one the day we met. So sexy."

I dug my head into the pillow, laughing. "You know, when you got it, flaunt it."

Sarah pulled away, her eyes taking me in. "Are you okay? With everything that happened today? Over the holidays? With Peter?"

"I'm on the road to being okay. Do you know what would help me right here and now?"

"What?" Her voice was heavenly sweet and supportive.

"Make love to me. I need to be close to you."

"Are you using sex to distract me from the couples therapy thread?"

"Depends." I ran my hands down her naked back.

She arched her brows. "On?"

"If it's working."

"What if it isn't? Working, that is?"

"Then it'd be an asshole move and completely out of character for me. We Petries, nothing but class." I gyrated my hip into her pussy.

"Yes, I'm picking up on that class." Sarah rode my hip.

"You didn't answer my question. Is it working or not?"

Sarah laughed. "What do you think, Einstein?"

I grabbed the back of her head, pulling her lips to mine, hard at first, easing into a sweet but sexy kiss, our tongues dancing in tune with the other.

Raising my hip higher into Sarah, her increasing wetness indeed was testimony my diversionary tactic was more than successful.

"Why do we ever get out of bed?" I asked during a breather from our lip lock.

"Life. Three kids. Jobs." Sarah hitched a shoulder as if implying it couldn't be helped.

"It's just so unfair. I want to stay here with you all the time."

"Don't you think you'd get tired of sex?"

I kneaded her left breast. "Not at all."

"You can be such a scoundrel sometimes."

"You're complaining that I find you sexy as hell and always want you naked in bed with me? Seriously?"

"For someone who wants to fuck all the time, you're sure doing a lot of talking instead."

"I'm waiting for you to fuck me. Was I not clear enough at the start?"

"Is that right? Do you have anything in particular in mind?"

"Oh my God, I have to do everything." I rolled Sarah onto her back, both of us laughing. "How about I show you what I like doing to you, and if you have the energy, you can replicate it?"

"Still talking, dear."

I kissed her much harder this time.

Sarah bit down on my lip.

I groaned into her mouth.

One of my hands snaked down her supple skin, slipping under her derriere, angling her slick pussy into my hip, hitting just the right spot.

"That's a move I really like." Her breath hitched, her back arching, showcasing her marvelous tits.

"It always works to my tit fetish." I clamped my lips onto her nub. It already was fully alive in my mouth. I tugged it. Nipped. Sucked. Teased.

Sarah's eyes closed.

One hand fisted the sheet; the other threaded its fingers into my hair.

Our bodies moved in unison, the urgency kicking up a notch but not quite to the *take me right fucking now* stage, allowing me time to explore more of her.

I slid my tongue from one nipple to the next.

Again, her breath hitched, her nails leaving marks on my scalp.

I bit down harder, both of us releasing an *oh Jesus* moan.

I shifted off her slightly, inserting two fingers into her wetness. So fucking incredible.

Sarah's muscles tightened, embracing my presence. "You always feel so good."

I groaned my yes, unable to articulate anything in recognizable English. Or in any language aside from the secret communication we'd developed over the course of our lives together. A language only the two of us would ever hear.

Hammering in deeper, I received Sarah's nonverbal *Oh fuck, don't stop*.

I didn't, my mouth now making its way to her epicenter, her scent guiding me home. Although, I took my time, licking and kissing her skin. Tasting her desire, love, wanting. The shortest distance may be from A to B, but life and longing resided in all the tangents along the way. One thing I'd learn being with Sarah was to enjoy every second we had together, because like she'd said earlier, life, kids, and jobs took us away from each other more than they brought us together. A fact of life no one explained.

These journeys showed me Sarah had one particular spot an inch from the right of her belly button that drove her insane, in a good way. All it took was a kiss or lap of the tongue to elicit the most satisfying groan. I loved making Sarah come, but that wasn't all that mattered in bed. Every moan, hitch of the breath, scoring of my skin, fisting of the sheets, gyration, scream, arched back—they all mattered and left indelible marks in my memory bank. When I replayed memories, more often than not, I cherished the aspects most would ignore or skip entirely. All of the steps created the memory, much like historical events. I caused her to feel this way. That was a gift not to be taken for granted.

I'd arrived at the spot.

Sucking in the deepest breath.

Flicking her bud with my tongue.

Moving further south.

Dipping inside.

Moving further south.

Running my tongue inside her left thigh.

Then right.

My fingers back inside, going in deeper.

My mouth finding her spot, once again, taking it fully into my mouth.

Then slowing it down, languorously lapping her throbbing clit, gorging on her passion. For me. Sometimes, that still knocked me for a loop. This stunning creature wanted me. Loved me. Needed me.

I was the luckiest clueless one on the planet.

It was time to show her my gratitude.

I drove in deep.

My mouth worked overtime.

Sarah's upper body lurched completely off the mattress, her hands cradling my head, holding me in place but also conveying her love. We did this together. Like we did everything. But this was the most magical.

Her body quivered.

I knew the exact move that would trigger the release she craved.

Her thighs clamped down around my head, her upper body crashing back onto the mattress, Sarah moaning for me not to stop. Not until she was spent.

I had no intention of letting her down.

Not in bed.

Not in life.

She was my one.

Fuck, I was the luckiest bastard on the planet.

Sarah came.

Hard.

Her body went limp, one of her arms attempting to pull me to her but not having the needed energy. I kissed her clit tenderly, as if saying until we meet again, and I snaked up her side, laying on top of her, both of us breathing heavily.

"I love you," I said, closing my eyes.

"Ditto."

I smiled. "Am I crushing you?"

"Not at all. I've always loved you on top of me."

"Good. I may fall asleep like this."

She kissed my forehead. "While I'd love that, I kinda have another plan in mind."

"What?"

She got me on my back. "You asked me to make love to you, remember?"

"That does ring a bell, but I thought you were content with being a pillow princess."

Sarah smiled. "You think you're such a comedian." Her fingers separated me below. "Oh my, you're wet. If I don't do something, you may explode." She plunged in deep.

CHAPTER FIFTEEN

I sat in the quaint coffee shop near the campus, waiting. Given that the spring semester hadn't started yet, and it was a snowy mid-January day, the place had an *end of the world* feel all the while exuding a warm and cozy vibe. It was extremely off-putting to the likes of the black and whiteness I preferred.

The short woman breezed in with a confidence that was difficult to ignore, and truth be told, I resented her a bit for it.

"Lizzie."

I rose and shook JJ Cavendish's hand.

"Can I buy you another drink?" She motioned to my half-consumed chai.

"Uh, sure. Why not? Chai, please." My heart was racing, but I wasn't certain if I could solely blame the caffeinated drink.

JJ marched to the register, placed the order, and paid with cash.

Soon enough, she was sitting across from me with an odd smile. "I've heard through the wife grapevine you've been going back and forth about the job offer. I'm serious. I do want to hire you for both writing and the show, which we're hoping to launch in late spring or early summer."

I laughed nervously. "Oh, I know the offer is real. It's just the accepting part that's... giving me heart palpitations."

"I love the honesty. Can you tell me why?"

A twenty-something woman with an eyebrow piercing called out the drink order behind the counter. JJ gestured for me to hold my thought while she fetched the drinks.

My brain seemed to be lacking any thoughts at the moment. Was this what it would be like when the cameras were on me?

JJ placed my chai in front of me.

I wrapped my fingers around the warm mug.

"You were saying," she prodded.

"Not much. That's the problem. You're asking me to do a job that's just not in my wheelhouse."

Her enigmatic smile returned. "Says the college professor whose students love her."

"I wouldn't go that far."

"I spoke with Jorie at the last music class. Her baby brother is adorable, but I'm digressing. She told me how much your lectures affected her."

"Jorie's a special case."

JJ shifted in her seat. "How so?"

"She's struggling with coming out, and I'm some type of lesbian role model for her." I waved, trying to imply the idea was preposterous given I wasn't the role model type.

"You think that's the sole reason why she connected with you?"

I shrugged. "It's what comes to mind, yes."

JJ sipped her drink. "I have a hard time believing in myself as well."

I hunkered down into my chair.

"No, it's true."

"I'm sorry, but you run an up-and-coming media company,

you've penned a best-selling memoir, and your nickname is literally The Miracle Girl."

"Guilty on all fronts. Doesn't mean I'm comfortable in my own skin."

"Why would your viewers want to hear me talk about anything? Jesus, I'm awkward at best, and there are some who are probably trying to figure out if I'm on the spectrum."

She looked at me quizzically.

"The autistic spectrum disorder."

"Are you?" Her voice was supportive.

"I... I don't think so. Just awkward. Ya know, Mom issues." I flicked a hand, implying *what can you do about that?*

"What's wrong with being awkward?"

"You are aware of the definition."

"Enlighten me." She leaned on the table, holding her drink with both hands.

"Lacking social skills, which strikes me as something required for the role you want me to assume."

"There's no set formula to the perfect TV personality."

"I don't really have much personality. That's what I'm trying to tell you."

"I totally disagree. I find you honest. Intelligent. Vulnerable. Passionate. I've read your books. You have a wonderful way of relating difficult concepts for the average person to evaluate without having to tax their brains too much, something most loathe. I bet if I sat in on some of your lectures, it would only reinforce my feeling that you're the perfect fit for the show. I want real people with informed opinions. I don't give a crap if you were the most popular chick in high school or the social outcast. That doesn't matter."

"And my connection to Peter Petrie?"

She leaned back in her seat, leveling her eyes on me. "He's your brother."

"I'm aware of that. How does my brother factor into your plan?" I circled a finger in the air.

"I'm an only child. I have absolutely no idea what it's like to be judged by my brother's crimes. But I do know what it's like to be judged for the shit I've done. It sucks."

"What does that mean?"

"How much do you know about me?"

"Not much," I confessed.

"How much do you want to know?"

"Is it a requirement? I'm not the type to really dig into people's lives." I shrugged.

"God, why can't the world be filled with people like you?"

"The human population would have died off centuries ago."

She laughed. "I've met your wife and twins. You have everything most would kill for."

I nodded. "I do. I'm a fucking lucky social outcast. If the world was filled with people like me, you wouldn't have a job and, honestly, history would be a lot less entertaining. Boring doesn't sell."

A sadness crept into her eyes. "I know."

"Why'd you go into media?"

"Curiosity. What about history?"

"The same. I wanted to figure out how people could be so cruel."

"What'd you find out?" Her expression had an underlying emotion I couldn't put my finger on.

"It's just how humanity is. Repeatedly." I made a circular motion with my index finger.

"That's a cheerful thought." Her eyes bored into mine.

"Do you disagree?"

She shook her head. "I've seen enough to know you're spot-on."

"People suck." I sipped my chai.

"Mean people, yes. But not everyone is mean. Some are just lost."

"Tell me about it." I stretched both arms above me and then cradled the back of my head.

"I'm starving. Do you want to go someplace to have lunch? We can continue this, because I'm really interested in your analysis."

* * *

AFTER LUNCH, I popped into the office to take care of some prep before the start of the semester.

"We missed seeing you on New Year's. How are you feeling?"

I looked up from my desk. "Dr. Marcel, happy New Year."

He ambled into the room and took a seat. "You too."

I set my pen down on a sheet of paper where I'd drawn a terrible sketch of my cat, Hank.

He leaned over to peek at the sheet. "Care to tell me what's bothering you?"

I sighed. "Not sure there's enough time in the day for that."

"I read about Peter."

"You and everyone else on the planet." I straightened in my chair. "I'm sorry."

"It's okay. If I were in your shoes, I wouldn't know how to act either when people mentioned my brother, who is arguably one of the world's least favorite people in the news. Is that what's causing your face to pucker like you've been staring directly into the sun for hours without blinking?"

"Peter is part of it. The other is a recent job offer."

His widened eyes clued me in I'd captured his interest. "What kind of offer?"

"It's not another teaching job." I placated with hand gestures to assure him I had no intention of leaving my teaching post. He only had one more semester left before retirement, and the last thing he needed was to find my replacement. "More like a part-time thing."

"Are you in need of it?"

"Define *need*?" I flicked my hand to suggest I was kidding, but I ended up threading my fingers on top of my desk to get my nervousness under control. It wasn't Dr. Marcel making me nervous. Just everything in life. "It's a TV show gig. If I'm understanding the job description correctly, they want me to lend my insight about the state of the world."

He relaxed into the chair. "That sounds like an excellent opportunity."

"Does it?" I ran a hand over my head. "I just never thought of myself doing such a thing. Being on TV. Fame isn't something I've ever chased or craved."

"No, I imagine not. Or if you did, the historian route was an interesting choice." He laughed at his own joke. "Life has a funny way of surprising even the most prepared. Since I've met you, you've worked your tail off to succeed at everything. You still do when it comes to teaching, being a wife, and mom. I have no doubt you'll put the same effort into this."

"If I accept."

His mouth curved up. "When have you ever turned down a challenge?"

I rolled my eyes. "You're going to play mind games with me?"

"Is that how you see it? Fascinating?" He waggled his brows. "I remember a time when you wouldn't have tossed that in my face, choosing to sit there with a forced blank expression instead. I much prefer it when you call me out on my shit. You're becoming more and more the woman I always knew was inside you."

"Which is?"

"Confident."

"Does this mean you think I should do it?" I reached for my pen and inspected it as if I'd never seen it before in my life.

"It means I believe you'd be great at anything you put your mind to. Also, if you have any ambition to advance in academia, which I know you do, this could be an excellent stepping stone. Take it from an old geezer; opportunities like this don't fall into your lap every day."

"The timing isn't great."

"It rarely is. As a historian, you know that."

"Yeah, but when dealing with this and Sarah wanting to have another child because her clock is ticking…" I released a puff of air. "I never thought I'd be raising four kids, have a cat, and now George's dog."

"Four kids? You've been busy since I last saw you before the holidays," he teased.

"One is Demi, Peter's daughter. And, well, Sarah and I are trying to get pregnant again." It was odd admitting this since I was the prude Sarah always accused me of, but later this week we had our first doctor's appointment to discuss the insemination process. I was bursting at the seams with excitement, along with the usual *am I ready to populate the world with another Petrie?* fear.

His fatherly grin widened. "I can't wait to tell Lydia. She'll love having more little ones to spoil. How'd you end up with George's dog? That's your neighbor, right?" He arched his brow in the way I knew indicated he wanted me to fill him in.

After I did, I stared at the newly tacked-up lighthouse wall calendar Sarah had given me. January's photo showed one being pummeled by the water on three of the four sides. Boy, could I relate.

Dr. Marcel whistled. "You do have a full plate." He chuckled. "I wish I could tell you it gets easier, but it never does. Life keeps chucking curveballs no matter what. Be grateful you have a wife like Sarah. Together, you two will deal with everything. Is this a bad time to mention I want you to take over another one of my classes?"

My jaw dropped.

He showed his palms. "Kidding. I couldn't help it. The look on your face." He slapped the arm of the chair. His laughing subsided some. "How can I help you? Arrange time in the studio for the show, perhaps?"

"That would be great if I take it on. I'll let you know soon, I promise. Oh, how do I go about starting internships for students to work at the local paper?"

His grin was the type I imagined a father wore on his daughter's wedding day. "You never cease to amaze me. I'll have Jean set up an appointment to walk us through the paperwork. What gave you the idea?"

"It's something I always wanted to do, but didn't have the opportunity."

"So you're creating it for others." He started to rise. "Take the job, Lizzie. You have a heart of gold. Share it."

CHAPTER SIXTEEN

I tramped into the kitchen, placing my laptop bag on the stool.

"How was your day?" Sarah asked with a sweetness in her tired voice.

"Okay. Yours?"

"Okay."

"You seem as tired as I am." I glanced about. "Where are the kids?"

"With Jorie and Bailey at the art table. Valentine's Day is just around the corner."

I groaned.

"Oh, don't be that way. Who doesn't love a fabricated holiday? My favorite part is the candy hearts."

I made a mental note to pick up some. "I'm sure flower companies helped shape it."

"Speaking of, Gabe is in your office hanging out in hopes you have time to chat."

I groaned again. "When did I become the Petrie headshrinker?"

"He's not a Petrie."

"Excellent point. Not a drop of blood connects us."

"And yet you love him. Amazing how that works." She motioned to the boxes on the counter. "Black or herbal? Kettle is already hot." Her smile didn't attempt to hide the fact she'd been plotting this. Had she requested Gabe wait for me in the office?

"Black." I slid onto the barstool that didn't house my bag. "Any idea what he wants to talk about, oh wise one?"

She chuckled. "Even you must have a general idea."

"Maddie? Relationships? If the Easter Bunny is real?"

"I hope for your sake it's the latter. Much easier to dissect."

"You'd dissect the Easter Bunny? All this time, I didn't know I was married to a sociopath." I drummed the side of my thumb on the counter.

"I did."

I started to laugh but stopped abruptly. "Do you mean you knew you were a sociopath or that I'm one?"

"You don't expect me to answer that question, do you? Sometimes you just have to puzzle things out on your own." She placed two steaming mugs of tea in front of me. "Time to face the executioner."

"Was that a hint that you're the sociopath?"

"I love you."

"You're confusing the fuck out of me today." I gripped the mugs and headed for the office.

Gabe sat at my desk with his laptop open, but I suspected from the canned laughter filtering from the speakers he wasn't working but streaming a comedy show.

"I hope black tea is okay."

"Perfect." He closed his computer and rose. "I hope you don't mind." He motioned to his station at the desk.

"Not at all." I set his mug down on the far side of the coffee table wedged between the two sofas and collapsed onto the one facing the desk, cradling the cup between my hands. The fire kept the room at a comfortable temperature, but I still felt chilled. Hopefully that wasn't a sign of how the conversation would go.

Gabe took a seat on the opposite one, looking pale and about ready to spew chunks. Sadly, I thought it was the result of emotions, not the flu. Slipping him Theraflu would have been a much easier task that involved minimal talking.

"Sarah mentioned you wanted to chat."

"I never told her that."

"She has a way of figuring shit out. It's annoying as hell."

He nodded.

"How's Maddie?" I asked.

"Pissed."

"So getting into a fistfight with her ex didn't impress her much. Go figure."

He squirmed. "I feel terrible about that."

"It seemed bound to happen, or at least that's what everyone keeps telling me. I do appreciate that neither of you destroyed my house. Maybe the family should take boxing lessons. That way we can have a professional supervise us as we smack the shit out of each other."

He chuckled. "Do you want to hit me?"

"Not at the moment, but it's still early."

"It's four in the afternoon."

"I meant in our chat. Who knows what you're about to tell me? This isn't my forte."

He gazed at me, his expression softening. "I don't know about that. You have a calming effect on me. I've always felt a kinship with you, considering we both had shitty fathers."

"That's true. Are you still in contact with yours?"

He shook his head. "He bailed on my mom as soon as he heard the news."

"Have you ever met him?"

He bobbed his head. "I think he had a moment of contrition

and reached out, but…" He shrugged. "Fatherhood isn't for everyone, I guess."

"Same for some mothers."

"Yeah, you got screwed on both fronts."

My laughter could cut glass. "It wasn't easy."

"I would have been lost without my mom."

"You're lucky."

"She really likes you, Lizzie." His eyes were kind.

I pressed my lips together.

"How did you get past it?"

Confused, I asked, "Past what?"

"Being abandoned by the very people who were supposed to love you unconditionally."

"What choice did I have?" I set my mug down on the side table. "I didn't even know I was getting past it or whatever. I just kept going. I was lucky to a certain degree, I guess. I loved learning things, so I tucked into books and history." I sighed. "It wasn't until I met Sarah that I realized I wasn't exactly managing my abandonment. More avoiding it."

"Abandonment," he echoed.

"An ugly word."

"You feel like your mom abandoned you?"

"Yes."

"And Charles—I mean, your dad?"

"Yes."

"I know you said you don't, but how do you not hate Allen? Or me?"

I sucked in a deep breath. "It's funny, but I don't. I was shocked when I learned the news, of course. Like I'd been whacked with a two by four. I'm envious, maybe, that you two had Helen." I gestured I had no idea. "Did I mention this shit isn't my strong suit?"

He grunted and sank back into the sofa. "I hated Peter for a long time."

"Tell me about that."

"He was the golden boy who'd been handed everything. I have no doubt Charles loves me, but I'll never be like Peter. His firstborn. The heir apparent."

"Do you want to be part of Dad's company?"

"I did."

"Not anymore?" That was hard to swallow given his obvious barbs about Peter and then literally picking a fight.

He shrugged. "Seems like a shitty way to realize it with Peter going to prison."

"Life is funny the way it presents opportunities." I thought back to what Dr. Marcel had said to me, and his words started to sink in more. I shoved it aside to focus on this conversation. "Has Dad talked to you about it?"

Gabe nodded.

"Recently?"

"Not that recently. I doubt he's had time to process everything with Peter. None of us knows for sure what happened or what to expect. Your father was always kind to me. He paid for my education. He offered me roles in the company." His eyes darted all over the place. Was Dad's retreat a big part of Gabe's current insecurity? Had Gabe thought if he played his cards right, he'd end up with a plum job? But the Peter wrench was ruining all his efforts, including his relationship?

"And you stayed with your mom's business because…?"

"She needed me. Allen has no interest in business, like you."

"How do you feel about Allen?"

A protective look replaced his initial flash of anger. "I really hated him in the beginning. Poor Mom didn't know what to do with me. She put me in therapy out of fear I'd kill him."

I raised my brows. "Was it really that bad?"

"It was just the two of us for years. Then your father,

followed by Allen. I'm ashamed to admit it now, but I didn't welcome either at first."

"I'm glad you met me later." I laughed. "I really didn't need a murdering stepbrother back in the day. I had enough of my own demons to battle."

"I could have helped you slay them. We may have made a great team." He waggled his brows.

I smiled at him. "We still can, Gabe. One thing I've learned from all of the shit swirling around us since meeting is it's better to open up." I leaned forward. "If you ever tell Sarah I said that, I'll kill you."

He mimed waving a white flag. "As long as you don't tell Maddie anything."

"Deal." I reached for my tea and took a bolstering slug. "Do you want to talk about the Maddie bit? That's the part that's really troubling you, isn't it?"

"You're good."

"Years of therapy. I can spot the signs I love to bury deep inside myself. I wonder if that's why therapists go into the business in the first place. It's much easier to fix others than yourself." I didn't mention I suspected Maddie was the same way.

"I don't think Maddie trusts my motivations at the moment."

"What do you mean?"

"She's accused me of wanting to be with her because I'm jealous of Peter and this is my way of really sticking it to him."

That explained a lot, and I felt foolish for not putting my finger on that sooner.

"Is she right?"

"No." He paused. "At least, I don't think so. I can't imagine I'd do that to her. I love her. Honest to God."

He had me until the last sentence.

"What does she want?"

"I don't know. I'm afraid to ask." His eyes fell to his lap.
"Okay, what do you want?"
"Maddie."
"Why?"
"I love—"
"Dig a bit deeper."

He rubbed his palms over his thighs. "It's hard to articulate."

I nodded, not wanting to lead him in either direction.

"I was so angry when I learned she'd slept with Peter after he was married."

An interesting tangent I wasn't expecting him to bring up, probably due to the fact I wouldn't personally want to talk about it. "Because?"

"You're kidding, right?"

"I honestly don't know what thoughts are going through your head. Do you?"

"I'm afraid she'll cheat on me."

"In general or with Peter?"

Gabe sucked in an exasperated breath, his nostrils widening with the effort. "Would it really matter?"

He had a point, but I was starting to see he believed Maddie would choose Peter in the end, which I didn't see happening unless Gabe pushed her away with his jealousy. From experience, women didn't like having their every thought or action questioned. I also knew how controlling the fear of abandonment warped everything, and sometimes it was easier to wreck things because, in a way, it gave a semblance of control.

"How do I let it go?" He slapped his forehead with the heel of his hand.

"Knowing Maddie slept with Peter?" I steepled my index fingers and chewed on the tips.

He nodded.

"I really don't know. Sarah had to forgive me when I made a pass at Maddie. Have you talked to Sarah about it?"

"Can I?"

"If she doesn't mind. I have no say over that."

He seemed to mull this over.

"Can I ask you something?"

Gabe motioned for me to shoot.

"Why'd you rush into asking Maddie to marry you?"

"I love her."

"Okay, but what's wrong with dating and getting to know each other more? Marriage isn't something that should be rushed. Sarah pressured me, and I did everything I could to sabotage us."

"Do you think Maddie will resort to that?"

"Perhaps. Or you. I have to wonder if proposing was your way of trying to end things."

"Let me see if I'm understanding. You're suggesting I asked Maddie to marry me to get rid of her."

"It's a theory of mine."

He stared at me. "That's the weirdest thing I've heard all day."

"No weirder than asking someone you don't trust to forever be your partner in life."

"I want to trust her!" His erratic breathing made it clear his mind was racing and he didn't know what to believe. "And I love her. No matter what." His voice lost steam.

"I don't doubt you love her. Really, I don't. Just consider slowing things down a bit. There's no shame in taking a step back and getting things right from the start." Or it'd crash and burn.

"What about Peter, though? You know them. Do you think she'll go back to him?"

What should I say? I'd also been wondering about the Maddie and Peter saga? It really wasn't my place to dive in between them, more than I had already done. I had a hard enough time managing my own life, but the lost look in his face propelled me to answer. "If you really want my advice, I suggest talking with Maddie. Laying everything out you've told me. Does she even know about your father? The whole story? You're reaction to Allen's birth? How much you hated Peter? These are vital pieces of who you are."

"Not all of it. What if some aspects push her away?"

"Honesty can be excruciating. I know this firsthand. I also know when I tried to hide the most embarrassing aspects of my past from Sarah, it nearly destroyed everything." A thought struck me. "They say therapy plunges you into the deep end of darkness until you can see your way out of it. It's not pretty. It sucks, actually, which you may remember from when you went as a child. I'm not sure what I'm saying." I leaned forward. "But I can't see your relationship with Maddie moving past this until you two talk to each other about how you got to where you are."

"Are you suggesting couple's therapy?"

I sighed because I knew how much I hated the process. I also understood I was married to Sarah because we had worked through our issues. "It may behoove you two, yes, but I'm not really the person you should be asking."

We remained silent for many moments.

"Now, I hear the kids are working on an art project for Valentine's Day. Do you want to join? I haven't had much of a chance to see them today."

"I'll be there in a minute."

"Take all the time you need." I rose. "I'm sorry if you didn't want to hear anything I said. I wouldn't have if I were in your shoes back in the day before Sarah and I settled down."

His eyes glazed over, and his smile was watery at best. "I don't know what to do."

"None of us does. No one really prepares children for adulthood, but if they did, Jesus, none of us would ever grow up."

"There's hope, then, that I'll grow up." He forced a smile.

"Sadly, you can't actually stop the process, but you do have control over whether or not you behave accordingly. It's not the sexiest thing, but it's kinda necessary if you want to bring children into the equation. Which both you and Maddie want to do. Stop rushing to the finish line, because it doesn't really exist. Every time you think you've made it, something else has to be conquered. You need a strong foundation to meet the challenges together."

CHAPTER SEVENTEEN

We got all the kids bathed and put to bed.

"Care for a drink in the library?" Sarah asked.

"Please."

"I take it from your eager tone the conversation with Gabe pushed you out of your comfort zone."

We bounded down the stairs.

"When did I become the grown-up in the room?" I asked when we reached the bottom.

She shook her head. "I'm just as baffled. The other day, I was with the kids at their music lesson, and when I looked around, I was the oldest in the room. I kept thinking if something happens, I'll have to take charge."

"Did anything happen?"

"No, thank God."

I kissed her cheek. "Let's get liquored up like the good old days."

"Yeah, you were the life of the party back in the day."

"Revisionist history is all the rage these days." At the bar in the library, I asked, "Wine or something stronger?"

"Grappa for you and seltzer for me. I'm weaning myself off booze for when we get pregnant."

"I see. Care to tell me about your day, *dear*?" I stressed the term of endearment. "Are you trying to get me drunk to break the news?"

"Nothing to report, really." She yawned and stretched her arms over her head. "You're the one leading the exciting life these days. Having chai with The Miracle Girl. A brother on the way to jail."

"I even had lunch with JJ. Then a tête-à-tête with Dr. Marcel."

"How is he? Did you say sorry for missing the party and reschedule a time to see them?"

"He's still spicy, and I didn't think to reschedule."

"I'll arrange with Mrs. Marcel."

I handed Sarah her glass and took a seat next to her. "Cheers." I carefully clinked our glasses.

"I talked to Gabe, and I think he has his sights on Dad's company. He claims he doesn't, but I think he's full of shit."

"Color me not surprised. Sons can be competitive."

I chuckled. "It's our daughter who's the competitive one."

"She is, but I hope when push comes to shove in the future, she's protective of Fred, not smacking the shit out of him over a girl."

"I think she will be. Just the other day, when Jorie brought Max over for a playdate when you had your spa day with your mom and Helen, Max stole Freddie's crayon. Fred didn't seem bothered by it, but Ollie shoved Max and took it back."

Sarah curled up against me, still holding her drink. "Is it wrong of me to be proud?"

"I was. I probably wasn't overly scoldy."

"Scoldy?"

I shrugged. "I'm going with it."

She sipped her drink, sighing deeply.

I rested my cheek against the top of her head. "Dr. Marcel thinks I should take JJ up on her offer."

"Dr. Marcel is a wise man."

"That's what I hear."

"But you're still struggling with the decision."

"I gotta be me." I laughed. "Can I stick with giving advice to Gabe or whomever and not deal with my own problems?"

"Wouldn't that be nice? Can I never be the grown-up in the room?"

I nodded. "Glad we're on the same page. No more adulting for us except for giving advice to others on how to be an adult. Simple!"

She snuggled closer to me. "Says the woman who's raising her brother's daughter."

"Says the other woman raising her brother-in-law's daughter."

"She's getting close to taking her first step."

"That figures. Peter did well before he was one."

"Did you?"

I shook my head. "No, I was the cautious one."

"You still are."

"It's how I'm wired. Mom used to throw it in my face."

"Being cautious?"

"Not taking my first step before I was one. For some reason, she took it as a personal affront." I laughed, not out of revenge but over the ridiculousness of the Scotch-lady.

"Your mom was an intriguing person in all the ways she could be mean."

"An interesting way to put that. I may have pushed Gabe a bit too much earlier."

"Time will tell."

"Don't you want to know what I said to him?"

"He cornered me already."

"Oh." I took a drink. "Are you mad?"

"I agree with what you said and told him so. He's going full steam ahead with the relationship, when it takes time to build trust. I don't think either of us is on his good side at the moment."

"I was never one of the cool kids."

"For that I'm glad, or you may not have gone into history and we may not have met in Dr. Marcel's office."

I rested my head against the back of the couch. "Who would have thought, that day, we'd end up here?"

"Would you change it?"

"Ha!" I pressed a finger into her thigh. "I thought we were past the mind-game stage of the relationship."

"Does that stage have an expiration? I'm so good at it." She batted her eyelashes at me.

"I stand corrected and slightly scared."

A girlish laugh bubbled out of her.

We fell into silence, Sarah wrapping her arm around my stomach. I set my drink on the table and pulled her into my arms.

"What are you thinking?" she asked.

"About having another."

Sarah started to stand, but I pulled her back down next to me.

"No, I meant—" I placed my hand on her belly.

Sarah melted against me. "I can't believe we're actually trying again. And this soon."

"Please don't tell me you're changing your mind."

"Nope."

"Good. Because I have my heart set on it."

"You're different this time around."

"How so?" I rested my head against hers.

"Not sure how to explain it without upsetting you."

I laughed. "Not off to a good start."

"You seem more excited by the prospect. The first time around, there was a lot more convincing involved."

"I remember."

"What's different?"

"You. Us. I mean all of us, including the little ones upstairs. We're all a well-oiled machine. Stronger together. I've learned some families can be a good thing, not—"

"Destructive like yours?"

"Exactly."

"I have a theory as to why you don't want to take the job. Do you care to hear it?" She fiddled with the string on my hoodie.

"How can I refuse when you put it like that?"

"It goes back to what you said earlier. About Peter walking first." She pulled away and looked me in the eye. "He's usually been first with everything, until his engagement with Maddie fell apart. You and I got married. Had the twins. All the while, Peter started making one mistake after another. Or his mistakes started becoming more apparent. We've watched him slowly fall apart, and I think it's hitting you hard." She paused and arched her brows as if asking if I wanted to chime in. I didn't, so she plowed on. "He wasn't a great brother the majority of your life, but I don't think you had it out for him the way he did for you. Even when you didn't talk to him, you loved him. Now, I think you're afraid to accept because you don't want to shove it in Peter's face. How successful you're becoming when he's unraveling before the world."

I remained quiet, and Sarah didn't push me to say a thing. Instead, she got up and fixed us another round: grappa for me and seltzer for her. After taking a seat, she finally said, "Mull it over, Lizzie fashion. We'll chat again about it when you're ready."

"I really do love that."

"The part of me that knows you need the time to process?"

"Why'd you phrase it as a question if you know it as fact?"

"That's another thing you need so you don't get upset with assumptions." She winked at me in her *I know you better than you do* way.

I laughed.

Gandhi rushed into the room and jumped onto my lap, settling down instantly. "Can we agree to no more pets?"

"We didn't set out to acquire either one. They keep finding us."

I scratched behind the little guy's ear. "How is George?"

Sarah nodded as if understanding I needed a change in the conversation or I'd never be able to process what she'd dumped into my lap. "He's stable. His nephew is looking into a home for him, and none of his family wants this adorable little guy." Sarah leaned over and kissed the dog's head.

"Poor George. Is a home necessary?"

"He can't stay on his own. They think he's suffered from several strokes. His mind is... disappearing."

I stilled my hand on Gandhi's back. "Can you just shoot me if I get that way?"

"Yeah, no. No shooting you."

"Okay. I'll ask Ollie when she's old enough."

Sarah jabbed her arm into my stomach.

"I was kidding."

"Not completely."

"How do you do that?" I flicked an exasperated hand in the air.

"Know when you're lying?"

"Or what I'm thinking, even before *I* know what I'm thinking."

"Magic."

"I've always wondered if you're a witch."

She rolled her eyes. "Don't try and be clever and say with a b or something."

"I wasn't going to. What am I thinking now?"

"Sex. You want sex."

"I always want sex."

"With anyone in sight or only with me?" She crossed her arms.

"You tell me." I shifted, causing Gandhi to jump off my lap and settle on his dog bed in front of the fireplace.

"Not sure I like that particular evasion."

"You're the one who said the mind-game stage wasn't over. And what do you expect asking a ridiculous question like that?" I shrugged.

"Careful, you may not get any tonight."

"Was it on the agenda? I don't remember that during the morning briefing." I mimed holding a clipboard and pen.

"You think you're so funny." She straddled my waist.

"Not something many say about me, actually. Usually, they get this look that suggests they can't tell if I'm being serious or not." I mimicked the expression to the best of my ability.

"That's pretty good."

"I see it a lot."

She freed a couple of her blouse's buttons. "What about these?"

"I don't see them nearly enough."

"Is that a fact?" She undid the remaining ones. "What should we do about this—?"

"Travesty."

"Oh, dear. Is it that serious?"

"I don't know how I survive day to day without a proper—" I buried my face into her cleavage, her silk bra caressing my cheeks.

"I feel a bit evil, denying you."

"You are. The evilest."

"That's saying something considering your specialty." She

laughed. "It's funny how your job creeps into even these moments."

"For the record, you brought it up this time."

She stared deeply into my eyes. "I love you, Lizzie."

"I fucking hope so because I can't go a day without you." I cupped her cheeks, pulling her lips to mine. She kissed me sweetly. The type that said she had no intention of ever leaving me.

A single tear snaked down my cheek.

She brushed it with her finger. "I doubt many know how sentimental you can be."

"Only you matter in that regard."

"It's a shame, but I do like knowing something about you no one else does."

"Oh, you know many things about me that no one else knows."

"Such as?"

"Take me upstairs, and I'll show you."

"Not so fast. We still have one task before bed." She placed a finger on my lips.

"Please don't say more talking," I whined and went limp on the couch. "I'm talked out."

"One of us has to take the dog out."

We both turned our heads to Gandhi, who perked up on his bed as if knowing it was his time to shine. The little guy loved to lift his leg.

"I got it." I rose. "Come on, Gandhi. I'll give you an extra rawhide if you're quick about it."

He let out an excited yip and circled my legs.

CHAPTER EIGHTEEN

I found Sarah leaning against the nursery doorjamb, smiling at the sleeping children.

She turned to me and whispered, "Quick work with the newest family member."

"He loves rawhides. If only that trick worked with everyone under this roof." I turned my attention to the kids. "Do you know any contractors?"

"For?"

"If I remember correctly, you wanted to construct a gym in the basement, and we'll need to turn the spare room into a nursery. Any contractors connected to the twins' music class? That seems to be the six degrees of separation for everything in our lives lately."

"I'll ask around. Maddie may know someone whose decent and reasonable."

"Do those people exist? And would they know Maddie?"

Sarah gave me her *behave* glare.

I whispered in her ear. "I want you."

In our bedroom, Sarah eased the shirt off her arms, standing in the middle of the room with only her bra and jeans. I was two feet away, frozen by her beauty. My eyes roved over her milky skin, red licorice bra, and soft flesh below her belly button.

"I love it when you do that," she said.

"What?" I remained rooted in my spot.

"Look at me that way as if still amazed you're seeing me naked or half-naked in this instance."

"I am. How did you and I happen?"

"I ask myself the same thing."

"You do?"

She crooked a finger. "Of course. You're quite the catch, Dr. Petrie. Just wait until you have groupies."

I slowly made my way to her, not wanting to rush. "I'll be sure to tell anyone who asks I have a smoking hot wife."

"What if that doesn't stop them?"

"Who?"

"Someone with a crush."

"Doesn't matter." My eyes locked on hers. "Besides, who's going to want to hook up with a woman with four kids and a brother in prison for being a Wall Street crook?"

"Good point." She encircled my neck with her arms.

My fingertips explored her skin. So soft and welcoming.

She rustled the hairs on the back of my neck, giving me goose bumps.

I kissed her right shoulder, nipping her skin with my teeth. My tongue made its way to her neck, working upward to her earlobe. I sucked on it, slipping inside her ear, making her squirm and release an excited moan.

Her fingers kneaded my lower back as she pulled me against her.

"Hold on." I lifted my shirt and sweater off in one go. "I need to feel you." I pressed into her, my lips on hers with a fervent desire to own her. Never did I want someone else to be able to do this to Sarah.

She pulled away. "You okay?"

"What? Yeah. I just… I don't want to lose you."

"Why would you think that now or ever?"

"I'm a Petrie. We hurt people."

Her eyes softened. "You don't have to be like them. You're a fighter, sweetie. Fight the Petrie factor."

I took a deep breath. "If I show signs, please let me know right away. Just say a word."

"Like a safe word?"

"Yes, but one that will keep my soul intact."

Sarah cradled my cheek with her hand. "You do love to torture yourself when you really don't need to. You aren't like them. That's why you didn't have contact with them for so many years."

"It scares me. The more successful I become, I worry it'll go to my head. Like Mom and Peter. Even Dad. He stayed with my mom because she'd threatened to bring down his business. I can't be like that." I rested my forehead against hers.

"Is that another reason you're struggling to make the decision about the job?"

"I think so, but I didn't make the connection until now."

"Timing has always been your thing."

"I'm sorry."

She shook her head, resulting in her forehead rolling against mine. "No apology needed. I'm always here for you when you need to talk. Do you want to talk?"

"Do you want to?"

"I want to do what you need."

I walked her backward to the foot of the bed and gently eased her onto the mattress.

"Right. We'll talk later." She flashed her sexy grin that connected to all the right spots in my body.

I shucked my jeans and then helped Sarah strip hers off. She repositioned on the bed, her head now on a pillow. I climbed on top of her. She unhooked my bra. I shoved hers off her breast, taking her nipple into my mouth. Her fingers dug into my back. I took my time working on her nipple. Kissing. Licking. Sucking. Biting.

Sarah reached under her and unclipped her bra. I slid the straps off her arms and went to work on her other nipple. My right hand moved up and down her torso, sliding over her supple skin.

Her hips started to move with mine.

Our breathing quickened together.

Our hands explored and pawed, eager to feel every inch of skin.

"I love you, Sarah Cavanaugh." I gazed into her eyes.

"You still think of me as a Cavanaugh."

"It's a compliment. Trust me. What do you think of the name Calvin if we have a son?"

"Not Charlie?"

"I just can't. I love my dad, but it's a complicated relationship, and I can't place that kind of baggage onto an innocent child."

"Calvin it is. If we have a son. I can't do that to a girl, no matter what Casey says about our hypocrisy over sexual politics."

I lay my hand on her stomach. "I wish we were already pregnant."

She placed her hand over mine. "Soon, hopefully."

"You'll be the sexiest pregnant lady."

"Is there such a thing?"

"You were last time. I mean look at these masterpieces right now." I massaged her breasts.

"I do wish your students knew you're a boob girl."

"That's a really weird wish to have."

"I have an unusual sense of humor."

"Now you're telling me? After agreeing to have another child?"

"You changing your mind?"

I kissed her, our tongues doing a sensual dance. Sarah writhed under me, while my hip gyrated into her pussy, its slickness painting my hip with her love.

We continued kissing as I moved my hand down to her center, easing two fingers inside. She was warm and so fucking wet. I groaned into her ear. Sarah's hips bucked, pleading for me to go deeper and harder. She clasped her hands onto my cheek, holding my face in place. I moved in and out of her, not taking my eyes off hers. I could tell she was fighting to keep them open, not wanting to break our connection. Not that she or anything could. I could stare into her eyes all day and night, though. The way they communicated the deepness of her feelings. Her love. Protection. Desire.

She edged closer to a release, and I managed to keep moving inside her and brushing her clit with the pad of my thumb. Her eyelids tapered, but she wouldn't quit. It was fucking hot and comforting.

I seared this memory into my vault, knowing I'd replay it over and over until the day I died. I mouthed, "I love you." Her adoring expression spoke volumes. Then her eyes closed, her head dug into the pillow, and she came hard.

CHAPTER NINETEEN

Friday morning around ten, the house was filled with laughter.

I sat in the leather chair in the family room, reading my notes for a lecture I'd prepped the day before, while Bailey and Jorie helped the twins and Demi build a pillow fort on the floor. Fred took the task seriously, carefully placing one pillow on his left flank. Ollie swung one in the air. If she was trying to start a pillow fight, no one else was engaging.

Sarah and Maddie, laughing about something, entered the room.

"How can you work with this going on?" Sarah parked on the arm of my seat.

"Used to it. Besides, with classes starting on Monday, I won't be able to enjoy these mornings."

"You could join in the fun." Maddie sat on the couch.

I eyed the five of them. "Not enough room."

"Coward." Sarah played with my ponytail.

"Ollie's armed. Can you blame me?"

Ollie bonked Fred on the head, but he giggled, putting his pillow wall back in place.

The doorbell rang, and Maddie jumped to her feet.

"This is the life. Having two nannies and Maddie who answers the door. Maybe we should hire more people." I shuffled to the next page of notes.

"Do you want me to feed you grapes?"

"Do we have some?"

Sarah swatted the back of my head.

"Oh, is it beat Lizzie day? Can I sign up?" Courtney smiled.

"Only those wearing my ring can, apparently. Hello."

"Hope you don't mind my crashing your Friday morning. Mads invited me over."

"I'm surprised you aren't chained to your desk." Sarah stood and gave her a hug.

Did I have to get up and follow suit? I remained put with my feet propped up on the ottoman.

"Coffee? Tea?" Sarah asked.

"No grog?" Courtney arched her brows mischievously at me.

I stroked my forehead. "Not today. Or ever again."

"Fun hater." She pivoted to say, "Coffee would be lovely, but only if you're making some for yourself."

"We live on caffeine in this house."

Sarah and Maddie trooped into the kitchen, and Courtney sat on the ottoman closer to the kid action.

Freddie closed one eye and took her in with his other.

Courtney laughed. "He doesn't seem so sure about me."

"He takes after me," I said.

She swiveled her neck. "Are you still deciding about me?"

"Absolutely."

"Let me know what you come to."

"Hope you aren't in a rush. I like to give everything careful consideration."

"I wouldn't have guessed that." She winked.

Bailey and Jorie laughed, and I felt my cheeks prickle with warmth.

"Now, it's time for a cuddle with Demi." Courtney plucked Demi from the center of the fort and held her close. "Are you as cautious as Aunt Lizzie, or do you take after your father?"

Demi clamped her hands on each of Courtney's cheeks.

"Uh-oh. Looks like you're in trouble, Lizzie. She likes having me around." Courtney blew a zerbert onto Demi's stomach.

Rising, I said, "I'll help Sarah."

In the kitchen, I whacked the back of Maddie's head.

She rubbed it. "What was that for?"

"I don't know yet, but my gut says you deserve it. Or will."

Sarah smiled.

Maddie shrugged one shoulder. "I gotta be me."

"What's the deal with Courtney? Are you two—?"

"Friends," Maddie filled in for me.

"With zero benefits?" I pressed.

"You really need to stop asking me these types of questions. It's weird."

"I will when you stop getting engaged to my brothers. It's that simple."

Maddie's jaw dropped, and Sarah had to smother her laughter with a hand.

"I don't know what to say to that." Maddie did indeed appear speechless.

"If you aren't sleeping with her, why is she in my house on a work day? This is the woman who prides herself on working a full day on Christmas."

Maddie conceded the fact with a nod. "If I tell you, promise you won't do a Lizzie?"

"What's a Lizzie?"

"Overreact."

I groaned, palming my face, more for show. "You *are* sleeping with her."

"Nope. She wants to sleep with your nanny."

"You're certain of this?" I'd seen signs that Courtney had her sights on Jorie, but I had hoped there was a 7.58 percent chance I was dead wrong. Or that the attraction had been forgotten as soon as Jorie was out of sight. Courtney wasn't the type to latch on for the long term, which is what had me worried for Jorie. She was young and inexperienced in this department and probably believed in the whole happily ever after fairy tale of relationships. It'd be a lot simpler if Maddie and Courtney were involved again. Not for Gabe, but...

"You'd have to be blind to miss it. And it's mutual." Sarah poured coffee into a carafe.

I sucked in a deep breath. "Jorie's just a kid."

"She's twenty-four."

"She's still an undergrad."

"She's an adult."

"And Courtney is still engaged to my sister-in-law's brother. Brothers. They're the link to all my woes." I collapsed onto a barstool.

"Court broke it off with Kit," Maddie declared with zero emotion.

"What?"

"She ended it with Kit."

I blinked.

"I can't tell if you aren't understanding the words or not believing them." Maddie slanted her head to get a closer look into my eyes.

"Both. We're talking about Courtney and Kit."

Maddie bobbed her head. "That sounds about right for you."

"Do you have solid evidence for this?"

"What do you want? Kit's broken heart presented in a box?"

"I'm not sure he has a heart. He's related to Tie, after all. Besides, they were never in love and the relationship was for show. Another reason why I'm doubting this news. They don't do things the way normal people do things."

"Considering the situation with Tie and Peter, you can't be that surprised. Courtney's family doesn't want the association."

"Ah, business." I made a check mark in the air, ticking an imaginary box I hadn't thought of. "I'm tired of rich people." Not that I wanted any contact with Tie's family, but it was difficult to accept none of them had reached out for Demi's sake. For the better, yes, but still…

"Keep having kids and you'll end up poor."

I gazed at Sarah. "But happy."

Maddie's face crinkled. "God, you two make me sick sometimes. So in love."

"How are things with Gabe?" I asked.

Her eyes shifted to me and then Sarah. "Okay at the moment. He's seemed to relax a bit about Peter." She shrugged. "That may be because he hasn't seen Peter since the dustup. Gabe is good at compartmentalizing."

Inwardly, I smiled, not wanting to let her in on the fact that I'd spoken to Gabe about their relationship. Maddie loved to butt into my life, but I wasn't so sure she'd appreciate it if I did the same with her.

Sarah's sly look confirmed I should stay mute.

Perhaps Gabe had seriously considered what we talked about and he was entertaining the idea of couple's therapy. I retreated inwardly when needing time to figure out the next step.

When we returned to the family room, Courtney, in her black suit, was on the floor with all three kids crawling over her, Ollie doing her best to smother Court with a pillow.

"Can a toddler be charged with murder?" I asked out of the side of my mouth.

"Maybe she and Uncle Peter can share a cell," Maddie offered.

Sarah gave Maddie the hairy eyeball.

"Oh, look at the time." I tapped my watch. "I should go to the office."

"I didn't know you were going to the campus today." Sarah's pinched face made it clear that wasn't acceptable. "We have a consultation this afternoon."

"I meant the library. I need to fine-tune Monday's lecture." I kissed her cheek in hopes to ease the furrow in her brow. I wasn't as successful as I would have liked.

"What happened to cramming in family time?" Sarah's smile made it clear she knew my motives.

"I did. And now that you two are about to have a conversation and Ollie's trying to kill Courtney, this seems like the perfect time to work, and Maddie oh so recently reminded me about the heavy weight of supporting a growing family."

"You're such a Petrie sometimes." Sarah ran one finger over the other, admonishing me, but her grin let me off the hook.

CHAPTER TWENTY

Rose, with Freddie on her hip, pointed out the window at a small bird. "Can you say bird?"

Freddie made a chirping sound instead.

"He's almost too clever for his own good." Rose kissed his forehead. "I can't believe it's spring but still so winter-like? The poor bird looks so cold in the snow." Rose turned and asked, "Do you have everything you need?" Her eyes panned the kitchen counters taking in all my supplies.

I shoved my hands into my pockets. "I think so. Thanks again for taking the kids for the night."

Troy, with the girls in his arms, kissed Ollie's head and then Demi's. "Are you kidding me? I love it."

Rose's eyes glimmered in the way only a grandmother's could. "If you have any questions or need help, I'm just a phone call away."

"Thank you. That means a lot." I briefly looked into her eyes.

"Sarah's going to be surprised by this." Again, she looked skeptically over the counter.

"Hopefully in a good way. Not in a..." I flicked my hands up in a disheartened gesture. "I'll grab the kids' stuff."

After seeing them off, I returned to the kitchen, wondering if I was up to the task.

"Alexa, find me a chocolate cake recipe."

She pulled one up, and I scanned the ingredients, which I'd already purchased but hadn't bothered printing because I had Alexa. Too bad she couldn't change diapers or grade essays and tests. My life would be so much easier.

"Alexa, tell me a joke."

It involved penguins referring to burritos as *brrr*itos. I'd have to remember that one for the next time Casey was over since I didn't think the twins were old enough to understand. I wondered if Alexa could curate World War II jokes for my students. Many might be surprised by all the ones I'd stumbled across in diaries and letters. Humor had helped many through the war.

I settled for asking her to select a playlist for me, the inept music person. I mixed the ingredients for the cake batter, humming along to a Pearl Jam song, one of Sarah's go-tos.

Soon enough, the cake was ready to go into the preheated oven.

Alexa pulled up a recipe for the red wine-braised short ribs recipe I selected earlier in the week for this adventure. It would take nearly five and a half hours in the crockpot. I consulted the clock on the microwave. Sarah was due home in six hours.

I got to work, losing track of time and enjoying the process of cooking for Sarah. Not something I thought I'd ever like.

"What are you doing?"

I looked from the cutting board to Maddie. "Slicing jalapeños."

"I see that. Which brings me back to my original question: what are you doing?"

"Making an appetizer for dinner tonight. Sweet and spicy jalapeño poppers."

Maddie turned her head as if she couldn't hear me. Then she sniffed.

The smell got my attention at the same time.

We both wheeled about to the oven, where smoke was billowing out.

Maddie rushed over. "Jesus. The oven is on fire!"

I reached for the handle but stilled because I didn't want to get burned.

"Don't open it!" Maddie was on her phone.

"Are you calling 911?"

"No, googling oven fires."

"But this is an emergency!"

She ignored me, her eyes glued to her phone. "Turn off the oven."

"It's on fire. I don't want to touch it."

Maddie grabbed a towel and switched off the oven. "Whatever you do, don't open the door. The lack of oxygen will put out the fire."

I stared through the glass from a safe distance, the flames still going strong. "Are you sure we don't need 911? This categorically seems like a 911 situation."

"Not completely. Do you have a fire extinguisher just in case?"

I grabbed the one Sarah stored under the kitchen sink. "Armed and ready." I aimed it at the oven.

"I think the fire's dying."

I still had the extinguisher ready to go. "You know, I've never used one of these before. Maybe we should test it out."

"You want to spray the oven as a test case?"

"It *is* on fire." I gestured to the flames.

"Inside. You'll make an even bigger mess. What in the world were you cooking, anyway?"

"A cake."

She placed a hand on my shoulder. "Only you can set a cake

on fire."

"I've got skills." I looked at the mess inside. "You're right. It's dying."

"One of you had to. Glad to see you get to live another day. A very close call. Luckily I popped by."

"Probably the first time I'm grateful for that."

She shoved my shoulder. "What made you think you could do this?"

"I wanted to show Sarah I was capable of pulling my weight around here. To help ease her mind about having another child."

Maddie's smile was somehow both heartfelt and sarcastic. "Not sure setting her house on fire was the best approach."

"Now you tell me."

"I really had no idea I needed to cover this base. Now, I do." She took the fire extinguisher from my hands. "I think I should be in charge of this."

"What about the rest of the dinner?"

She eyed the jalapeños. "I don't think you can make those if they need to be baked."

"They do." I looked at the oven. "I think I need to buy a new one."

"Maybe. Or just don't use it again."

"Would Sarah be opposed to hiring a cook, do you think?"

"I'm all for it."

"Me too. I've been watching cooking shows all week, and not one set the oven on fire."

"The shows or cooks?"

I laughed. "Listen, wiseass, will you help me or not?"

"I already did. I saved your house."

"True," I said with honesty. "Sarah would never forgive me for burning down her house."

Maddie rolled up her sleeves. "Okay, talk me through what you were planning, and I'll see what we can salvage." She sniffed. "After we open up all the windows. What's the occasion anyway? You usually have more than one reason for things."

"Besides showing I can pull my own weight? I wanted to apologize for us having to postpone our trip to Berlin over spring break." The vacation had been my Christmas gift, but with Peter's sentencing rapidly approaching, we'd come to the decision this wasn't the best time to leave the country.

"Yeah, the year really hasn't gone according to plan for the Petries. How was your conference last weekend?"

I gazed at the oven. "It was okay. I probably wasn't on my A-game." I hitched a shoulder. "It sucked that Dad and Allen weren't able to join me like we'd planned over Christmas, but with Peter… I never knew Boston could be so fucking cold in March."

"I'm tired of cold weather." She scanned the counter top as if hoping someone would appear to fix the situation I'd gotten myself into.

"It's okay. You don't have to help me. I'll figure this out."

"Sarah would never forgive me if I left and let you finish the job you started with the cake. Besides, I wanted to chat with you."

"About?"

"Gabe."

I suppressed a sigh. It'd been many weeks since my conversation with Gabe, and as far as I could tell, he had forgotten my advice. Or he and Maddie were secretly going to couple's therapy. This was Maddie, though. If she was going to therapy, we'd know about it. "Shoot."

"Let's get a plan together first about this."

"Are you stalling?"

"Most definitely."

"Points for honesty." I made a slashing gesture with my finger as if ticking an imaginary board.

After we got everything squared away, I poured us some

iced tea, since Maddie had to drive and I wanted a clear head for breaking the oven news to Sarah.

We sat at the kitchen table as if neither one of us wanted to be too far just in case there was another emergency.

I waved for Maddie to start talking.

She sipped her drink.

"Oh, geez. Is it that bad?"

"No. I just don't know how to begin."

"Shall I ask some questions to get the ball rolling?"

"Okay." She sneezed. "I think I'm allergic to your cooking."

"Low blow. Is it Gabe?"

"Is what Gabe?" She lowered her eyes.

I slanted my head to make eye contact. "The reason you can't look at me."

"Possibly."

"Are you wanting to end things with him?"

Her head snapped up. "Not at all!"

I showed my palms. "Then why are you being so bashful around me? This thing you're doing"—I circled a finger in the air—"isn't you."

"I just don't know how to get us back on track."

"Before Peter got arrested?"

"Before Christmas. We were fine until we got engaged. Things were good. There wasn't any pressure. I miss that."

"Is that the only change? The ring on your finger?" I pointed at the diamond.

"No."

"Going to need more." I waved for her to fill me in.

"He's insanely jealous about Peter. I'm not positive, but I think he tried to guess my pin to unlock my phone."

I let out a whoosh of air. "Why me?"

She bunched her brow. "What?"

"Why are you talking to me and not Sarah?"

"Because I know Gabe talks or talked to you."

I placed a hand on my chest. "And you think I'll betray his trust?"

"No, but I'm hoping you can lead me in the right direction. Drop a few hints."

"Do I have to? You just said he's insanely jealous of Peter, and when Peter was arrested, you rushed home to do the thing you always do. Stick your nose into things in an effort to help." I sipped my drink. "Helen made him go to therapy after Allen's birth."

"What?"

"Fuck. I didn't mean to share that." Had I?

She shook her head. "You must think me a fool. Thinking I could be happy with Gabe."

I reached for her hand. "I don't think you're a fool. I think you love Gabe, and I believe he loves you. But for the life of me, I can't figure out why you two don't talk to each other. Both of you have sought me out to talk."

"Maybe we need you there."

"Uh, no. I'm not trained for this. I suggested couple's therapy."

"To Gabe?"

I nodded.

"He never mentioned it."

"Let's be honest. Not many jump up and down when thinking of therapy. I agreed to go with Sarah because I knew if I didn't, our relationship would be over."

"I think we're at that stage. Gabe and me. I'm not secretly dating Sarah." She attempted to laugh at her lame diversion, but it died quicker than the oven fire.

I smiled. "Do you want a recommendation for a couple's therapist?"

Maddie hesitated. "We haven't even been together a year."

I stayed silent, not wanting to ask, "Then why are you engaged?"

"I just wish we could go back to dating."

"Why can't you?"

"Because."

"There's no rule that says you can't go back to dating."

"Wouldn't that be considered a failure?"

"To whom?" I couldn't understand why that would be her thought considering everything the family had been through lately.

"Everyone."

"The only two people who matter in this situation are you and Gabe. Do what you two need to do to be happy. Who gives a shit what people think?"

"How do I tell him that?" Her sigh was heavy.

"Gently and if you want to save the relationship, stress that part about how it's necessary. Make it clear to him you want to be with him. Not Peter." I paused. "Do you want to be with Gabe?"

She nodded.

"One hundred percent?"

Another nod.

"I think he needs to hear that loud and clear. And tell him if he ever tries to break into your phone again, it's over. No relationship can survive that." I tapped the screen on my phone. "I still recommend therapy. It totally sucks. Lots of touchy feely shit. You'll eat it up. Gabe will probably squirm. But it does work if both of you want it to."

"Can you not tell anyone about this?"

"About therapy?"

"No. That I came to you for advice and you actually gave it to me straight. I prefer people thinking you're the idiot."

"Trust me, that's what I prefer. It's much simpler than everyone coming to me with their problems." The screen on my phone lit up. "Sarah's on her way. Maybe we can get a discount for group therapy." I looked to the oven, sighing.

CHAPTER TWENTY-ONE

Sarah walked through the kitchen door from the garage. "What's that smell?"

I stood, wearing an apron, with flowers in my hand for her. "Dinner?" It sounded more like a question than statement.

"That burnt smell is dinner?"

I nodded, stalling for the right way to put things. "Sadly, the cake portion of the evening didn't make it."

She cocked her head. "What does that mean exactly?"

"It's more than crispy."

"You burned the cake."

"And oven." I hadn't meant to say that and pressed my lips together.

Maddie returned from the bathroom. "Oh, good, you're here. I have plans but didn't want to leave Lizzie alone. She needs adult supervision."

I glared at Maddie. "I do not."

Maddie glanced over her shoulder at the oven. "The oven says you do. Well, my job here is done." She wheeled about to Sarah. "How much do you pay for babysitting?" Maddie stuck out her paw. "The design biz has been slow."

Sarah kept her eyes glued to the oven. "How much damage has been done?"

So much for Maddie's attempt at humor to shield me. "Do you remember when you said you wanted a new oven?"

"I don't remember ever saying that."

"Too bad, because I'm buying you a new one." She had a stony expression as she processed the information, so I decided to distract her. "How was your massage? Feeling all relaxed?"

"Not anymore," she said.

I waved for Maddie to take her leave before things got worse because Sarah's rigid stance was intimidating.

Maddie whispered something in Sarah's ear and then bolted from the scene.

Sarah set her purse on the counter and took off her jacket. "Care to walk me through everything that's happened today? Wait." She glanced around. "Where are the kids?"

"With your mom." I added, "For the night."

She massaged her forehead. "I can't even go to lunch with friends and spend the afternoon at the spa without you shipping off the kids and then destroying the house."

"Sure, you can. Maddie arrived in the nick of time. The flames never got out of the oven. Miranda is scheduled to come over tomorrow to clean the kitchen from top to bottom. Dinner is about to be served, minus the appetizers and cake. And you get to do one of your favorite things: shop. An entire kitchen remodel if you so desire. I'm chalking this up to a win. And, I would like to add, I arranged to have your mom take the kids so we could have a romantic night together. I didn't ship them off because I was overwhelmed."

"Do you remember when you tried grilling steaks for me years ago?"

"Yes, I couldn't get the grill started. I had no idea baking a cake was the way to create massive flames." I tapped my head as if filing that nugget away for future use.

She sorta smiled.

"On a related note, would it be weird if we hired a chef or someone to make prepared meals we can toss in the oven—the new one?" I jerked a thumb over my shoulder. "This one scares me."

"Will you be able to heat up dinner without causing massive damage?"

"Only one way to find out."

"You know how many husbands' have a mancave? I think you literally need to live in a cave. Less chance for destruction."

"Is that the Sarah version of being in the doghouse." I tapped my chin with the side of my finger. "Hey, wouldn't I need to start a fire to stay warm? So not a viable option. Fire isn't my friend."

"What am I going to do with you?"

"Love me. That's all I want."

"For some unexplainable reason, I do."

"That's great. Any chance I can talk you into giving me a massage? Cooking did a number on my back." I jumped back in case she attempted a strike.

She rolled her eyes. "Considering you ruined all the work the therapist did on my shoulders, I think you owe me one."

"Pretty sure that can be arranged. Are you interested in dinner at all? Or shall we go straight to bed?"

"It's only six."

I stifled a yawn. "Does smoke inhalation make you groggy?"

"Poor baby. Did you learn a lesson today?" She crossed her arms very mom-like.

"I should never ever cook."

She grimaced. "That's the lesson you got from this?"

I nodded.

The crinkles in her forehead set in more.

"What message do you think I should have received?"

"Maybe it's time for you to take some cooking lessons."

"Wh-why?" I stuttered, glancing at the oven, which seemed like solid evidence that I should never cook again.

"Consider it part of your punishment." She recrossed her arms, but the smile she wore was working on me.

"My punishment for setting the oven on fire is more cooking? You either have a death wish, or I don't know what."

"You're almost forty. Don't you think it's time you learn to cook dinners for your growing family?"

"I already came up with the perfect solution. Hire a cook."

"That's the Petrie way. Hiring others to do things."

"It's how I survived to almost forty," I said forthrightly.

"You're cute when you get worked up, you know that?"

"Does that mean you're only trying to wind me up and not really suggesting I take cooking lessons?"

"Oh, no. I'm signing you up for some. With Maddie."

"Why Maddie?"

"I don't have time." Her mood swings were confusing the hell out of me, but I didn't want to press considering I was the cause of the problems.

"And I do? Is it really necessary for me to learn how to make cherries jubilee?"

"I had my hopes set on more functional meals like meatloaf. It's hard to mess up meatloaf."

I scrunched my face. "I don't like meatloaf. Besides, it's not like you cook all that much, either."

She crooked an eyebrow. "Oh, I'm sorry. Raising three kids doesn't give me much time."

"We have two nannies. Why is it okay to have two nannies but not a cook?" I raised two fingers in the air, which probably wasn't the best choice.

"You're going to take cooking lessons!" She raised her voice to the level she used when scolding Ollie.

"I don't want to!"

"Then what was the purpose of all this?" She waved a hand over the mess.

"To surprise you!"

"Mission accomplished."

"You don't seem happy about it."

She started to say something but zipped her lips shut.

"I'm sorry." I hung my head and whispered, "I never meant to cause this much trouble."

"I know." She opened her mouth wide and seemed to take a few cleansing breaths. "Would learning how to cook for your family really be all that bad?"

"I'm not good at it."

"Not yet, no. But I believe in you."

"I do hate it when you try to trick me like I'm one of the twins."

"Point taken. I…" Her voice trailed off, and she massaged her forehead. "I'm sorry. I don't know why this has hit me hard. It's not like I even like cooking. You and I survive mostly on takeout. The kids' meals are much easier to prepare."

"It can't be nice to come home to a ruined kitchen."

"It's not the worst thing that's happened to us lately."

I laughed. "Oh, boy. That says a lot, doesn't it? We need a break."

"We just cancelled Berlin."

"Rescheduled," I corrected. "I'll make sure that happens. I don't know when, but it will. And since we can't flee the country with everything going on, how about we head out for a weekend. You like skiing. The kids love the snow. What about a weekend in Vail or Aspen? It's been such a bad winter snow-wise, and I read in the paper the slopes are staying open a month longer than normal. They might have a cooking class I can take while you ski. Bailey or Jorie might want to come along to help with the kids. Or Allen."

"You'd take a class?"

"I'd like to have sex with you again."

She laughed. Really laughed.

My shoulders started to relax.

She opened her arms. "Come here. I'm sorry I'm being such an ass."

"I'm sorry I ruined the oven."

We hugged.

"Shall we eat dinner? I think it actually turned out okay thanks to Maddie. Hey, what'd she whisper in your ear?"

"To go easy on you."

"Huh. And you decided to take the opposite track?"

"So it seems. Shall we have dinner?"

"Perhaps makeup sex after that." Might as well plant the seed now.

"I suppose I owe you that."

"Don't sound too excited about eating my pussy."

"I have to do the work."

"Cooking is exhausting." A thought struck me. "I'm starting to see the allure of cooking lessons."

"You're terrible."

I waggled my brows. "Punish me in bed later."

CHAPTER TWENTY-TWO

The following morning, I was in the kitchen making herbal tea for Sarah, when she strolled in dressed in a bathrobe and her hair resembling Medusa. The image was off-putting to say the least.

"Were you serious about a weekend away with the kids?"

I nodded, not liking the grave expression on her face.

"Did you mention it to anyone yet?"

"I texted Bailey. She's in."

"We're here!" Rose shouted from the entryway.

"In the kitchen," Sarah called back in a cheerier voice, but her shoulders still had the *oh shit* hunch going on.

Troy held Demi in his arms, but the twins tottered in on their own.

Sarah hunched down. "There are my babies."

"Momma!" Each twin thrust themselves into her arms.

"What's that smell?" Rose's nose curled up.

"Lizzie baked a cake last night," Sarah said in a voice that suggested, *Please don't ask questions*.

"I see." Rose's eyes meandered to the oven and then skittered to me before returning to Sarah. "What's this I'm hearing about a family trip to Vail?"

I held the teakettle over Sarah's *Coffee because adulting is hard* mug. "Can you define *family*?"

Rose started to reply, but Sarah butted in, "Let's have coffee and tea in the family room with everyone sitting down."

"Does this have to do with what you were about to tell me?" I asked Sarah.

She ignored me. "Mom? Troy? Coffee?"

"Uh, sure," Troy said, holding Demi a little tighter.

Rose nodded, but I sensed she didn't like the underlying shitstorm brewing.

Sarah shooed all of them out with a hand clap, resulting with frantic finger-pointing.

I still held the teakettle midair. "Define *family*."

"Really, Lizzie. You're the word lover."

"In this situation, I meant immediate family."

"Define *immediate*," she countered.

"You. Me. Fred. Ollie. Demi. Five total. Well, Bailey to watch the kids so we can have some alone time. Jorie couldn't make it."

"Add seven to your five, and you have it exactly right. Well, unless others decide to come."

"*Decide to come*," I parroted. "This is our getaway! I get to decide who can and can't come."

"If I remember correctly, you also implied Allen could come if Bailey did. That messed up the earlier equation." She started to count on her fingers.

I ignored that part. "I don't mind Allen coming because he's a sweetheart. I actually like him, and I can't think of one problem he's caused."

"He is a sweetheart, and he feels absolutely terrible that our Christmas was ruined."

"It was. By the Petries. I used to spend Christmas all alone working, and those times were far more enjoyable than the one we barely survived not so long ago."

"I think Allen wants to make up for the Christmas that shall never be remembered."

"Oh, I remember it." I circled a finger around my temple. "I'm going to need lots more therapy to recover."

"Just remember that you like Allen. He means well."

I set the teakettle down. "Please, just fucking tell me so I can scream or die. Hoping for the latter at the moment."

"No dying."

I waved for her to get on with it.

"Allen decided it would be nice to invite the whole family to Vail to show you that everyone can actually get along. Since we always host the holidays, everyone wants to lift the burden from us."

"But part of why we're leaving Fort Collins is to escape everything, including my family, to have time with the kids."

"Yes, I understand that. Allen didn't get the memo."

"Wait? What holiday are we talking about?"

"Easter."

"Are you saying the Petries are getting together for Easter?"

"Yes."

"Was that our plan? I don't remember Easter being discussed." I went over the conversation the previous night.

"It kinda morphed into a getaway for Easter while you were sleeping last night."

I growled loudly enough that Hank, who'd been sleeping on the mat by the back door, fled the room. "Can I kill some of the family members three days before the trip and see if any of them are resurrected?"

"Not sure it works that way, and remember the recent rule about not getting arrested?"

I closed my eyes.

"It's going to be okay. Really, what can happen that hasn't

already happened?"

"Donner Party. Hatfield and McCoy feud. The Battle of Bastogne. D-Day—"

She moved around the counter and pulled me into her arms. "Stop."

"I'm only getting started."

"I know. But—"

"I just wanted time away to sort through my thoughts." I rested my head on her shoulder. "Not have any drama. Everything turns into drama. Even baking a fucking cake. I'm so tired, Sarah."

She squeezed me tighter. "It's okay. You can hide in a bedroom with a fireplace and read. Not associate with them at all."

"Them," I spat out. "Why do they like me so much now?"

"It's a mystery."

I laughed, which came out garbled.

"Is she still in shock?" Rose asked.

Sarah gazed into my eyes. "Are you?"

"Denial. So much denial." I glanced out the window. "Maybe I should go for a bike ride."

"It's snowing," Sarah said.

I nodded. "It'll be invigorating."

"Remember when I said no dying. I'm holding you to that."

"Are you saying I can't go for a bike ride?" I pouted.

"Yep. Put on your big girl pants, and let's have coffee and tea and plan a wonderful weekend away." Her voice dripped with sarcasm.

"You're the planner. Not me. I'm the bike rider."

"You haven't been on your bike for weeks."

"Exactly!"

She pressed her iPhone screen and then held it up. "They're forecasting six to eight inches. No bike ride!"

I took her phone. "Fine. I'm ordering a stationary bike."

"Great. It'll be here in two days. Now get your ass in there!" She jabbed a finger to the family room.

"I don't wanna."

"Me either, but dammit, we don't have a choice."

"We do, though. Let all of them go, and we can stay here. Change the locks. Build a moat. Can you buy supplies for a moat online?" I googled how to build a moat. "The kids will love the drawbridge and alligators. Or do you fill a moat with crocodiles? Both? Do alligators and crocodiles get along?" I searched again. "Oh, the Florida Everglades is the only place where they coexist. We should move there. Now, I need to work on supplies. Will I need the state's permission, you think?"

Sarah's horrified expression softened some. "On second thought, why don't you go read in the library or something? I got this."

"Can the kids come with me?"

"Yes. Absolutely."

"Great." I kissed her cheek. "Freddie will love helping me dig a big hole. Massive. It's right up his alley. And Ollie—she'll love feeding the crocogator babies. That is if they can have babies. Casey. She'd know the answer to this. Must call Casey." I made a tick in the air as if concocting a mental list of things to do to realize the moat dream.

"I know I've said this before, but she's a weird one." Rose's voice followed me into the family room.

"Kids, let's build a moat in the library. Troy, you may want to join us."

"Sounds like fun." He started to whistle "Chain Gang," much to Fred's delight.

As I led the tiny engineers, with Demi in my arms, to the library, I spied Sarah's concerned face. A small part of me felt a twinge of remorse. The rest was bullied by the prospect of carving out a Petrie-free zone.

* * *

An hour or so later, there was a knock on the library door.

"Come in," I barked.

"Oh, wow. I wasn't expecting this." Sarah gaped from the doorway.

The drapes were closed, and the only lights in the room were two strands of Christmas lights I scavenged from the boxes that hadn't been stored in the attic yet. All of the furniture had been pushed to the fringes of the room, and in the middle was a fort made with practically every pillow and cushion we had in the house with two sheets over it. The lights lined the entrance. Demi was sound asleep inside the tent in the far corner. Freddie was curled up with a picture book. Ollie wandered the library, perhaps in search of something to destroy. Troy and I sat outside the tent flaps, enjoying the quiet.

"This is amazing," Sarah whispered.

Freddie perked up.

Sarah got onto her knees and crawled in, Ollie following her. "Did you two build this?" she asked the twins.

Freddie nodded.

"Yes," Ollie said, without really pronouncing the S.

Sarah glanced over her shoulder, smiling. "What happened to the moat?"

"Sadly, we didn't have the right tools. Troy suggested this."

"Troy wins the best grandfather award for the day."

He gave an aw-shucks shrug.

"Does this mean Mommy has lost her home office for good?" Sarah asked the twins.

"I can probably adjust to working in a tent with three beautiful little helpers," I responded. "Much better than the cave idea you proposed last night."

Sarah laughed. "All right. Who wants lunch?"

CHAPTER TWENTY-THREE

Later that night, in bed, I set my book on the nightstand, rolled over, and placed my arm across Sarah's stomach. "I'm sorry about earlier."

She eyed me cautiously. "Which part?"

"The wanting to build a moat and stocking it with reptiles."

She smiled. "Were you planning more than crocodiles and alligators?"

"I may have researched the venomous water moccasin snake."

"Because that would be good to have around children?"

"Are you saying crocs and alligators are kid-friendly? Because I do think the moat idea has potential."

"Yes, that's exactly what I'm saying."

"Something tells me you're being sarcastic."

"Can't imagine what."

"The frown lines in your forehead. Pinched lips. Crossed arms. Oh, your tone." I climbed on top of her.

"And all my signs say I may be in the mood for nooky."

"No, all your signs say I need to get you in a better mood."

"Can we chat about Easter weekend?"

I rolled off. "If you didn't want to have sex, you could have just said that."

"I didn't say no. I'm saying, let's chat first about the holiday plans."

"Since it's Easter, I doubt we can get rooms for the entire family."

"Nice try. Your dad booked a place."

"Like hotel rooms?"

"No, a house."

"All of them under one roof again." I tossed my arm over my face. "I'm not going."

"I think that would be noticed."

"Yes. That's the point."

"Does it make it easier knowing Peter won't be there?" She uncovered my face. "Tie won't either. No George. Not even Ethan, Lisa, or Casey."

"Peter won't be with Demi on Easter?" I asked, knowing the answer but still shocked.

"Your dad doesn't think it'd look good in case anyone got a photo of him skiing or whatever days before his court date. He's going to spend some time up here with us before."

I nodded. Peter had been traveling our way once or twice a week, when he wasn't dealing with Dad or the attorneys. "Why can't Ethan and his family come?"

"Do you want them to? That's easily arranged if they're free."

"They're my family, the branch I like, and no holiday is the same without them."

"Because they're not related by blood?"

"Because no matter what, they love me. Ethan has seen me do many a stupid thing and hasn't turned his back on me. Not like my family, anyway."

"He has, and they do love you. I think you'll find the others do as well. Give them a chance."

"I have. Repeatedly."

"That's family."

"It's the definition of insanity."

"That's family."

"But that makes no sense."

"That's family."

"You keep saying that."

"You won't change my mind. Listen." She straddled my waist. "Christmas was bad. I won't sugarcoat it. The situation with Peter is terrible. The fight between Peter and Gabe was surprising, but also not really. Don't even get me started on Tie. Any mother—" She closed her eyes and took what seemed to be a cleansing breath. "At the end of the day, they're still your family. And there may come a day when you need them. Don't turn your back on those who love you."

"But they turned their backs on me."

"Out of the people coming this weekend, only your dad did."

"Your mom hated me for a long time."

"Hate, no. She wanted to strangle you, but she still came to our wedding."

I sighed.

"It's just two nights. Most of the time, the adults will be skiing, which you don't do, so you'll be safe with the kids."

"Maybe they'll help me make a snow fort."

"Fred would love that. What kind of creatures will guard your snow fort?"

"Ollie is the only protection I need."

"So you have an architect and bodyguard. What role does Demi play?"

"That's a good question. She's cute as a button."

Sarah rolled her eyes. "Are you saying she's a decoration?"

I shook my head. "Not at all, but it doesn't hurt to have

deep blue eyes, killer eyelashes, and dimples. She's going to break a lot of hearts."

"You have two out of three." Sarah tapped my cheek with two dimples.

"Have I mentioned you're cheating with your coercion technique?"

"Oh, really. How?"

"Getting me to agree to the weekend while sitting on top of me, completely naked."

"You set the rules that we have to go to bed in our birthday suits."

"I did. It was a no-brainer considering..." I massaged her tits.

"Are they the only reason?"

"Oh, there are so many reasons I wouldn't even know where to start."

"You seem to always start with the girls."

"Name one person who doesn't like boobs."

"Ethan."

"Really? I'm not sure if I've ever asked him." I pondered this. "The majority of the time when dealing with them, there's no liquid involved." Ethan had an odd aversion to fluids.

"Casey's adopted. Lisa never breastfed."

"Right. Excellent point."

She stared into my eyes. "Do you really want to discuss whether or not Ethan is a boob person with me while I'm... well?" She waved, indicating she was now grinding into my pussy.

"Who's Ethan?"

Sarah bent down and kissed me, her tongue making it clear she was in charge and if I was good, she'd fucking rock my world. There was a part of me that wanted to tempt fate and see what type of punishment she may inflict.

Her hip jammed harder into me, and I realized it wasn't the time to push those buttons.

She moved on to my nipple, taking it into her mouth, and the flick of her tongue made a direct connection to my nether regions. Her hand ran down my side, tickling me in such a delicious way. I tried to control the squirming but failed, which only encouraged her to tickle me more.

"Problem, Lizzie?" she asked in a seductive voice.

"N-nope," I stuttered.

She tickled me more. "Are you sure? I can stop touching you."

"Never stop touching me."

"What about the tickling?"

"It's a fun distraction."

"Distraction, huh? What's this?" Her tongue trailed to the nipple that had been neglected until this moment.

I moaned.

"What? No words?" She asked with my nipple mostly still in her mouth.

"Who needs words when you're doing this?"

Her hand stopped tickling, roving down the outside of my thigh. Then the top of my leg. Down my leg. Up along my inner thigh, causing me to writhe more in anticipation of her end game. She ended up bending my leg over her ass, and I tightened my grip on her, needing her body as close as possible to mine.

Sarah bit down harder on my nipple, while her fingers entered me.

I gasped.

She drove in harder, and my muscles tightened around her fingers.

"You feel so good," she panted.

I tried to ditto but could only pronounce the D since she added another finger.

Her mouth made the familiar trek down my body, but it felt like the first time. It always did with her. I think that was one of the reasons why we worked so well. The way we made the other feel. As if nothing else mattered but being with each other in the most intimate of moments.

She didn't stop until she was on my clit. Like her kissing earlier, she announced with her actions she intended to make me come. Hard. Fast.

Her fingers were in deep, curling upward. Her tongue lapping my clit. There was no controlling my body at the moment. Sarah was in complete control of my bundle of nerves and emotions. If she asked me to quack like a duck right then and there, I would have.

She took my clit completely into her mouth, sucking it hard. Releasing it and then lapping it with her tongue.

Jesus, I was close.

"Oh, Sarah, don't stop."

She didn't.

I felt a surge of juices.

Then my body started to tremble.

My back arched.

I bit down on my bottom lip to keep from crying out.

I cradled Sarah's head with my hands as she brought me well beyond the finish line. Spent, I crashed back onto the mattress.

Sarah climbed on top of me, her wet chin perched on my chest, and she stared deeply into my eyes.

"What?" I asked.

"I love you."

"I love you, but why do you look so serious?"

"Feeling a bit emotional." Her eyes misted.

"Honey, are you crying?"

"No."

I wiped my own eyes since orgasms tended to fog my

contacts. "You are crying. What's wrong?" I pulled her into my arms.

"Nothing's wrong. I just really love you."

"Okay."

The tears really started to stream down her cheeks.

"No. There's something wrong. Is it the oven? The moat?"

"No."

"Are you sure? You got kinda mad last night and kept insisting on classes."

"It's cute, really, that you can't bake a cake."

"Does that mean I don't need to take classes?"

"Only if you want to."

"And the moat?"

"Hard no."

I laughed.

She laughed and then cried again. "This is ridiculous. Why am I so emotional? What's the date?" Her face lit up, and then she bounded out of bed toward the bathroom not waiting for an answer.

"Are you sick?"

She didn't answer.

I followed her and watched her take a box from the bathroom drawer and head for the toilet. Everything started to click in my mind. We'd had the insemination appointment back in February but had been warned not to test too early only to receive a false positive. We were well past that date.

Unable to speak, I stood guard while she hovered over the toilet and peed on the stick.

We moved into the main part of the bathroom and sat on the edge of the jetted tub. Neither of us spoke as she held the pregnancy test in her hand.

The seconds ticked by in what seemed like super slo-mo.

Sarah reached for my hand and held on.

I squeezed it, my intake of air almost slow enough that I wasn't actually breathing.

Sarah held the stick so we couldn't see the result, her eyes on the clock on the wall by the closet. The second hand circled once. Twice. Again. After the third revolution, Sarah slowly turned over the pregnancy test in her hand.

CHAPTER TWENTY-FOUR

The Friday night before Easter, I pulled the car into the drive of the place Dad had rented.

Sarah hunched down in the passenger seat to get a load of the rental. She whistled. "I have to give it to your dad. When he does something, he doesn't do half measures."

The ten-bedroom manor looked like it'd been plucked from the Swiss Alps and placed in Colorado—from the stone façade, gabled roof, wraparound porch, decks off some of the second story rooms, and isolated drive tucked away with the slopes in the background. The sun had already set, but the porch lights and some interior lights made the place feel warm and inviting. Poor house. Didn't know the Petries were about to descend upon it.

"Looks like we're the first to arrive. That means we get to pick our room." Sarah rubbed her hands together.

"Dad has assigned the rooms."

Her shoulders slumped some. "Of course, he did."

"He gave us the biggest room with a room off to the side for the makeshift nursery. I'm pretty sure the cribs and every possible thing we'd need has been set up, including a stocked fridge."

"How does he find the time considering Peter isn't by his side anymore?"

I killed the SUV's engine and looked at her. "You don't think Dad made any calls, do you? This is his assistant. She's amazing."

"You've never mentioned her before."

"Never needed to, I guess. She's the type that totally stays in the background." I shrugged.

"Can we hire her? Forget the chef."

"Now there's a thought, but I haven't given up on the chef idea." I peered into the back of the vehicle. "All of them are asleep."

"That was the plan. It's almost their bedtime."

Ethan's vehicle pulled up behind us, and he immediately shut off the lights.

I got out of the car and motioned for him to come quietly. "Can you grab Freddie without waking him?"

"It's a skill I've mastered."

The three of us got the sleeping kids inside in record time without waking one of them. After setting up the video monitors, we went to the great room with a stone fireplace in the corner, arched ceilings, western-style couches and chairs, plus the typical framed photos of wildlife that was popular in this part of Colorado. I wondered if it was the law every rental had to have at least one shot of a moose standing in a lake.

"Lisa, how are you?" Sarah gave Ethan's wife a heartfelt hug.

"Thanks so much for inviting us."

I noticed she didn't answer Sarah's question, which wasn't all that unusual when asked about your well-being during a greeting. But my gut said she didn't want to talk about her mother's death, and I couldn't blame her. It'd only been a handful of months, and she'd been close to her mom.

"Where's Gandhi?" Casey asked.

"He'll be here soon with Allen and Bailey."

Casey, Sarah, and Lisa drifted to the kitchen.

"Are Bailey and Allen sharing a room?" Ethan asked me.

I shrugged. "I try to stay out of those aspects of my brother's life."

"I bet Janice knows."

"She's in California. How would she know if her cousin is sharing a room with Allen?"

"Women talk. Not you. But normal ones do." Ethan wore a *duh* expression.

"We'll know soon enough." There was another SUV pulling into the drive.

Ethan looked out the window. "How is it that your brother who isn't old enough to drink has a nicer car than both of us?"

"He's a Petrie son."

Ethan spun around. "Your dad won't buy you a car?"

"He would, but I like to do things on my own."

"See where that's gotten you."

My eyes found Sarah across the room, chatting with Lisa and Casey in the kitchen while Sarah rooted in the fridge for snacks. "Yes. I'm happy."

Ethan crossed his arms and looked me up and down. "You are. Just in time for your family to arrive and send you into the corner crying."

"That's why you're here. To provide cover."

He stood in his best Superman pose. "I got you."

I laughed. "I'll be glad when everyone hits the slopes or whatever tomorrow. Just me and the kids."

"And me."

"You don't ski?"

"It's the southern in me. Skiing is unnatural. Besides, I

want to read next to a roaring fire. Casey is signed up for lessons in the morning. Was that you're doing?"

I furrowed my brow. "No. Alice, my dad's assistant, probably."

"Casey's excited. I've never met your dad's assistant, but"—his eyes roamed the digs—"I like her style."

"She's been with him for decades. Dad can't live without her."

"He seems to be that way with women."

I started to say something but needed to chew on that thought more.

"What's Lisa's dad doing for the holiday?"

Ethan bobbed his head in a helpless way. "He's with his brother's family. When school's out for the summer, we're heading out there for a couple of weeks."

"Are you meeting up with Casey tomorrow afternoon?"

"Nope. Lisa's going to take her to lunch for *mother and daughter* time. She's been big on that lately."

Maddie burst through the front door. "Where's Jeeves with the wine?"

"Let me get on that." Ethan made his way to the kitchen, and I wondered if he did so I wouldn't press about his being excluded tomorrow.

Gabe set their ski bags and luggage next to the door.

"Oh, I should get the rest of the luggage," I said to myself.

Outside, I bumped into Allen and Bailey, who had taken their time exiting the car. Gandhi, in an adorable fleece-lined jacket, zipped past me and into the house.

"Hey, did you two get lost on your way in." I gave each a hug.

Allen's face went up into flames.

Bailey laughed nervously.

Had they been canoodling or more?

"Anyhoo, I need to get my shit." I mentally added *together*.

"I'll help once I get our stuff inside," Allen said.

"No worries, most of the kids' stuff is already inside. I just need to grab Sarah's bag, a dog bed, and the stuff for Easter morning."

I regretted turning down Allen's help once I hefted Sarah's bag out of the back of the SUV. After I manhandled it into the house, and then hauled in the other loot, I gave Sarah, who was still in the kitchen, my best *you couldn't pack lighter?* look.

She grinned and waggled her fingers in the air, which looked like a friendly greeting, but I was willing to bet it meant *next time you pack for two adults, three kids, and a dog for a holiday weekend*. It effectively shut me up.

Within the hour, Dad arrived with Helen, Rose, and Troy.

With twelve adults and Casey, the volume significantly increased in the room. Quietly, I worked my way over to the coat rack and grabbed my parka. I slipped it on and made my way to the porch with a cup of hot chocolate.

I sucked in a mouthful of brisk mountain air.

"Care for some company?"

I turned and smiled at my dad. "Sure."

He had his jacket on and a beanie, making him look vulnerable somehow. "I should have thought ahead." He motioned to my hot chocolate.

"Here, take this one. I'll be right back."

"I couldn't—"

"It's not a problem."

Soon enough, I was back outside. Dad stood at the far end of the deck, staring into the blackness. On this side of the property, there wasn't another house or street in sight, and at this time of night, it made everything peaceful in an eerie kind of way. Or maybe the Petrie factor added the dose of eeriness.

My boot crunched on the packed snow, causing the boards to groan in protest.

Dad turned slowly, his eyes softening when he saw it was me. "It's something out here, isn't it?"

"So quiet."

He nodded.

I stood next to him at the railing, looking out into the same darkness. "How are you handling everything?"

"It's not something I've ever experienced."

"No, I imagine not. Unless you have more kids you haven't introduced me to yet."

He chuckled. "I never knew you were so funny."

"Not everyone appreciates my sense of humor." I shrugged *What can you do?*

"I like Ethan. He's a good friend to you."

"Always has been. Even when giving me shit about my mistakes."

"That's a mark of friendship, when able to say how things really are."

I nodded, taking a sip of my hot chocolate.

"Helen noticed Sarah's only pouring tonic water into her G and Ts. She's not drinking any of the champagne either," he said.

"Nope."

"Are you telling anyone yet?" He glanced at me out of the corner of his eye.

"It's still early, but I'm not sure how we'll be able to keep it quiet."

He whistled. "You've really become a remarkable woman."

"Thanks. It's hard to fathom, though. And, with Demi—that was a surprise."

He sniffed. "Yes. She's lucky to have you and Sarah step in."

"She has Peter's eyes and smile, but she's kind."

Dad laughed. "She didn't get that from either of her parents."

"What do you think will become of Peter?"

Dad took a drink, which I gathered had gone cold given he dumped the remaining contents over the deck railing. "I hope he learns from this and applies it to whatever he'll do when he gets out. He's never had to deal with consequences before. That's partly my fault."

I couldn't disagree.

"I can't believe he's being sentenced this week." Dad held onto the railing, his knuckles whitening. "With everything going on, Helen wants me to retire. She's worried about my health."

"What will you do?"

"She wants to travel."

"Oh. Will she give up the shops?"

Dad shook his head. "No. Either Gabe will take them over, or we'll hire someone to."

"Gabe wants to work for you. He says he doesn't, but I think deep down, that's his goal."

"I know."

"But?"

"Look how it turned out with Peter. It's a dirty way to make money. I know that now."

I rested my backside against the railing. "You didn't before?"

"I did, but I didn't know it'd ruin my son."

"Tie played a part."

"Yes, but they have other things on Peter. He played fast and loose." Dad held onto the railing but rolled back on his heels, as if stretching out his arms and back. "God, Lizzie. He's screwed. Prison. And then what?"

His voice didn't break, but I could tell he was close to tears.

"Then we help him rebuild."

"Yeah," he said without much belief.

I placed a hand on his shoulder. "He's going to be okay.

Wanting to take care of his little girl will give him the kick in the ass he needs."

He grunted in his *dad* way. "Children have that effect. What's this I hear about you being on TV soon?"

"Oh, that. An interesting side project that seems to excite everyone else but me."

"You don't want to do it?"

"It terrifies the shit out of me."

He snorted.

It was becoming more apparent that I'd picked up my communication skills from him.

"Why does it scare you?"

"Oh, I'm afraid I'll look like a complete ass in front of the entire world."

"Glad to see you aren't putting too much pressure on yourself." He offered a rare smile.

"I'm not used to failing. Part of me wants to back out."

"Not trying is another form of failing. If you give it your all and it doesn't work out, it's a lesson you can learn from, not a failure."

"Sounds like a greeting card for graduates."

"That's my secret side business. To support all my secret kids."

I chuckled. "We have such a strange family."

"That we do. Maybe Helen's right. It's time to close up shop and travel. Keep in touch via postcards."

"Coward."

"Come with us. The kids may learn more by seeing the world. School bored the shit out of me."

"And I couldn't get enough of it."

He blushed some. "I forgot. I'm surrounded by teachers."

I ticked them off. "Me, Ethan, Troy, and Sarah."

"Don't forget Rose and Helen. Teaching children to be good people is the most important role in society."

"Is this your way of saying Allen's your favorite since he had Helen?"

He rubbed his chin. "I hope he's a good man. He's hard to get through to sometimes. Locked up in his own head like you."

"The sensitive souls can be fragile. I worry about Fred."

"Not Ollie?"

"Oh, I do. In a different way. She has a bit of Uncle Peter in her."

"Be kind to her. Peter wasn't treated the way he should have been." He made eye contact. "Neither were you. I hope this weekend away will make up some for Christmas."

I laughed. "I have to admit when I heard everyone was coming, I wanted to cancel."

"I don't blame you one bit, but thanks for giving us a chance. Again."

"Sarah said I had to."

He laughed hard enough to shake his belly. "Helen's the same way."

"You mentioned Helen wants you to retire. Is that what you want?"

His gaze landed on mine. "I think we should go back inside."

"Go ahead. I'll be inside in a minute."

I wasn't alone long.

"Are you hiding?" Gabe bumped my shoulder.

Not well enough. "Nah, just soaking in the atmosphere. What about you?"

"Maddie sent me out to see if you'd be interested in playing charades."

"She doesn't know my answer?"

Gabe tossed his hands up but then tucked them into his armpits since he hadn't bothered to put on a jacket.

"How are things between you two?"

"Weird."

"I take it you haven't broached the whole couples therapy idea."

"No. Not yet."

"But you plan on it?"

He shrugged.

I kicked a mound of snow, breaking the chunk into smaller pieces. "Not to be too indelicate, but it might be time to shit or get off the pot."

"You sound like Maddie."

"She does love that phrase." I rested a hand on his shoulder. "Don't lose her because your scared to face your fears or from stubborn pride. Perhaps both. I firmly believe women like Maddie come along only once in a lifetime. Peter blew his chance. Don't make the same mistake."

"I'd never cheat on her."

"Can you prove that you're willing to fight for her, though? And vice versa?"

CHAPTER TWENTY-FIVE

The following morning, Sarah woke early.
I poured her a cup of Rooibos tea. "Promise me you won't get on skis."

"I won't. I volunteered to take Casey to her lesson so Lisa can ski. I think she needs this. We didn't even bring my skis."

"I know. I just don't like you out of my sight these days."

"Nothing will happen to me."

"What if there's an out of control skier and—" I pointed to her belly.

"Calvin will be fine. I'll be fine. Trust me. I'll never let anything happen to any of my children."

"How do you know it's a boy?"

"Mother's intuition." She blew into the mug.

"Dad knows your pregnant."

"So does Mom."

"I think the rest are just being polite, even Maddie. Do you think she feels okay? Usually, we can't prevent the woman from blabbing."

"I think she has a lot on her mind." She ate her toast and

drank a third of her tea. "I think the rest of the troops are rousing. What are you planning today?"

"Getting some work done this morning before I spend the afternoon with the kids. And thanks for arranging for the kids to go with Bailey to art classes so I could get some stuff done."

"Wasn't me."

"Alice strikes again."

"Seriously, hire her."

"I might be able to. Helen's trying to convince Dad to retire."

With only one arm shoved into her jacket, Sarah said, "What will he do?"

"He says travel."

"Oh, dear. That doesn't sound good. Not for your father. Don't take this the wrong way, but he's a lot like you. Downtime doesn't really exist."

"I'm planning downtime today."

"Which will involve writing a lecture."

"That relaxes me. Oh, I get what you're saying." I tapped my noggin. "I think it's more about Peter. Dad feels guilty that he didn't rein in Peter's Peterness before, well, ya know." I kissed her cheek. "Please be careful." I leaned down and kissed her belly. "Take care of your mom."

Casey bounded into the room. "I'm ready!"

Within an hour, everyone else was out of the house, except Ethan and Gandhi, who was napping by the fire in the main room.

I found Ethan in the kitchen, sitting on a barstool in pajamas and what can only be described as a dad's robe, reading a paperback while sipping a cup of coffee.

"Good morning."

He grunted and turned the page.

I made another cup of tea. "Do you hate mornings, or are you in a bad mood?"

"Is there a difference between the two?"

"That was my way of asking if everything is okay with you and Lisa."

"Oh." He scratched the top of his head, making his bedhead even worse. "It's okay. We haven't talked much about us since she got back. I don't think she can handle anything other than grieving for her mom right now."

That made sense. I didn't even like my mom, but her death did a number on me. "Whatcha reading?"

"*The Underground Railroad* by Colson Whitehead."

"Oh, I've heard of that one. Good?"

"Very." He closed the book. "Are you making coffee?"

"Was that your way of asking me to make you another cup of coffee?"

"Was I not clear?" He grinned. "How far along is Sarah?"

"I fear we're not doing a good job keeping it quiet." I chewed on my bottom lip.

"Lisa was the one who noticed the tonic water trick."

"Helen picked up on it as well and told Dad."

"My guess is you'll have another daughter and you'll never be able to get away with a thing."

"That would be my luck. A house with four females." I filled the reservoir for Ethan's coffee.

"Poor Freddie. He may have to live with me."

"Well, there's a chance Peter will have to live with us when he gets out."

"Really?"

I shrugged. "Not sure what his parole will entail or if he'll want to be alone with Demi. Not to mention, all his assets have been frozen. Dad has mentioned selling the house. We're not sure Peter can keep such a large place going on his own when he's released. My greedy sibling is going to be penniless."

"Your life keeps getting more interesting."

"Tell me about it."

"Are you happy about the baby?"

I grinned. "Very."

"What if you get twins?"

I tossed up my hands. "Not even that thought scares me."

"It would serve you right for knocking her up."

"Uh, you do know that it wasn't literally me." It wasn't even my eggs this time.

"Not for a lack of trying. It makes me ill to think of all the sex you two have."

"Oh, hey, that reminds me. Do you like boobs?"

Ethan's jaw tightened.

"I know you don't like fluids, but what about boobs?"

"Are you asking in general or about yours?"

"Why in the fuck would I ask if you like my boobs?" I looked down at them.

"I don't know why you're asking at all."

"Because the other night, I made a comment that everyone likes boobs and Sarah said you didn't. So, do you, or don't you?"

"I'm more into brains."

"Come on. That's a cop-out." I placed my hands on the counter top and did some calf raises, a recent habit I'd developed while waiting for the kettle to heat up.

"Are you saying you don't appreciate your wife's intelligence?"

"I do. Very much so. I also love her tits."

"You're a Neanderthal."

"No, I have a pulse." I placed two fingers on my wrist for emphasis.

"Stop gabbing. Coffee. Then I'm going to read again."

"Interesting. Even boob talk gives you the willies. How'd I not know this?"

"It's weird to talk about boobs." He moved around as if covered in a cobweb.

"Says no straight guy ever, but you."

His eyes darted upward. "You may be surprised to know I'm not the only guy who thinks this way."

"If you say so. Okay. Coffee for you. Tea for me. Then I need to work on a lecture about Kristallnacht."

"When the Nazis destroyed Jewish shops and such?" His forehead creased.

"Yep."

"That's a weird subject for a weekend away."

"You're reading a novel about slavery."

He shrugged. "It won a Pulitzer."

I laughed.

Ethan settled into one of the chairs by the fireplace, while I camped out at the table with my books and journals.

Around eleven, Bailey and Allen returned with the kids for lunch.

"Do you two want to hit the slopes? I'm on kid duty for the afternoon." We'd planned this as a surprise for Bailey, who'd been putting in extra hours this semester.

Bailey slanted her head. "You're a weird boss."

"Ethan's been lecturing me all day about slavery."

"I have not. I haven't said a word. It's been delightful." He chomped into a grilled cheese sandwich after dipping it into his tomato soup.

"You wouldn't mind?" Allen asked as he slipped Gandhi some cheese. The dog had mastered a begging face that was impossible to ignore.

"Not at all. Besides, they'll be napping soon. Ethan will be here if all heck breaks out."

"Did I not mention I plan to nap after lunch?" Ethan said.

"Even better. You can sleep on the floor with the kids and the dog." I jostled his arm with my elbow.

"Somehow that didn't work out in my favor." He returned his attention to his book.

Bailey pushed up her glasses. "Janice wants to know when she should visit."

"Whenever she has the time."

Bailey gave me a look that implied *cut the act*. "You know what I mean."

"Not sure she does," Ethan piped up. "Use clear, short sentences."

"Right. When is the baby due?"

I groaned. "Jesus."

Fred said, "Baba."

I smiled at my son. "Does everyone know?"

Even Allen nodded. "You guys did announce you were planning it on the night that shall not be named."

"True. It just happened a lot quicker than we anticipated." Apparently, Sarah was extremely fertile. I kept that thought to myself.

"Kids have a way of doing that." Ethan wiped his hands on a napkin. "You going to eat the rest of your sandwich?" He motioned to mine.

"Go ahead."

"Someone has to gain weight with Sarah." He broke off a small piece for the Yorkie.

"Yeah, you're a champ like that."

"And, I don't objectify her breasts."

Allen choked on his Coke.

Bailey arched her brows.

I glared at Ethan, who wore a Cheshire cat grin.

Gabe burst through the door. "Lizzie and Allen, you two need to come with me!"

I shot out of my chair. "Is Sarah okay?"

"It's your dad. He's in the hospital."

"Can you guys watch the kids?" I asked Ethan and Bailey.

They waved for me not to waste another second.

In the car, I asked, "What happened?"

"They think heart attack." Gabe backed out of the drive.

"How bad?"

"Don't know. Sarah didn't want either of you to drive."

"Is she at the hospital?"

"Everyone is. He started to complain about tightness in his chest, and Mom didn't mess around."

Sitting in the passenger seat, I looked out the window. The snowy tree branches zoomed by. Just like the thoughts zipping through my mind.

Sarah greeted me as I walked through the sliding glass doors, putting her arms around me in a way that concerned me.

"Is he okay?" Allen asked.

"Yeah, he's fine."

"Then why the *prepare yourself* hug?" I leaned into her more.

"Pregnant. Emotional." She made a circular motion that it was all connected.

"Right."

"You're pregnant?" Gabe blurted louder than necessary.

"You didn't know? It seems everyone else does," I said.

"Did you tell everyone but me?"

"What?" Sarah squeezed Gabe's shoulder. "No. We haven't told anyone. But apparently when I don't drink, everyone assumes that can be the only reason."

"They were correct." I smiled.

"Oh, man. This is exciting!" Gabe hugged Sarah with exuberance. "Oh, sorry." He relaxed his hold.

Helen waved us over. "We can all go in."

"Really?" I asked.

Helen didn't look like a woman who was worried her husband was dying. "I'll let your father tell you himself."

That seemed odd.

Dad was in a hospital bed, still in his own clothes, saving me from seeing him in a hospital gown. From a cursory look, he wasn't hooked up to any machines, and he seemed quite grumpy.

"Hey, Dad. How are you doing?" I asked.

"I'm ready to leave."

"Is that wise?"

He nodded.

I studied Helen, who was struggling to keep a straight face.

"What am I missing?" I whispered to Sarah.

She shrugged.

"What happened, Dad?" Allen asked.

"Helen overreacted."

"You were having chest pain," she defended.

"I told you it wasn't anything to worry about," he grumbled.

"How was I supposed to know for sure?"

"Because I told you."

"Seriously, Cap, I had no idea you only had gas."

Gabe burst into laughter but tried to pretend he was coughing.

"Can we go?" Dad started to get off the bed.

"We're just waiting for your discharge papers."

A man in a white coat walked in. "Wow. You have a big family. Is this everyone?"

Define everyone.

"Can I go now?" Dad said in what I imagined was his CEO voice.

"Sure thing." The doctor quickly dispensed some do's and don'ts.

After the man left, Sarah said, "You know, Lizzie farts in her sleep."

My gaze fell to the ground, and I hoped the linoleum would open up and swallow me.

"Does gas run in the family?" Maddie asked in a somewhat normal tone.

My father and I exchanged a look.

Gabe tossed an arm over my shoulder. "I didn't know you had it in you."

"Not for long since she releases it," Maddie explained oh so helpfully.

"You know, now that I'm in town, I may get some shopping done. Christmas will be here before you know it." I made for the door.

"It's spring."

"Time's a ticking."

"I'll go with you," Dad said.

"Great."

"Don't forget to buy gas medicine," Gabe said as Dad and I left the room.

Outside of the hospital, I asked, "We don't really have to shop, do we?"

"I'd rather donate a kidney. I could use a drink. You?"

"Are you allowed?"

"Probably not, but… you know. Just don't tell Helen," he whispered.

"Does that work? Sarah seems to know when I don't follow the rules."

"Oh, I have a feeling Helen won't say anything tonight. Tomorrow is a different story."

"Where to, chief?"

"I have a place in mind, but we'll need a car." He got his phone out, and I wondered how long we'd have to wait for Matthew, his chauffeur.

When a Toyota Corolla pulled up and Dad opened the door, I realized my father, the multi-millionaire actually used Uber. I was learning a lot about the man.

Inside a dark bar that was much more rustic than I was anticipating, we found a table with two uncomfortable chairs in the corner.

Dad asked, "What can I get you?"

"A Coke without a straw. They're bad for the environment, and I'm not drinking alcohol while Sarah's pregnant."

His eyes crinkled. "That's so you on both counts."

"I don't think you should have booze, either, in case you were wondering."

He sniffed. "I know. I just needed an excuse to process what happened."

Soon enough, he returned with a Coke and a tea.

"Did you want to process alone, or do you want to talk about it? I'm praying you don't want to talk about my flatulence issue."

He chuckled. "I'm pretty sure everyone does that."

"It's still embarrassing when your wife announces it to your family."

"I can relate at the moment."

"How does your chest feel now?"

He shifted in the wooden chair. "It's fine. I just think it's time."

That sounded ominous. "For?"

"A break to give me the strength to rebuild."

"Not retirement?"

"Not sure that's in my DNA."

"I feel the same way. Which is one of the things that worries me about Peter when he gets out."

Dad nodded.

I sipped my Coke, enjoying the cold fizz of the bubbles on my face in the warm bar. "His dream of being a pilot won't get him far. Workwise. It may get him to different places."

"I knew what you meant. Some, like you, are survivors. Peter isn't, I fear."

"That's pretty blunt."

"Do you disagree?" His voice seemed hopeful.

"I don't know. Not sure I'm ready to write him off completely, though. He wasn't the best brother, but I have noticed some significant changes over the past year or so. I'll do what I can to help him adjust."

Dad leaned back in his chair and crossed his arms. "How did you come from me and your mother?"

"Please don't make me think of that." I wiggled in my seat.

"Yes, every kid imagines the immaculate conception."

"Kinda works for my kids."

He chuckled again. Gas made him soft.

"Does Helen really expect you to retire?"

"I think she does."

"Are you going to break it to her that you don't want to?"

"I don't know how."

"Sarah likes me to use words." I mimicked Sarah's voice to the best of my ability. "Use your words, Lizzie."

"I'm sure Helen feels the same way, but she won't like what I have to say."

"Which is?"

"Work is an important part of my life. She'll think I'm choosing it over her."

"Are you?"

"No, but how can I walk away from it when I spent my entire life building my company up from the ground? With Peter—it's under threat. I need to right the ship. I don't trust anyone else to do that."

"I understand. I have a feeling Helen would to, if you told her."

"I don't like these types of conversations."

"Gabe's in a similar boat." I slapped a hand over my mouth.

"Something I should know?"

"I'm not sure I should say more."

"You might as well so I can help. Gabe can be a stubborn shit, and it may take another person to try to talk some sense into him."

CHAPTER TWENTY-SIX

We returned to the house right before dinner, Sarah pulling me to the side immediately.

"I'm so sorry." She kissed my cheek and then hugged me, her fingers playing with the stray hairs on my neck.

"Any other ways you plan to throw me under the bus during a family situation?" I was only partly teasing.

"I honestly don't know. Being pregnant isn't helping my decision-making." She rested her head on my shoulder.

"You weren't pregnant when you announced to everyone I kissed Maddie."

"True. Are you mad? About earlier today?"

"Not really. I'm getting used to it. Dad and I ended up having a good talk, so there's that."

"Is this the best time to mention I have good and bad news?" She still had her head on my shoulder, so I couldn't see her face to determine if she was trying to wind me up or if she was serious.

"Has there been another visit to the hospital or anything?"

"No." She stared into my eyes, her arms still around my neck. "That makes two pieces of good news."

"Go on. Rip the band aide off."

"We need to go shopping!" she said in a singsong voice.

"Is that the bad news?"

"Nope. The good."

I closed my eyes and counted to five. "Okay, what's the bad news?"

"I forgot the Easter eggs I prepped for tomorrow morning, and we have to buy all new plastic eggs and goodies that go inside or the kids can't have their egg hunt."

"Right." I bobbed my head, doing everything in my power not to scream at my pregnant wife, who usually was more on the ball. "You look exhausted." I rubbed the puffiness under her right eye. "Is this something Maddie and I can handle while you stay here?" I placed a hand on her belly.

"You'd do that?"

My curmudgeonly feelings melted. "Yes. I would. You're growing a human. Seems like the least I can do." I scouted the main floor for Maddie. Making eye contact, I beckoned her with a crooked finger.

Maddie slinked over. "That may work with Sarah but not me."

"You came over, so it does."

Maddie swore under her breath.

"We have an Easter egg emergency and need to go to the store," I whispered so little ears, Casey's in particular, wouldn't hear.

Sarah rattled off the shopping list to both of us, and I prayed Maddie was taking better mental notes than I was. I tried jotting things down on my phone but gave up since my fingers were cold and Maddie seemed to be nodding as if in control.

We went shopping after dinner and returned around eight. The kids were down for the night, aside from Casey, who was curled up on the couch with Ethan and Lisa, watching a movie. The remaining adults were at the table playing poker. From the pile of poker chips in front of Helen, she was cleaning everyone's clocks.

Sarah set her cards down and approached us. "We should do this in our room so…" Her eyes landed on Casey.

In our suite, there was a small table with some chairs. Maddie dumped out the contents of the shopping bags on the bed.

"Oh good, you got sparkly plastic eggs in addition to the regular ones. Okay, the sparkly eggs are for Casey, and those should be filled with the chocolate and jelly beans. The other ones are for the twins and should be filled with the toddler snacks. Did you get them?" Sarah sorted through the pile. "Yes. These." She held up a plastic container with toddler puffs. The label purported the snacks melted in the mouth and aided with eye and brain health. I believed the melting part and thought the rest was a crock of shit, but I kept that thought to myself.

Soon enough, Maddie and I set up an assembly line of sorts.

There was a knock on the door. Sarah, who had been sitting on the bed assembling the Easter baskets, got up and answered it.

"Do you need help?" It was Bailey and Allen, each with a mug of hot chocolate.

Sarah waved them in, and soon enough, everyone was brought up to speed, getting all the eggs filled.

By the time Casey went to bed, the adults got into the spirit of hiding all the eggs.

"Remember folks, the sparkly ones should really be hidden, but the other ones need to be in plain sight for the twins to find on their own," Maddie instructed in her impression of take-charge Sarah who was in bed, hopefully asleep.

I swallowed a comment that I'd be finding all the eggs in plain sight with the twins.

* * *

"Look, Fred. Here's a bright pink one." I held my son's hand in mine.

He glanced around, his attention focused on the bowed table legs, not the egg on the shelf at the bottom of the furniture. I guided his hand to the egg, and his face lit up when he scooped it up and then dumped it into the basket. We'd only found a handful of the neon eggs.

Sarah assisted Ollie, who had a much larger pile of loot.

"Aha!" Casey found one of hers in between the couch cushions.

"How many more are there?" Ethan asked me, his eyes bloodshot.

I shrugged. "No idea. We probably should have counted."

"This could take all morning," Gabe said. "I know Casey hasn't found any of mine yet."

I stifled a groan. "Why is that?"

"I hid mine outside."

"But it snowed overnight."

Gabe's eyes lit up. "I know. It's going to take her forever!"

I twirled around. "Casey, get your jacket on. Uncle Gabe is going to help you with the outside portion of the hunt."

She squealed.

Gabe in flannel pajama bottoms, T-shirt, and slippers scowled at me. "I've only had one cup of coffee."

"I haven't had any. For weeks," Sarah said in her *don't argue with the pregnant lady* voice.

"Right." Gabe set his mug down. "Let me get my boots and jacket."

"I'll help you." Allen seemed much more cheerful about the activity.

Casey zipped around to get her own boots and jacket, squealing again when she found an egg in each of the toes of her shoes.

Ethan prepared as well, and I wondered if this was his way

of confessing he'd also had the brilliant idea of hiding some of the eggs outside. There'd been quite of bit of alcohol involved for the majority of the adults.

Maddie rubbed her temples. "Should I get started on brunch?"

"Please," Sarah said, resting on the couch, while Ollie sat on the floor, her legs in a V, as she played with the eggs in her basket. Fred was next to his sister, trying to stack his eggs. Gandhi snoozed in his bed in front of the fireplace.

"I'll help you," I said to Maddie.

"Uh, Charles, did you have to pay a huge deposit for this place?"

"I don't know." He shuffled in his slippers. "Why?"

"Lizzie can't be trusted with ovens," Maddie announced with a mischievous grin.

"I can make toast and pour orange juice."

"Maybe I should help instead." Lisa rose from a chair. "I heard about the oven."

"Traitor," I said to Maddie.

Bailey also helped in the kitchen while I got Gandhi dressed in his jacket and booties for a short walk outside so I wouldn't have to get up during brunch. The dog had impeccable timing for needing to relieve himself, and I was doing my best to pick up on the signs.

Out front, Allen and Casey were still hunting eggs, while Ethan and Gabe stood in the corner of the deck, deep in conversation. From the expression on Gabe's face, it wasn't a pleasant chat.

"Come on, Gandhi." I patted my pocket to ensure I had a plastic bag just in case.

We walked down a narrow-shoveled path leading to the back of the house, the sky now a brilliant blue, but darkening clouds gathered in the west. Gandhi zipped from one side of the piled snow to the other, leaving his trail of yellow patches.

A brisk wind blew loose snow into my face and covered the Yorkie, who tucked tail and headed back to the front door. Before I had a chance to open the door, I heard a shriek inside. I busted through the door, my heart pounding in my chest.

Ollie stood in the middle of the room, her face covered in black, red, and green colors with matching smudged fingerprints on her white shirt.

"How'd she get a hold of jelly beans?" Sarah asked.

I inspected the eggs in her basket and found the source of the problem. "Uh, we must have messed up last night." I dumped jelly beans out of two more of her eggs.

"She could have choked."

Ollie giggled and held her hands up. "Bean!"

I filled her hand with the toddler snacks instead.

"No! Bean!"

"Check Fred's," Sarah barked, which I did while Sarah calmed Ollie down.

Fred helped me open his eggs, seeming to pick up on the goal: not eating the jelly beans. He handed me a black one. "Thanks, Little Man." I kissed his forehead.

Everyone came back inside, Casey chatting excitedly with Ethan.

Gabe went into the kitchen, with a determined face, perhaps in search of more coffee.

After getting the egg mishap under control, I started to collect the empty egg halves, putting them back together and tucking them into a bag for next year.

There was another shriek.

My eyes found Sarah and then Ollie, but neither of them was the source this time. Freddie had curled up on the couch with Sarah, snoozing.

"You want it back?" Maddie shouted.

Gabe stood at her side, with a guilty expression. "Not permanently."

"You can't give a woman a ring and then ask for it back without the woman thinking it was permanent."

They had everyone's attention now.

"Why are you so upset? We've been talking about this. Simplifying the relationship to take the pressure off. You were onboard about going back to dating before I was." Gabe's voice wavered.

"Maybe we should give you two space." Helen rose from the table where she'd been playing bridge with Dad, Rose, and Troy.

"No. Don't go." Maddie glared at Gabe. "Why do you have to ask for it back, though? Why not ask me to take it off, but allow me to keep it for… if…? And to do it this way. It's so insulting! It seems final." Her voice shook, and it was clear she was having a hard time holding her emotions in control.

"Maddie," he reached for her hand, but she yanked it away. "Please, Mads. Don't take it the wrong way. I want things to work out between us. This"—he shook his hands in the air indicating the space separating them—"whatever this is between us is killing me. I love you. I want us to get back to where we were before everything… happened. I thought this would help."

"How would taking away my hope help?" Maddie tucked her hands into her armpits as if warding off his attempts to pry the ring from her finger.

"It hasn't been the same since you put it on. It's cursed or something."

"Do you plan on buying another one?"

"What? No. Well, I can if you want, but Lizzie, Dad, and Ethan told me—"

Maddie whirled about. "You all told him to take the ring back?"

The three of us stuck our hands in the air and shook our heads.

Maddie narrowed her eyes. "What did you tell him?"

It was clear no one else was going to say anything. "I just said maybe it'd be better for you two to date and to consider speaking to a professional. We talked about all this when you saved me from burning down the house. The fire is like a real-life metaphor for your relationship now that I think of it."

Sarah winced, and I replayed my words and tone. Whoops.

"Why can't I have my happily ever after?" A tear streamed down Maddie's cheek.

"You can," Gabe said, a pained look in his eyes. "I want us to have that. That's why I think we should go to therapy."

"But..."

"We need a stronger foundation," Gabe's voice was hard to hear over Maddie's deep intakes of air.

Maddie slipped the ring off her finger and placed it on the counter. "Here." She ran to the back of the house.

Sarah, Helen, and Lisa followed.

Gabe stood in the middle of the kitchen, completely frozen.

I sat on the couch, Freddie snuggling close to me in his sleep. Ollie grinned as if enjoying the scene.

The fire alarm went off, and Dad rushed into action, unplugging the toaster, while Ethan waved a dishtowel to clear the smoke, and Troy climbed on a chair to remove the device from the ceiling.

"Happy Easter," I muttered under my breath, comforting Freddie, while Rose scooped up Ollie, who seemed to take delight in the chaos.

CHAPTER TWENTY-SEVEN

We returned Sunday night, exhausted and slightly grumpy. The kids were taken straight to bed.

"Do you think it confuses the shit out of them? Falling asleep in one place and waking in another?" I asked as I sat down on the couch in the library.

Sarah settled next to me. "Maybe, but they should feel lucky. We have to manage all the steps. They just wake for the fun stuff."

"True. Not sure they'll appreciate that until they have their own kids." I massaged my temples. "Does my accepting the TV job make you think I'm choosing my career over you?"

"Whoa. That's coming from left field."

"Sorry. My conversations with my dad over the weekend have done my head in. Not to mention the whole Gabe and Maddie fiasco."

"Go on about your dad."

"Helen wants him to retire. He doesn't. Ever, apparently." I sighed.

"Will he scale back at least?"

"Not sure. He built the company from the ground up, and

with Peter out of the equation, I don't think he can hand it off and walk away. I doubt he'll trust anyone for some time."

"If Peter wasn't"—she raked a hand through her hair—"in his situation, would he be able to?"

"Ah, you're asking a historian to make a projection about what could be."

"I know. Humor me." She moved so she could place her foot in my lap, and I started to massage it. "Oh, that feels good."

I continued. "He may have stepped back some."

"Yeah, that's what I think." Sarah closed her eyes.

"Does my drive upset you? I do take after him." I pressed deep into the arch of her foot.

She let out a happy sigh. "It can frustrate me, but it's also one of the things I admire. You're not like your dad, Lizzie. You love your family."

I flinched.

"I didn't mean for it to come out like that. What I mean is you think of us first." She bonked her forehead with a palm. "Damn, that came out wrong as well."

"I'm not so sure. If honesty was your goal, you nailed it."

"I was hoping to spare your feelings some."

I started to work on her other foot. "Don't worry. I'm aware my parents sucked, and I don't want to be like them. Which is why I'm asking if taking on this TV role will be a mistake. I'm already teaching, which includes the history club, publishing articles, and, for some insane reason, working on a novel, which I can't keep on the back burner forever. I think I should start looking for an agent."

She opened her eyes. "Really?"

I nodded, not feeling overly confident now that I'd spoken the words aloud.

"That's exciting."

"And terrifying."

"True. Have you already contacted any agents?"

"Nope. I don't want to repeat the last mistake."

She wore a sheepish grin. "I still feel terrible for how I handled finding out about the novel."

"You mean by accusing me of having an affair with my evil ex. Yeah, that wasn't your finest moment."

She jabbed an elbow into my side.

"What did I do this time?"

"Haven't figured it out yet."

My eyes darted to the ceiling. "Not sure you've noticed, but I've been on my best behavior lately. I even started giving you a foot rub without you having to ask, besides you plonking your feet in my lap, which wasn't that subtle."

She chuckled. "You are getting better about some things."

"With Gabe's performance today, you can't complain about a thing."

"Poor Maddie." She tsked.

"How'd they leave it?"

"Good question. They drove back together, so…" She crossed her fingers. "Back to you, though. Are you nervous about juggling everything when the TV job starts?"

"On a scale of one to ten?"

She nodded.

"An eleven."

"I see. But before the talk with your dad, you weren't as nervous?"

"I was, but I don't want to get myself in his situation. So involved with work I can't stop."

"I don't think you will, or if you were getting close to that point, I think you'd open up to me. Lately, most of the time I don't even have to prompt or yell at you to let me in. It's annoying."

"Why?"

"I kinda liked yelling at you sometimes. A great stress reliever."

"I can stop if you want."

"Don't you dare." She jabbed a finger at me. "I'll yell at the kids."

"I hope you're kidding. I'm not fond of you yelling at me or our innocent children."

"Innocent?" she muttered. "Today, Ollie—"

The ring of the house phone interrupted her.

I moved her feet and went to my desk. "Hello?"

"Lizzie, can I come over?"

"Courtney?"

"Yes."

"Uh, sure. We're still up."

Sarah raised a questioning brow.

"I'll be there in fifteen," Courtney said.

I shrugged. "See ya in a few."

"What's that about?" Sarah asked right when I put the phone down. "How did she get our house number?"

"Dunno." I fished my phone out of my pocket. "My ringer was off."

Sarah checked hers. "Mine too. Must be important."

"Since when is Courtney on the list of people we have to put back together?"

"She did help you in the past when dealing with the Meg issue."

"You see, this is the problem with letting people in. The quid pro quo aspect."

"Yes. We should cut everyone off and never leave the house."

"Now you're talking." I rubbed my hands together, miser-like.

"I can't tell if you're kidding. Please tell me you're kidding."

I rubbed my forehead.

"Do you want me to handle her?"

"I haven't forgotten you have a crush on her."

"Oh, please. I'm preggo."

"The first time she hit on you, you were pregnant. Maybe that's her thing. Hormonal ladies."

"Lizzie!"

"Pregnant. Clearly, I meant *pregnant*. I've never considered you unbalanced or anything. My head hurts. I can't think straight."

She closed one eye to inspect me in her special way as if trying to determine whether or not my head really hurt or if I was lying. "Is she driving from Denver?"

"She said she'd be here in fifteen. Maybe she has meetings here tomorrow."

"Or she was with Jorie. A little bird told me they've gone on a few dates."

"Another situation I'm not thrilled with." I yawned.

"We can't tell our nanny who she can or can't sleep with."

"It would be a better world if we could. Can't I just tell everyone what they can and can't do? Rule number one: leave me alone." I held a finger in the air.

"I'm thinking maybe you should change your specialty. You're starting to sound a little too Hitlerian."

"I don't want to kill people. I just want peace and quiet." I placed my hand on my forehead, the tightness behind my eyeballs building.

"Sure. That's how it starts."

"I need to pee and find some headache pills."

"Interesting tactic. Go. We'll talk about your dictator traits later."

I stayed hidden upstairs until I heard the front door open. Sarah must have sat in the bay window to spy Courtney before she had a chance to knock or ring the bell.

Getting off the bed, I tromped downstairs, ready to face the music.

When I entered the library, Sarah was pouring a glass of

white wine for Courtney, who looked about as pale as the beverage. Great, just what I needed.

"Hey," I said.

Courtney nodded a hello and accepted the glass from Sarah.

Sarah raised the grappa bottle with a questioning brow.

I shook my head.

Sarah didn't seem convinced that was the best course of action.

"Shall we sit?" Sarah said, clearly unable to come up with anything else.

Courtney sat on one of the couches, and Sarah and I took the one facing her.

"How was Vail?" Courtney asked.

"One trip to the hospital, perhaps a broken engagement, and the fire alarm only went off once, so a good weekend away for the Petries." Sarah forced a laugh.

I offered a tight-lipped smile.

"And no arrests," Courtney offered.

"Yeah, that's a new thing on the checklist." Again, more forced laughter from Sarah.

"How is Maddie? She texted me but hasn't filled me in completely."

Sarah shrugged. "It's been a rough few months for her. I'm not sure she knows what she's thinking, and then there's Gabe's surprise maneuver today. She's got to be questioning everything."

Courtney nodded, not pressing about the Gabe situation.

"Did you come over to chat about Maddie?" I asked, annoyed because it could have waited until tomorrow.

"No, I didn't. I heard from Kit," Courtney said.

"Oh. How is he?" Sarah's face relaxed some, but I felt my shoulders tense.

"Uh, not good." She set down her wineglass, and it was

then that I realized she hadn't taken a sip. "I don't know what to do, really. Or how to say this?"

Sarah reached for my hand. "This doesn't have to do with Demi, does it? Tie gave up her rights. She signed the papers."

"Yes and no."

"Please. Just tell me." Sarah applied more pressure to my hand.

"Tie's dead."

Oh, good God, did someone in my family kill her?

I couldn't catch a fucking break.

"Wh-what?" Sarah asked as if she had the same thought as me. That perhaps Dad or Peter had played a role.

Or was it Samuel? Was he cleaning house?

"It was a terrible accident." Courtney leaned forward, resting her elbows on her knees.

At least they'd done a good job. Was that why Dad was so uptight this weekend? And did he use us as an alibi? Oh, Jesus!

"An accident?" Sarah spoke slowly, her voice wavering.

"Yeah. According to Samuel, she accidentally dropped her phone into the trash shoot in her building. Tie went to the basement to dig it out of the… the trash thingy and ended up falling in."

"And that killed her?" Sarah's hand covered her mouth.

"She couldn't get out when it started to compact."

I sat next to Sarah, putting my arm around her shoulder.

"She got trash compacted?" Sarah's watery eyes peered into mine.

Courtney nodded.

"That's the most bizarre thing I've ever heard," I blurted. "Who dies like that?"

"Tie," Courtney said matter-of-factly.

I let out a rush of air. "I didn't see this coming."

"Poor D-Demi," Sarah was sobbing now. "H-how do we tell her that her mom gave her up and then died like that?"

It did seem fitting to a certain degree. Tie was a piece of garbage. Not that I could say that aloud. "We don't ever have to tell her that Tie renounced her parental rights." Again, I stopped myself from saying her death saved us from that conversation.

Sarah sniffled. "Yeah, right. That's good."

"And we don't need to tell her anything yet. She's too young to understand anyway. Maybe by the time she's old enough, we'll know what to say. Or Peter will."

Sarah gave me her *be serious* face.

I shrugged. "He does have a say."

Sarah turned away from me. "How is Kit handling all of this?" Her tears started to flow again.

"He doesn't know what to think. Kit likes to play people, but he was never cruel like Tie. I think he's struggling with his own identity at the moment. Not wanting to turn out like Tie."

"Oh, I get that. Seriously, Sarah, can we change our last name?"

Sarah's expression made it clear this wasn't the time for that conversation. "We need to pull together. All of us. That little girl upstairs deserves to have us be there for her. No matter what."

That was true.

It didn't make anything easier, though.

"I'm going to call my mom." Sarah got up and left.

"How are you doing?" I asked Courtney.

"Is it terrible if I admit I'm kinda relieved? Tie knew a lot of things about me."

"Was she blackmailing you?"

"I wouldn't go that far. Let's just say she liked to keep me on my toes."

I pressed the heels of my hands into my eyes. "How are people like Tie created, and why do they keep finding me?"

There wasn't an answer.

"Does Peter know?" I asked Courtney.

"I don't know. Kit said the police tried to inform him, but he's not answering his phone or the door. Her death hasn't hit the news yet, thanks to her dad, but it's only a matter of time given her connection to Peter."

I rose. "I should go to his place."

"You're exhausted." Sarah had just returned.

"I'll drive." Courtney stood up.

Sarah shook her head, obviously not happy with the situation but unable to mount a good reason as to why I shouldn't go. "Will you stay the night there?"

"Should I?"

"It's already late. The conversation will be difficult. Peter's angry with Tie, but she was his wife and the mother of his daughter."

"I don't want to leave you alone all night," I protested.

"Mom and Maddie are on their way over."

"That was quick work," I said amazed, trying to picture if she'd used some type of device like the Bat-Signal.

"You can stay at my place if you want," Courtney offered.

"I guess I should pack a toothbrush or something. Give me five minutes."

In the upstairs bathroom, I rested my palms on the edge of the counter and gazed at my reflection in the mirror. "Okay, Lizzie. All you have to do is tell your brother, who's going to prison soon, that his estranged wife was killed in a tragic dumpster incident. Totally normal." Yeah right. Even a death was truly bizarre in the Petrie family.

CHAPTER TWENTY-EIGHT

Courtney pulled into Peter's driveway. None of the exterior lights were on, and I couldn't spy any sign of life inside. No wonder the cops didn't try to break the news themselves.

Courtney turned the car off but didn't make a move to get out. "You ready?"

"I think I can do this. You don't have to come in."

"Are you sure?" Her voice made it clear she doubted my abilities.

I puffed out my cheeks and swished the air from side to side, thinking. "Yeah. I really should be the one to talk to him. I'll call you if I need backup."

"There's an IHOP near here. I'll go there for an hour or so. If you need me, don't hesitate to call."

"Thanks." I stared at the door handle. "Now or never." I bucked up my courage and bounded out of the car, nearly slipping on a patch of ice. If I fell in my brother's driveway, could I sue as a way of getting back my inheritance from my uncle that Peter stole?

Knock it off, Lizzie.

Carefully, I made my way to the front door. Peter hadn't shoveled all winter, apparently, and I wondered how many threatening letters he'd received from his HOA. Not sure what kind of leverage they had over a man facing prison time. Could they send any unpaid fines to a collection agency while Peter was incarcerated?

I rang the bell.

Nothing happened.

I knocked.

No one stirred.

I resorted to banging my fist on the door, shouting, "Peter! Let me in!"

It took well over a minute and more knocking coupled with shouting before the door creaked open less than an inch.

"Peter?" I asked, feeling foolish.

"Lizzie?"

"Yes. Can I come in?"

He hesitated but slowly opened the door.

Even in the bad light, I could see his mountain-man beard, and he smelled like he'd been trekking the Oregon trail for months. It took everything I had to give him a hug.

"Sorry. I wasn't expecting company." He seemed to pick up on my revulsion. Or possibly he noticed I was taking sparing breaths.

"I wasn't intending to come over tonight, either. But…"

"What?"

We still stood in the entryway with the door open.

"Tell you what. Go shower. I'll make some coffee. Then we can talk."

He raked his beard. "Is Demi okay?"

"Yes. Rest assure on that front. Now, go shower, and don't make me pull rank."

"I'm older."

"I'm a mom. We have special powers. I'd rather play nice."

Without a word, he headed upstairs, presumably to his bathroom.

In the dark, I bumbled into his kitchen, wondering if I should turn on the lights or not. Probably best to. Normalcy. Peter needed normalcy. Or I did and was forcing it on him.

His coffee machine, which probably cost more than my newly purchased oven, was more complicated than any of the gadgets in my home, and I ended up watching a two-minute YouTube video to figure it out.

After ten minutes, I started to wonder if Peter had shimmied down the side of his house. I set an alarm on my watch for five more minutes. If he didn't appear then, I'd round up a search party of one.

Wait, should I call Courtney now and give her the heads-up? Or text, "Um, I've seemed to have lost Peter. Can you help me find him?"

I couldn't help thinking about how uncomplicated my life had been back in the day when my family shunned me and vice versa.

"What are you thinking about?"

His voice scared the crapola out of me.

"Uh, nothing important. Now that I've figured out your machine, would you like a Lizzie special?" I made a ta-da motion.

"Sure. Something tells me I won't be sleeping much tonight."

"Have you been sleeping at all?"

"Yeah. A ton. And I'm all caught up on *Keeping up with the Kardashians.*"

"Time well spent then."

"Have you heard of them?"

I nodded. "Maddie likes the show."

"Yeah, she used to try to get me to watch it. And the Real Housewives of whatever." He sat on a barstool while I went about making coffee for him. "What's so urgent you had to get me out of bed?"

I pressed a button and turned around, resting my back on the counter. "Can you wait until we can have a seat?"

He shrugged. "I have a lot of time these days. How was Vail?"

"Dad has gas." I opted not to mention the Maddie news.

"Oh."

"Helen thought he was having a heart attack, but it was just—"

"Gas."

"Yeah. Embarrassed the hell out of him when we all rushed to the hospital."

"Worse things can happen."

"I see you're keeping the beard. It still takes me by surprise."

He ran his fingers through it. "I like the way it feels."

"It's looking good."

He laughed. "No, it doesn't. I'm hoping it makes me look like a crazed person to keep people away when I'm in…" He didn't finish the sentence. Not that he had to. "How's Demi? You promise this has nothing to do with her?"

Of course, it did, but I couldn't seem to bring myself to deliver the news about Tie quite yet. Not in the kitchen. "She's good."

His coffee was done. "Shall we sit in the family room?" Without waiting for a reply, I carried his coffee and a can of Coke I found in the fridge. The man didn't have any tea that I could find. How did one live without tea? Although, if I was facing prison, I'm not sure I would keep my pantry stocked for unexpected visits.

The family room had a distinct odor of pizza and Chinese food. Not surprising given the stacked pizza boxes and Chinese cartons scattered about. Maybe I should send Miranda here to do a deep clean. Would she need help?

Peter flipped open the lid of a box. "You hungry?"

I shook my head. "Go ahead."

He chomped into a slice of pepperoni, and I had to wonder how long it'd been sitting on the leather ottoman. "The suspense is killing me." He didn't appear interested in anything other than Demi.

"It's about Tie."

Peter swallowed a bite without much chewing as far as I could tell. "What's she want?" He swallowed some coffee. "More money? A nicer apartment in the Big Apple? She'll have to talk to Dad. I'm tapped out."

"I'm not sure how to say this."

"Quickly."

We shared this similarity, wanting bad news delivered without much fanfare. "Dead. She's dead."

"*Dead*, dead? Not just dead to the family?"

"*Dead*, dead," I confirmed.

He stared at the TV, which wasn't on. "Oh."

If there was ever a doubt that Peter hated his wife, his lackluster *oh* confirmed it.

"How?" he asked. He stiffened as if something seemed to click in his head. "Wait. They don't suspect me, do they? Did the bitch set me up even more?"

More confirmation Peter hated the woman.

"It was an accident from what I've been told."

"By whom?" He looked in the direction of the front door as if waiting for the police to barge in. Again. Although, they'd barged into my house, not his.

"Courtney delivered the news to me. Kit told her. I believe Samuel was present when it happened." I tapped my thumb against three fingers in succession to ensure I got the chain of events correctly.

"Did he do it? Samuel?"

I couldn't tell if Peter believed Samuel capable of murder, and I didn't have the energy to open that floodgate. "I don't think so." This was a lie since the thought niggled in my brain during the entire car ride, but I didn't want to go down that rabbit hole at the moment, so I explained it in the fewest possible words to avoid looking like I was mocking the poor woman's demise.

"She always was a piece of trash."

I clamped my lips shut, knowing this had been my first thought as well and sensing it wasn't the time to remind Peter she was also Demi's mother. Nothing would ever change that fact. And given Peter's self-imposed retreat from society except an occasional visit with Demi, I didn't think he was in the frame of mind for a *come to Jesus* talk from me. Maybe Dad could get through to him. Quite possibly, he just needed time. Would the prison have a therapist or programs to help him deal with his new reality?

I drank some Coke, the sweetness and long day causing my stomach to swirl.

"I'm being sentenced on Wednesday," he said.

"I know. I plan to be there." Dr. Marcel was going to teach my classes that day.

Peter shook his head. "Please, don't."

"Why would you want to go through that alone?"

He gripped the armrest closest to me to face me. "I was never there for you, so why would you be there for me?"

I took it as a good sign that he still had some sense of pride in a warped way. "Because I'm a bitch like that. I'm going to be there. So are Dad and Helen. Allen and Maddie—"

"Promise me, Lizzie, you won't let either be there. Allen is too young for this. And, Maddie—that would kill me. Besides, she needs to realize I'm not right for her. I'm not good for anyone."

"Uh, I'll try to convince her not to come," I said without much confidence I could talk Maddie into not showing up. Maybe we could put her in a disguise.

"Dad must hate me."

"Why do you think that?"

"I've destroyed the reputation of the firm. Dad's reputation."

How to answer? "It doesn't change the fact that you're his son. Firstborn, no less."

"Mom must be rolling over in her grave."

"Well, she's probably rolling over the fact that I'm going to be a mom again. She never quite agreed with the lesbian lifestyle." I exaggerated all the syllables like she used to.

"What?"

"Oh, with everything, I forgot you don't know. Sarah's pregnant."

His eyes widened. "Wow. Congrats. Is that welcome news?" he whispered.

"It's hard for lesbians to have accidental pregnancies."

He blushed and actually laughed some. "Yeah, right. Stupid question. It's just—"

"It doesn't change a thing with Demi. Know that she'll be loved and taken care of."

"I do know that. It's just I wish none of this was happening. I wish she had a mother who loved her. And a father who wasn't… me. She's the best thing I ever did. I don't want her life ruined because I fucked up."

"Hey now. With Tie gone, you're going to have to step up." I glanced around the detritus of the room. "You can only wallow for so long."

"My lawyers think I'm going to get at least two years."

"I thought with the plea you'd get less time."

"I am."

What all had he done? Did I really want to know?

"Hey, Tom Hayes, a trader in London, got fourteen years for manipulating bank rates to improve his performance. Two years in comparison—it'll be a breeze. Although, Martha Stewart only served five months, so…" He hefted a shoulder.

In addition to watching crap reality TV, had he been researching all financial crimes and subsequent prison terms?

"Demi will be walking and talking by then," he said.

"She can visit."

Again, he shook his head, seeming to shrink in stature in the chair. "No. Don't ever bring her there."

I agreed to this one.

"Do you want me to tell Dad about Tie? I'm assuming there'll be some things on his end that'll need tidying up."

"I can call him. In the morning. Are they sure it's only gas pains? He's not going to… you know?"

"I think it'd take a lot more to remove Charles Allen Petrie from this life. He survived Mom." I added, "So did you, Peter."

"Yep, I'm living the dream." He waved his arm.

"You still can. Lots of people rebuild their lives."

He swallowed.

I had to fight the urge to google books on how to rebuild your life.

He yawned.

"I'm keeping you up." I started to rise.

"Don't go, yet. I'm not… Would you like to watch TV with me?"

I settled back into my chair. "Sure."

"How about *Orange is the New Black*? For research?"

How was I supposed to reply?

Luckily, he flipped on the TV, not waiting for a response. I texted Courtney, letting her know I'd be staying with Peter for the night.

CHAPTER TWENTY-NINE

Matthew, Dad's driver, dropped me off outside my house Wednesday night.

I stood in my driveway, one hand gripping the strap of my messenger bag, looking at the lights inside the mini-mansion. No matter how hard I tried, I couldn't seem to get my legs to move.

Sarah opened the front door. "You're going to freeze. More snow is expected. It's the winter that keeps on giving even though it's spring."

I nodded.

"I heard the news. You okay?"

"Three years."

She nodded.

"Is anyone else here? I'm not in the mood for…"

"Just me and the kids, who are asleep, but I don't have the monitors on me, so you may want to come inside."

That lit a fire under my ass.

When inside I said, "I'm going to kiss the kids goodnight."

Another nod and what seemed like a silent plea not to wake them, leading me to believe Ollie had been a handful yet again.

In the nursery, I kissed the twins and then lifted Demi out of her crib. She didn't wake, but I needed to hold her in my arms. "Your dad sends his love," I whispered. She stirred, but her eyes never opened. My nose burned, and my eyes started to water.

Sarah joined me, staying silent. After several minutes, I tucked Demi back in and stood there watching her. Sarah sidled up next to me and threaded her fingers through mine.

I wiped my right eye. Soon enough, I had to repeat it with the left.

Sarah nudged me out into the hallway and then took me into her arms. "Everything's going to be okay."

"It's not fair."

"What isn't?"

"She's just a baby, with no parents. Do you know what that feels like? I do to a certain degree. It's not fair."

She tightened her grip on me. "She has us, the twins, grandparents, aunts, and uncles. She won't be alone, Lizzie. Not like you were."

"But why was I?"

I wasn't sure how Sarah managed, but she held me tighter.

"I'm sorry. This isn't about me. I need to be stronger." I sniffled.

"There's nothing wrong with feeling emotions, and it's no wonder this is hitting you, considering everything. Come on. Let's have a drink."

"The baby."

"I'll have herbal tea, and you can have a gin and tonic. Jesus, if my brother was sentenced to three years, I'd want one every hour on the hour for the next week."

"It'd be cheating. I'll have herbal tea with you."

"Can you have a gin and tonic for me? That's what I want but can't have."

"You want me to cheat for you?"

"I want you to stop overthinking it. Go into the library. I'll be there soon."

Sarah didn't lie. She came into the library with a steaming mug of tea. Without a word, she prepped me a gin and tonic, heavy on the gin. Although, I didn't taste anything when I swallowed a quarter of it in one go.

"He has two months to get his affairs in order. He's giving us power of attorney over his accounts, what's left of them, and Demi."

Sarah nodded.

"He doesn't want us to visit."

"Ever?" her voice was higher pitched than normal.

"That's what he says."

"But why?"

"Pride, I imagine."

"I understand not wanting Demi to see him that way, but us? Has he said this before?"

I shook my head. "I didn't want to argue the point with him. Give him some time to adjust."

"Three years. The twins will be in kindergarten and Demi in preschool."

"Yep." I swallowed more of the drink

"We'll have to teach Demi to say *dada*."

I rested my head against the back of the couch. "I won't lie; I used to hope for Peter's downfall when Mom doted on him all my life, but now that it's happening on such an epic scale, I feel sorry for the poor bastard. Just when he was starting to change for Demi's sake."

"Will he have access to a computer?"

"How would I know? The only time I've set foot in a prison was when doing research for a high school project."

"If he does, we can send videos of Demi. Maddie will help."

"Oh. Maybe." I traced the lip of my glass with the pad of my thumb.

"Not maybe. We will."

"I don't doubt your dedication, sweetheart. I'm thinking of Peter. Would that be too hard on him? Seeing everything he's missing?"

"If I were in his shoes—"

"If I can't die, you can't get arrested." I tossed the rest of the drink back.

Sarah took the glass from me and headed to the bar. "I'll do my best. As I was saying, if I were in Peter's shoes, I'd want to be as much a part of Demi's life as possible."

"Peter's different."

"He's her father!"

"Was." I reclined on the couch, stretching out my legs.

"No, he's still Demi's father." She motioned for me to lift my legs so she could sit, and then she handed me the refreshed glass.

"He wants her to know him as Uncle Peter."

Sarah winced as if slapped across the face. "He can't do that."

"He's thinking of her future, or so he says."

"No, he's thinking of his fucking pride."

"That too, I'm sure." I pinched the bridge of my nose, the burning sensation returning.

Sarah took a slug of her tea with an expression she wished it had brandy or something. "I don't know what to think."

"Join the club."

"What does your father say?"

"He didn't say a word when we huddled with Peter and his attorney after court."

"Typical," she spat out.

"Please don't be mad."

"I'm not mad at you. Or your dad." She wiped her brow. "I'm not even mad at Peter. It just sucks. For Demi." She peered at the baby monitors.

"True, but at least she has Ollie to protect her. And Fred adores her."

"He tried giving her his lunch today."

I laughed. "You see? Demi fits in here."

"You look so tired."

"I am."

We sat quietly as we finished our drinks.

"Come on. Let's put this day in the books. Who knows what tomorrow will bring?"

"Please, don't ever say that again. Not in this family."

CHAPTER THIRTY

I stood in the kitchen in what Sarah called my professor clothes, black slacks and a silk short sleeve shirt with a floral print. My attention was focused on the front page of the paper, Peter's glazed eyes staring back at me. "Why do news organizations always use a mugshot?"

"Because it's not a good look for anyone and makes them seem guilty as shit."

I tossed the unread edition in the trash.

"What time are we expecting your father and Helen tonight?"

"Eightish. My last final for today ends at four, and then we have that thing."

"Is it okay if Mom and Troy are here this evening?"

I nodded. "Of course, they're family. I should get to campus. Not sure it'd be kosher for me not to show up to administer final exams." I drained my tea. "See you later."

Sarah pulled me into her arms. "It's going to be okay."

"I can't stop thinking it's his first day there. What's happening to him? What's going through his mind?"

"I know, sweetie." She kissed my cheek. "One day at a time."

I nodded.

In the family room, I kissed the top of the twins' heads and then gave Demi a cuddle.

Jorie watched me with a look of helplessness as if she wanted to impart some pearls of wisdom but failed to think of any.

"Do you have any finals today?" I asked in an attempt to ease the awkwardness.

"Nope. All done."

"If I don't see you before you leave for your vacation, have a good time."

"Thanks. And best of luck, with everything."

I was sure she didn't mean grading or anything to do with school.

On campus, everyone in the history department went out of their way to stop me in the hallway or come by my office to chat about the weather, which was much warmer than normal for this time of year. I did appreciate that no one mentioned Peter, nor did they avoid me like the plague. In their own ways, they showed their support.

Jean, the admin, popped her head into my office around five. "You ready, Lizzie?"

I rose. "Yep."

On the table in the department's conference room was a going away cake for Dr. Marcel. All of the professors and some of the grad students were crammed into the space.

The man of the hour hadn't arrived yet.

Jean nodded at me, and I picked up the phone in the room and dialed his office phone. "Hey there, can I chat with you in the conference room?"

He quickly agreed.

When the door opened, everyone shouted "Surprise!"

Dr. Marcel placed a hand over his heart. "Are you trying to kill me?" He was laughing.

His wife made her way to him. "You've always loved being the center of attention."

"Quite true." His eyes misted as his gaze traveled through the room, taking in all of the professors to see him off. When he stopped on me, I had to dig deep to smile instead of cry.

Someone popped the cork of the first champagne bottle. Several more were opened and glasses were filled. That was when the speeches started.

When it was my turn, I said, "I've been trying for days to think of the right words to express my gratitude for all that you've done for me. I'm not sure I'd be standing here if it wasn't for your guidance during my grad school days. You always had a way of making me believe I could do anything. It's not just me who you've helped, either. Over the years, you've guided hundreds of students as they bridged the gap between adolescence and adulthood. I can't speak for all of them, but I, for one, will miss your presence in these hallowed halls." I raised my flute. "To the kindest ment—" I stopped myself from saying mentor, opting instead for, "friend."

There was some hooting, and Jean started cutting into the cake.

Dr. Marcel gave me a hug and then kept his hands on my shoulders. "You know you aren't getting rid of me so easily. Sarah's already sent us an invite for the Fourth of July."

I laughed. "I have my fingers crossed this holiday doesn't have an ounce of Petrie flair."

His expression softened. "How are you doing?"

"Nope. No talk of that on your special day."

Lydia slipped her arm through her husband's. "Is he trying to slip in one last history lecture?"

"I wish. I'm going to miss them."

"Come over anytime," he said.

Another professor approached, and I took the chance to slip away.

* * *

When I walked into the house via the kitchen door, I was greeted with laughter.

Sarah beamed at me. "Hey, honey."

"What'd I miss?" I set my bulging bag down on one of the stools.

Maddie started to say something, but Sarah said, "Nothing. Lots of grading to do?" She motioned to the bluebooks poking out of my bag.

Maddie raised her brows but remained silent.

"Yes, but not tonight."

"Everyone else is in the living room if you want to head in there. Maddie and I are getting the food ready."

"Okay." I didn't budge.

"Or you can hide in here if you need to." Sarah popped a green olive into her mouth.

"Is that what you two are doing?" I swiped a meatball and nibbled on it, licking my fingers clean.

"I would never." Sarah placed a hand over her heart.

Gabe strutted in and wrapped his arms around Maddie's waist, and she leaned back into him.

"Are you two getting along?" I asked.

"I hate him." Maddie laughed.

"I hate you back." Gabe kissed her cheek.

I looked to Sarah, who made a *roll with it* motion with her hand. I'd heard they started therapy, but I hadn't expected much improvement so soon.

"It's been noticed that the food hasn't arrived yet." Gabe held Maddie tighter.

"Oh, really. Who's noticed?" Maddie asked, rolling her head back to stare into his eyes.

"Allen." Gabe tossed his brother under the bus, but his growling stomach made it clear Allen wasn't alone. "I didn't have dinner," he explained, spearing a meatball with a toothpick.

"Let's get this started." I picked up the tray with roasted peppers, hummus, four types of olives, marinated mushrooms, a bowl of pistachios, and pitas. Gabe grabbed the one with meatballs, tabbouleh, stuffed grape leaves, and French bread.

The living room had been set up with the couches and chairs positioned conference style around the coffee table. Everyone took to the food like half-starved hyenas.

Once the hubbub died done some, Dad cleared his throat. "Thanks for having all of us over tonight."

Sarah leaned into my side, and I nodded.

"This isn't the happiest of days for the family, but it's good to know with everything going on, we can all still pull together." Dad placed a hand on Helen's thigh.

Gabe held Maddie with one arm.

Allen popped a stuffed grape leaf into his mouth.

I smiled at Sarah, who returned it.

"Peter has made his wishes clear. Our number one goal is to take care of Demi, and I know everyone in this room is dedicated to the precious girl." Dad locked eyes on mine and then Sarah's. "I want you two to know you aren't alone in this."

"I know," I said.

Sarah rested her hand on her growing belly. "Demi will never want for siblings."

"Are you having twins again?" Allen asked.

"No," Sarah answered.

"Are you going to tell us yet?" Maddie was practically bouncing on the couch cushion.

Rose looked just as eager, and I was amazed Sarah hadn't shared the news with her mom. Troy patted her knee.

"We kinda want it to be a surprise," Sarah continued.

"No fair." Gabe shook a finger at her.

"What do you think, Lizzie?" Sarah turned to me.

"I've been terrible at keeping secrets lately."

Sarah seemed torn.

I squeezed her hand.

She continued to rub her belly.

"Don't feel pressured," my dad advised.

"It would be good to focus on positive changes." Sarah's determination was wilting. Again, she queried my face, and I nodded. She cradled her baby bump with both hands. "Everyone, meet Calvin."

AUTHOR'S NOTE

Thank you for reading *A Woman Undone*. If you enjoyed the novel, please consider leaving a review on Goodreads or Amazon. No matter how long or short, I would very much appreciate your feedback. You can follow me, T. B. Markinson, on Twitter at @IHeartLesfic or email me at tbm@tbmarkinson.com. I would love to know your thoughts.

ABOUT THE AUTHOR

TB Markinson is an American who's recently returned to the US after a seven-year stint in the UK and Ireland. When she isn't writing, she's traveling the world, watching sports on the telly, visiting pubs in New England, or reading. Not necessarily in that order.

Her novels have hit Amazon bestseller lists for lesbian fiction and lesbian romance.

Feel free to visit TB's website (lesbianromancesbytbm.com) to say hello. On the *Lesbians Who Write* weekly podcast, she and Clare Lydon dish about the good, the bad, and the ugly of writing. TB also runs I Heart Lesfic, a place for authors and fans of lesfic to come together to celebrate and chat about lesbian fiction.

Want to learn more about TB. Hop over to her *About* page on her website for the juicy bits. Okay, it won't be all that titillating, but you'll find out more.

Printed in Poland
by Amazon Fulfillment
Poland Sp. z o.o., Wrocław